ANGELS OF DARKNESS

THE DARK ANGELS Space Marines are amongst the most devout of the God-Emperor's servants. Their loyalty is beyond question and their faith almost fanatical. But the Chapter harbours a dark secret that stretches back over ten thousand years, to the time of the Horus Heresy. In this terrible time, the Space Marine Legions turned on each other in a blood bath that nearly tore the Imperium apart. Many deeds of darkness were done, and the Dark Angels' mission is ever to safeguard their reputation by hiding the sins of their past.

When Dark Angels Chaplain Boreas captures and interrogates one of the Fallen, the past collides with the future with tragic consequences. Gav Thorpe's classic Dark Angels novel is re-presented in a new edition, complete with an afterword by the author.

ANGELS OF DARKNESS

Gav Thorpe

Thanks to Rick Priestley,
Andy Chambers and Jervis Johnson

A BLACK LIBRARY PUBLICATION

First published in Great Britain in 2003

This edition published in 2008 by
BL Publishing,
Willow Road, Lenton,
Nottingham, NG7 2WS, UK.

10 9 8 7 6 5 4 3

Cover illustration by Mark Gibbons.

A CIP record for this book is available from the British Library.

ISBN 13: 978 1 84416 655 8
ISBN 10: 1 84416 655 4

See the Black Library on the Internet at
www.blacklibrary.com

Find out more about Games Workshop
and the world of Warhammer 40,000 at
www.games-workshop.com

Printed in the UK by CPI Bookmarque, Croydon, CR0 4TD

IT IS THE 41st millennium. For more than a hundred centuries the Emperor has sat immobile on the Golden Throne of Earth. He is the master of mankind by the will of the gods, and master of a million worlds by the might of his inexhaustible armies. He is a rotting carcass writhing invisibly with power from the Dark Age of Technology. He is the Carrion Lord of the Imperium for whom a thousand souls are sacrificed every day, so that he may never truly die.

YET EVEN IN his deathless state, the Emperor continues his eternal vigilance. Mighty battlefleets cross the daemon-infested miasma of the warp, the only route between distant stars, their way lit by the Astronomican, the psychic manifestation of the Emperor's will. Vast armies give battle in His name on uncounted worlds. Greatest amongst his soldiers are the Adeptus Astartes, the Space Marines, bio-engineered super-warriors. Their comrades in arms are legion: the Imperial Guard and countless planetary defence forces, the ever-vigilant Inquisition and the tech-priests of the Adeptus Mechanicus to name only a few. But for all their multitudes, they are barely enough to hold off the ever-present threat from aliens, heretics, mutants – and worse.

TO BE A man in such times is to be one amongst untold billions. It is to live in the cruellest and most bloody regime imaginable. These are the tales of those times. Forget the power of technology and science, for so much has been forgotten, never to be re-learned. Forget the promise of progress and understanding, for in the grim dark future there is only war. There is no peace amongst the stars, only an eternity of carnage and slaughter, and the laughter of thirsting gods.

'Since the founding of their Legion at the birth of the Imperium, the Space Marines of the Dark Angels have been dreaded by their enemies and held in awe by those they protect. Stubborn and relentless in battle, ever vigilant and zealous in their pursuit of their duties, the Dark Angels are among the Emperor's most faithful servants. Yet, it was not always so. For ten millennia the Dark Angels have harboured a sinister secret, an act so terrible and shameful it threatens everything the Dark Angels hold most dear – and may yet bring them eternal damnation.'

– Inquisitor Bastalek Grim

THE TALE OF ASTELAN
PART ONE

WITH THE WHINE of the shuttle's engines dying behind him, Astelan stood on the landing apron looking at the large, ornate gates in front of him. They were wrought from black metal in the design of a winged sword that was mirrored on each side.

In the dark, cavernous room beyond, he could see ten giant figures swathed in thick white robes. They were standing in the shadows between the guttering circles of flame cast by tall candles set around the chamber's walls. Each figure bore a two-handed sword, held upright across its chest and face, the sharp edges of the weapons glinting in the erratic light. The ruddy glow flickered off thousands of skulls adorning the walls and ceiling of the vast sepulchre, gleaming in eyeless sockets and shining off polished lipless grins. Many were human, but most were not: a mix of subtle, elongated features; brutal, bucket-jawed aliens; eyeless monstrosities; horned, twisted creatures and many other contorted, inhuman stares looked down upon the assembled Dark Angels.

The solitary toll of a bell brought the assembled guard to attention. The great gates in front of Astelan opened inwards, another clanging of the bell drowning out the hiss of hydraulics and creak of ancient hinges, and he took a few steps forward. Suited in his heavy black power armour, he was still taller by a few centimetres than the assembled Space Marines. He wore no helmet, and his dark eyes calmly gauged the gathered warriors from beneath a heavy brow, the candlelight reflecting off his shaved head. He looked back at the Space Marine who had accompanied him on the shuttle, the one who had been referred to as Brother-Chaplain Boreas. He too wore heavy white robes, but unlike the honour guard, Boreas was still armoured. His face was concealed behind a helmet fashioned in the shape of a death's head skull, decorated by tarnished gilding. The dead eye-lenses of the helmet regarded him without emotion.

'I did not expect an honour guard,' Astelan said, glancing at the Dark Angels who stood unmoving around him.

'You were right not to, they are here to honour me, not you,' Boreas replied quietly and evenly, his tone slightly distorted by his suit's vocal projectors. He then raised his voice to address the others in the room. 'Form up for escort!'

Five of the Space Marines turned and took up position in front of Astelan, while the others fell in behind the newly arrived pair. At another command from Boreas, they started a slow march forwards. Astelan felt Boreas shove him from behind, and he fell into step behind the others. As they passed from the chamber into a wide but low corridor panelled with slabs engraved with names, Astelan felt a flicker of recognition.

'We just passed through the Memorial Gates, did we not?' he asked Boreas, who did not reply. 'I am sure. It all seems so familiar. The reception chamber used to be

hung with banners of the families of Caliban whose
lords had fallen in battle.'

'Perhaps once, but not any more,' Boreas conceded.

'But how can that be? I saw from the transport that this
is not Caliban, it is some form of space station,' Astelan
said. 'And the Memorial Gates were used to get to the
tombs in the catacombs beneath the citadel. It was a
place for the dead.'

'That is correct,' Boreas said.

Perturbed and confused, Astelan carried on in silence
as the Dark Angels led him further and further into the
bowels of the disturbing place. Their journey was lit by
torches that burned with smokeless flame, held in
sconces at regular intervals along the walls. Other corridors branched left and right, and Astelan knew from
memory that they were passing through the tombs of the
ancient rulers of Caliban. And yet he could not reconcile
the sight he had seen upon his arrival with his memories.
He was on an armoured fortress hanging in space – he
had seen the many towers and emplacements built upon
what he had taken to be a gigantic asteroid.

They turned left and right on occasion, weaving
through the labyrinth of tunnels, surrounded by tablets
proclaiming the names of Dark Angels who had died in
heroic combat. They seemed to go on forever in all directions. Underfoot, the dust was thick, having lain
undisturbed for many years, perhaps decades or centuries. Small alcoves set into the walls held relics of the
past – ornately decorated shoulder pads, the hilt and half
the blade of a broken power sword, engraved skulls, a tarnished gauntlet, glass-fronted ossuaries displaying the
bones of those who had fallen in battle, a plaque
beneath declaring who they were in life. He felt draughts
and chill breezes on his face emanating from side chambers, and occasionally heard a distant sigh, or the clank
of a chain, all of which added to the macabre aura of the
crypt, which did little to ease Astelan's unsettled mind.

Turning right at one particular junction, a peripheral movement caught Astelan's eye and he glanced to his left. In the shadows he saw a diminutive being, no higher than his waist, almost hidden in the darkness. It was little more than a small robe, but from the depths of the black hood two eyes glittered with a cold, blue light as the strange creature regarded Astelan. As suddenly as he had spotted it, the watcher in the dark faded back into the shadows and was gone.

His confusion growing as they continued to march into the bowels of the sepulchre, it took Astelan a moment to realise that they had stopped. The other Dark Angels turned and filed out by the way they had entered, leaving him and Boreas in a circular chamber roughly two dozen metres across, its circumference lined with windowless iron doors. All of the doors were closed except one, and Boreas directed Astelan towards it with a pointing finger.

Astelan hesitated for a moment and then strode forwards into the room beyond. He stopped suddenly as soon as he entered, stunned by what he found inside.

The room was not large, barely five metres square, lit by a brazier in the far corner. A stone slab dominated the centre of the room, pierced by iron rings from which hung heavy chains, and to one side a row of shelves was stacked with various metal implements that menacingly caught the light of the glowing coals. There were two more robed Space Marines awaiting them, their faces hidden by heavy hoods, their hands concealed beneath studded metal gauntlets. As one took a step forward, Astelan caught a glimpse of bony white under his hood.

The door slammed shut behind Astelan and he turned to see Boreas had stepped inside. The Chaplain removed his skull-faced helmet and held it under his arm. His piercing eyes regarded Astelan just as coldly as the flat features of the armoured skull had done. Like Astelan, his head was also shaven and marked with faint scars.

His left cheek was tattooed with a winged sword, Chapter symbol of the Dark Angels, and his forehead pierced with service studs.

'You are charged as a traitor to the Emperor and Lion El'Jonson, and I, as an Interrogator-Chaplain of the Dark Angels Chapter, am here to administer your salvation,' Boreas intoned. Astelan laughed harshly at the man's overly sombre tone, the sound echoing off the bare stone walls.

'You shall be my saviour?' snarled Astelan. 'And what right do you have to judge me?'

'Repent the sins of your past, accept the error of your Lutherite ways, and your salvation shall be swift,' Boreas said, ignoring Astelan's scorn.

'And if I do not?' asked Astelan.

'Then your salvation shall be long and arduous,' Boreas replied, pointedly glancing at the blades, tongs and brands on the shelf.

'Has the glory of the Dark Angels been so forgotten that you are reduced to barbarian torturers?' Astelan spat. 'The Dark Angels are warriors, shining knights of battle. And yet, here you skulk in the shadows, turning upon your own.'

'Do you not repent of your actions?' Boreas asked again. His face was intent, and his voice was tinged with anger.

'I have committed no wrong,' Astelan replied. 'I refuse to answer your charges, and I refuse to acknowledge your right to accuse me thus.'

'Very well, then we shall endeavour to relieve you of the burden on your soul,' Boreas stated with another glance at his torturer's instruments. 'If you will not repent freely and earn a swift death, then we must exorcise the sin from your soul with pain and misery. The choice is yours.'

'There is not one here amongst you who could lighten the weight I have borne upon my shoulders,' Astelan declared. 'And there is not one in this room who shall lay a finger upon me without violence.'

'That is but the latest error of judgment you have made.' Boreas smiled grimly and gestured to one of the other Dark Angels. 'Brother-Librarian Samiel shall set you right.'

The Space Marine pulled back his hood to reveal a dark, weathered face. Tattooed above his right eye was the winged sword symbol, its pommel in the shape of a glaring eye. His head was also shaven to the scalp, and criss-crossed with scars and branding marks. There was movement in Samiel's eyes, and it took a moment for Astelan to realise that they were tiny sparks of psychic power.

Astelan took a step towards Boreas, fists raised to attack.

'*Arcanatum energis!*' Samiel spat. Blue bolts of lightning leapt from the psyker's fingertips and struck Astelan full in the chest, hurling him across the room to slam into the wall. Ancient stone cracked and splintered under the impact and Astelan grimaced with pain from the blow. Flickers of blue sparks danced over his armour for a few more heartbeats as he pushed himself to his feet.

'You call me traitor, you who have brought a witch into your own ranks!' Astelan growled between gritted teeth, staring with loathing at Boreas.

'Be still!' Samiel barked, his voice cutting into Astelan's mind, hammering at his senses as much as the psychic bolt had hammered into his body. He resisted for only the briefest of moments before he felt the strength sapped from his limbs and he slumped within his armour, its servos whining to keep him upright.

'*Sleep!*' Samiel exerted his will again, and this time Astelan's resistance was stronger and he fought off the urge to close his eyes for several seconds. His gaze caught that of the Librarian, and in that moment, the full force of the psyker's mind was unleashed. Astelan felt his own thoughts being twisted into a whirl, his vision spun and a roaring filled his ears. He tried desperately to shake himself free of Samiel's burning gaze, but could not move. His attention was locked and he felt his will draining away, leeching into the witchfires that burned in the psyker's eyes.

'Sleep…' Samiel repeated and Astelan fell into unconsciousness.

WHEN HE AWOKE, Astelan was not surprised to find himself chained to the interrogation slab. Looking at the thick links of iron binding his legs and arms, he knew instantly that even with his prodigiously enhanced strength he would have little chance of breaking his bonds. He had been stripped of his armour, and he lay naked upon the stone table. His skin was tight across his corded muscles, marked by dozens of surgery scars where he had undergone his transformation into a Space Marine. Across his chest and abdomen a second skin glistened a dull black, broken in places by steel fittings for wires and cables, which allowed him to interact with his power armour when armed for battle. Now the metal sockets and circuits lay dormant, and his body felt cold where they pierced his flesh.

Glancing around the room, Astelan found himself alone. He wondered how long it would be before his torturers arrived. It mattered not, he knew well that he could block out whatever pain they dared visit upon him. Pain was a weakness, and as a Space Marine of the Dark Angels, he had no weaknesses. He reminded himself, as he lay there waiting, that he had suffered many wounds in battle and had continued to fight on. Even now, fettered in the prison of those who had forsaken the heritage he had left them, he would continue that fight.

Others had warned him that the Dark Angels were not as they had always been, that they were now ruled by suspicion and secrecy, but he had not truly believed them.

Had he realised what they intended, he would never have surrendered himself to them on Tharsis. He had spent the last few weeks in a state of constant turmoil. First, the Dark Angels had attacked the world he had commanded, forcing him to fight back. It was only after considerable bloodshed that, against the advice of his subordinates, Astelan had relented in his defiance and allowed his attackers entry to his bunker.

The first Space Marines he had seen had seemed very wary, and were confused. Soon they were recalled and the Chaplain, Boreas, had arrived, flanked by Space Marines in white heavy Terminator armour. The unconventional form of their livery and the barbaric decorations of bones and feathers had only added to Astelan's confusion, as had the term Boreas had used to describe them – the Deathwing. He had not resisted, in his ignorance, when they had manacled his hands with thick chains of titanium, so that even in his armour he could not break the links. A gunship, also in the colours of the Deathwing, had landed directly outside his command centre and as he was hurried on board he saw no sign of any other Space Marines.

From then on, he had been kept in total isolation. When he had been transferred from the gunship to a cell aboard the Dark Angels' vessel he had been hooded with a black sack, his mouth gagged with thick cord. He had received no contact other than when Boreas had introduced himself and brought him food and water. Astelan was unsure how long the journey had taken, several weeks at least, before Boreas had returned with the gag and the hood, and the shuttle had brought him to the hidden landing pad.

Now he was due to be tortured by those who falsely imprisoned him. He knew that in their ignorance they thought him a traitor, and in their own superstitious way they believed they were saving his soul. It was a mockery of everything he held dear, of everything the Dark Angels once represented to the galaxy. As his anger grew, Astelan resolved to show them the error of their ways, to demonstrate to them how far they had fallen from grace in the eyes of the Emperor.

While he waited, Astelan let himself fall into a trance, calming his mind. As he had been trained to do, he detached himself from his physical body, allowing the catalepsean node implanted into the base of his brain to control his mental functions. In a partial slumber, he remained aware of his surroundings and alert to any threat, but his brain also rested itself, redirecting neural signals from dormant areas to those still awake.

In his dreamlike state, his perceptions shifted focus, so that the room became bright and full of colour for a few minutes, before turning stark and grey as his consciousness transferred through the different lobes of his brain. Sound came and went, memories flooded his mind and then were lost, and he felt as if he were floating in the air, swiftly followed by the crushing weight of the air pressure around him. Through all this, the inner eye of his mind watched the door, awaiting the return of his jailers.

ASTELAN WAS AWARE that a considerable time had passed, perhaps several hours, and he eased himself back into full consciousness. His augmented hearing picked up the sound of approaching footfalls from outside the room. It had been this that had pricked his subconscious mind, forcing him to return from his mesmerised state. With a rattle of heavy keys, the lock was turned with a loud clanking, and the door swung open. Boreas entered, followed by Samiel, and the Chaplain swung the door shut behind him. He had divested himself of his armour and now wore a plain white robe, its front opened to reveal the Space Marine's massively muscled chest.

Boreas turned and hung the keys on a hook by the door.

'I hope you used your time of solitary peace to consider your thoughts carefully,' Boreas began, standing to Astelan's right. Astelan watched Samiel circle the room to stand on the other side of him.

'Your threats are meaningless to me, surely even you can understand that,' Astelan replied, turning his head to meet Boreas's gaze.

'If you will not recant your evil deeds, we must proceed according to the ancient traditions of my office,' Boreas intoned, beginning the ritual of interrogation. 'Tell me your name.'

'I am Chapter Commander Merir Astelan,' he replied with a note of indignity in his voice. 'Your treatment of me has taken no account of my esteemed rank.'

'And who do you serve?' Boreas asked.

'I once served the Emperor's Dark Angels Space Marine Legion,' Astelan told the Chaplain, dropping his gaze to the floor.

'Once served? Who do you serve now?' Boreas demanded, stepping forward.

'I was betrayed by my own lords,' Astelan replied after a moment of painful recollection, still avoiding Boreas's stare. 'They turned their backs on me, but I have endeavoured to continue the great task that the Emperor created me for.'

'And what is that great task?' Boreas leaned close, his eyes narrowing as he glared at Astelan.

'That mankind might rule the galaxy, without fear of threat from within or without,' Astelan replied fiercely, meeting the Interrogator-Chaplain's stare. 'To fight proudly at the forefront of battle against the alien and the ignorant.'

'And so how is it that you fought against the Space Marines of the Dark Angels on the world of Tharsis?' Boreas asked.

'Once more I was betrayed by the Dark Angels, and again I had to fight to defend myself and to protect what you would unwittingly destroy.' Astelan raised his head to look straight at the Interrogator-Chaplain, and the Chaplain recognised the hatred in his eyes.

'You enslaved a world to your own selfish whims and needs!' Boreas spat, reaching down and clamping a hand around Astelan's throat. The muscles in the prisoner's neck corded as he fought back against the pressure of the Dark Angel's powerful fingers. There was loathing in Boreas's voice when he spoke next. 'You betrayed everything you were sworn to uphold! Admit it!'

Astelan said nothing as the two gazed venomously at each other. For several minutes, they were locked together in their mutual disgust, until Boreas eventually eased his grip and stood back.

'Tell me how you came to be on Tharsis,' the Chaplain said, crossing his arms, acting as if he had not just been trying to squeeze the life out of the man chained in front of him. Astelan took a few deep breaths to steady himself.

'Tell me but one thing,' Astelan said, glancing first at Boreas and then at Samiel. 'Tell me where I am, how this place can be so familiar and yet so different, and I may consider listening to your accusations.'

'Has he not yet worked it out?' Samiel said, looking in amazement at Astelan. There was a flicker of a frown on the Chaplain's face before he looked down at his prisoner.

'You are in the Tower of Angels, renegade,' Boreas said.

'That cannot be so,' protested Astelan, trying to sit up but raising his head only a little against the strength of the chains. 'I saw nothing of Caliban when we approached. This cannot be our fortress. Why do you mock me?'

'There is no mockery,' Samiel said quietly. 'This fortress is all that is left of our homeworld of Caliban.'

'Lies!' Astelan declared, trying to sit up, his muscles bulging as he fought against the chains. 'This is just a trick!'

'You know we speak the truth,' Boreas said, forcing Astelan down again with a hand on his chest. His eyes bored into Astelan's as he spoke his next words: 'This is all that remains of Caliban, our homeworld that your treachery destroyed.'

NO ONE SPOKE for several minutes as Astelan absorbed this information. A chill began to seep into his flesh from the stone slab he lay on. Astelan watched his breath coalescing into a faint mist in the air as he breathed heavily, his chest rising and falling quickly. In all the years he had sought out information of his former masters, he had never heard of such a catastrophic event taking place. Perhaps it was a trick to weaken his resolve? He fast dismissed the notion though, as he considered the evidence he had witnessed since his arrival.

He was indeed in the catacombs below what had once been the glorious fortress of the Dark Angels Chapter, now somehow ripped from the planet and sent into space. It was this thought that prompted him to speak.

'Is this why you attacked me, unprovoked, on Tharsis?' Astelan asked, 'Was it misplaced revenge for the loss you have suffered, to destroy my new home?'

'Your new home?' Boreas repeated scornfully. 'A world full of soldiers and slaves, all sworn to be loyal to you. Can you not admit the heresy of your actions?'

'Has it now become heresy to rule a world in the Emperor's name? Is it wrong of me to command an army again, as I once did?' Astelan said, looking first at Boreas, and then quickly at Samiel.

'We were created to serve mankind, not to rule them,' Boreas rasped, leaning forward and wiping a bead of sweat from Astelan's brow with his thumb.

'You deny that we ruled Caliban?' laughed Astelan. 'You forget that a million serfs toiled in the fields of our homeworld to keep us clothed and fed, and in the forges and machine shops to arm us, and on our ships and in the factories.'

'A world does not exist to be enslaved to a single Space Marine,' Boreas said.

'We are all slaves of a kind, some of us willingly serve the Emperor, and some must be forced to,' Astelan told him.

'And which are you?' Samiel asked suddenly, stepping forward. 'Was it not you and your kind who refused to serve, taking it upon yourselves to usurp the Lion and betray the Dark Angels?'

'Never!' spat Astelan, thrashing at his bonds. 'It is the rest of mankind who betrayed us! I watched you fight on Tharsis, and I was appalled. My armies were great, worthy to be led by the Emperor himself, and trained well, but against the might of the Dark Angels that I fought alongside, the battle would have been swiftly lost. Now, they have pulled your teeth, scattered you across the stars. This I have learnt these last two hundred years.'

'You are wrong,' argued Boreas, pacing back and forth, his eyes locked on Astelan's like a predator. 'The Legions were broken up so that no single man could wield that kind of power again.'

'An act done by weak-willed men who were jealous of us, and afraid of what we were,' said Astelan, moving his head to keep Boreas in sight. 'I commanded a thousand Space Marines, just one of many Dark Angels Chapter commanders, and whole worlds fell before our wrath. I would have taken Tharsis in a single day, but you waged war upon me for ten times as long.'

'The power you wielded has corrupted you, as it has corrupted many others,' Boreas said, turning away. 'It was that temptation that could not be allowed to exist.'

'Corrupt? You call *me* corrupt?' Astelan was shouting now, his voice ringing around the small cell. 'It is you who have become corrupted, hiding out in this dark cell, slinking in the shadows, afraid of the power you possess. I remember this place as one of celebration and victory. A hundred banners flew from the towers, and the great festivals lit these rooms with fires by the thousand as we revelled in our glories. I remember when the Dark Angels cut across the galaxy as the Emperor's own sword. We were the first and greatest, never forget that! We never once knew defeat as we followed the Emperor, and even when we were given Caliban and El'Jonson became our leader, we were still the lords of battle. It was that time of glory that we should be living in again. We exist for battle, and I forged an army to continue the Great Crusade.'

'The Great Crusade ended ten thousand years ago, when you and others like you turned on the Emperor and tried to destroy all that he had built,' Samiel said. Boreas still looked away, brooding silently.

'I do not accept your accusations,' replied Astelan. Again the cell was silent for a while, until Boreas turned and loomed over the slab, arms crossed over his bulky chest, his biceps straining the cloth of his robe. 'If you are not a traitor, then explain why you commanded your army to resist us on Tharsis,' the Interrogator-Chaplain asked calmly.

'You left me little choice,' Astelan replied bitterly. 'I had reports from my ships and outposts of a vessel breaking from the warp, and I sent them to investigate. Your strike vessel opened fire without replying to their hails, destroying one of my ships. It is only natural that others in the patrol should attack, when assaulted without provocation. You showed no mercy, killing nearly a thousand of my men!'

'And yet, when the battle-brothers landed and you saw that it was the Dark Angels you faced, you did not surrender, nor order your army to give us free passage,' Boreas continued.

'I told them to resist at all costs!' spat Astelan.

'It was your guilt that commanded them!' roared Boreas. 'Fear of facing justice for your evil deeds!'

'I did it to preserve what I had created,' Astelan replied, his voice dropping to a whisper. 'Once before, the misguided had turned their guns upon our great works. I would not allow it to happen again.'

'What great works?' sneered Boreas. 'A world that laboured for your pride? Ten million souls in chains to fuel your ambition? Indentured workers, conscript soldiers, all the fettered minions of your greed.'

'I have learnt that the realm of the Emperor stretches over more than a million worlds,' explained Astelan, as he pictured the vast factory-cities of Tharsis. 'The numbers of humanity are beyond counting, millions of billions of them teeming across star systems, in space ports and on ships. Crammed atop each other in the hive cities, scattered beneath the rocks of the mining worlds, imprisoned in floating reformatories. I say again that we are all slaves to the will of the Emperor.'

'To the Emperor perhaps, but not to you,' countered Boreas. 'You were created to serve, not to rule. You are a warrior, not a governor. It is your duty to obey and to fight, nothing more.'

'I am an instrument of the Emperor's will, his weapon and his symbol,' Astelan replied, looking again at his interrogator. 'How can you not see the hypocrisy in your own words? You accuse me of resisting you. How could I not, when your gunships razed the fields that fed my people, when your cannons destroyed their farms and towns, when your battle-brothers slaughtered them like livestock at the cull?'

'We did what your actions forced us to do,' Boreas said, pointing an accusing finger at Astelan. 'It was your arrogance that brought misery and destruction upon the servants of the Emperor. It was you that sent them against us. It was you that condemned them to death, sacrificing their lives to protect yourself. You are a traitor, you have destroyed everything you have come across. Your sins have cursed you so that death and blood follow in your wake.'

'My army fought bravely to the end, as I had trained them to,' Astelan said, closing his eyes. He could picture his troops parading through the capital, thousands of them in rank after rank, banners held high, the martial drumbeat accompanied by the crash of booted feet. He remembered their last stand at the command bunker, as they threw themselves at the enemies outside, swamping them with their bodies. Not one had spoken of surrender, not one of them had baulked at their duty. 'It was their love for the Emperor that drove them to such acts of desperation. It was their fear of what you represent that gave them the strength to continue, to thwart your parasitic plans.'

'You call us parasites! Who lived in luxury while the people of your world starved and your soldiers fought over scraps?' Boreas shook his head as he spoke. 'You are an abomination, an abhorrent travesty of a Space Marine. Where you see strength, I see cruelty. Where you profess to greatness, I see despotism of the worst kind. Your heresies are beyond comprehension. Just admit to your sins, cleanse your soul of their burden, and you shall be free.'

'You call this freedom?' Astelan laughed bitterly, nodding to the instruments of torture on the shelves. 'You call this the Emperor's works? The Dark Angels were the first, the proudest Legion. We carved a path of light across the stars in the Emperor's name, and now you surround yourself with shadows and deceit. Your mighty warriors ravage a planet for a single man, whilst star systems fall to the alien and the unclean.'

'You dare to accuse me!' Boreas spat the words. 'I swear by the Lion and the Emperor, you will admit your crimes and repent your sins. I will learn everything you have done, every wrong deed, every evil act you have committed.'

'I shall tell you nothing!' Astelan insisted.

'You are lying,' Samiel said, staring into Astelan's eyes. 'You are afraid. There are secrets locked inside your mind, knowledge you would try to keep from us.'

'Get thee behind me, warlock!' Astelan roared, the chains biting deep into his flesh as he tried to lunge at the psyker. 'Do not pollute my soul with your magic.'

'Your soul is already polluted,' Boreas said, pushing Astelan's head back against the sweat-covered stone of the slab and holding him there. 'You have but one chance to save it, and I offer you that chance. Repent of your Lutherite ways, beg forgiveness from the Lion and the Emperor. Your life is forfeit, but your soul can still be saved. Confess your wickedness and salvation shall be yours without pain, without regret. Resist and I shall be forced to save you from yourself.'

'Do your worst, torturer,' Astelan said slowly, closing his eyes and turning away from Boreas.

'It is Interrogator-Chaplain, and I do not need your fear, only your compliance,' Boreas said, turning away and crossing the cell to the shelves.

He picked up a brand, its head shaped as the double-headed Imperial eagle. He walked slowly to the brazier and held the brand in the flames, turning it occasionally to heat it evenly. Lifting it, he blew softly on the head, the dull glow burning brighter, wisps of smoke dissipating into the air. He held the brand hovering over Astelan's right arm, and he could feel the heat from it prickling his skin.

'Have Space Marines become so weak over the cold millennia that they fear fire, that mere burning will cause them pain?' Astelan sneered.

'There will be little pain to start with,' Boreas explained. 'But even you, physically perfect and yet spiritually corrupt, will begin to feel the touch of the flame, the caress of the blade, after the hundredth day, the thousandth day. Time is inconsequential. The purification of the soul is not an instant and rash process. It is a long, arduous road, and you and I shall travel it together.'

Astelan gritted his teeth as the brand burned into his shoulder, filling his nostrils with the stench of charring flesh.

THE TALE OF BOREAS
PART ONE

THE FLAMES FROM the immense fire leapt high into the night sky, bathing the natural amphitheatre in a warm red glow. The circular wall of rock rose over a hundred metres into the sky, an ancient volcanic caldera several hundred metres across that was pock-marked with dozens of cave dwellings accessed by an intricate web of rope ladders and bridges.

The constant pounding of drums echoed off the surrounding cliffs, resonating with the howling chants of the gathered villagers dancing and leaping around the central fire. Strange six- and eight-legged beasts turned on long spits over the many fire pits dug into the arena's floor, the smell of roasting flesh mixing with the aromatic smoke of the ritual pyre.

From the rim of the caldera the jungle spread out for many kilometres. As the noise and light of the barbaric celebrations dissipated with distance, they were replaced by the hisses and growls of nocturnal predators, the

alarmed shrieks of their prey and the constant stirring of
the wind through the thick dark jungle canopy. Above
the treetops, the night sky spread across the heavens, layered with thick clouds of sulphurous smoke from Piscina
V's many volcanoes. The underbelly of the clouds was lit
with a constant red hue from the glow of the planet's
countless volcanoes, as rivers of molten rock poured continuously over the world, sweeping away tracts of jungle
in fiery outbursts of the planet's inner turmoil.

A tiny pinprick of light appeared in the gloomy heavens, bright yellow and moving fast. It swiftly blossomed
into a crisp glow as it neared, and the roaring of the gunship's engines barked out over the sound of the wind.
Plasma engines trailing fire, the Thunderhawk dived
steeply towards the jungle, vaporous whirls trailing from
the tips of its stubby wings, its blunt, faceted prow cleaving forcefully through the dense atmosphere.

Alert to any possible danger, multi-barrelled weapons
tracked back and forth beneath the gunship's wings as it
pulled up from the screaming dive and levelled out
barely ten metres above the tops of the trees. The Thunderhawk raced over the heaving sea of flat leaves, its
backwash shuddering the upper branches of the jungle as
it passed.

The engine roar slowed to a whining growl as the aircraft fiercely braked, the glow of plasma from its main
engines dimming, to be replaced by the blue glare of
landing thrusters. Descending on azure pillars of flame,
the Thunderhawk dropped into the caldera, scattering
the terrified tribesmen beneath it as it dropped down
from the night sky close to the central fire.

For a moment, panic gripped the villagers who
frantically ran to and fro to avoid the burning jets, until
their leaders called out, telling them not to be afraid. By
the time the gunship settled heavily on its landing feet,
sinking deep into the soil that covered the floor of the
crater, the chieftain and his best warriors had assembled

a welcoming party close to the landing craft. The engines cut out and left a still, tense silence for a few seconds before the front ramp lowered with a grinding of hydraulics.

The ramp reverberated with a clang of heavy booted feet as Boreas stepped out of the Thunderhawk. Clad in his black power armour, he was an imposing sight. Thick plates of dense alloys covered with ablative ceramite protected his entire body. Beneath the crushing weight of the armour, bundles of muscle-like fibres expanded and contracted in response to his every moment, allowing him to move as swiftly as if unencumbered. His skull-helmeted head was flanked by two immense shoulder pads, mounted on actuators that constantly changed their position, allowing him free movement and all-round visibility, but providing a near-impenetrable shield against attack from the flank. All of this was powered by the backpack plugged into the spine of his armour, linked directly into his own nervous system so that he could regulate the power to his suit as effortlessly as he controlled the beating of his twin hearts or the combat stimulants his armour could pump into his bloodstream at a moment's notice.

Even without the strength-boosting properties of his armour, Boreas's genetically enhanced physiology made him many times stronger and faster than a normal human. Armoured for battle he could crush a man's skull in his fist and punch through the armour of a tank. Hundreds of relays within the armour bolstered his already acute senses, feeding him a constant stream of information from extra senses, his specially developed brain assessing them all subconsciously as a normal man might look with his eyes and hear with his ears.

Boreas paused for a second and looked at the villagers who were gathering close by, the auto-senses of his skull helm casting a red tinge on the proceedings. Olfactory filters allowed him to identify the contents of the atmosphere – mostly oxygen and nitrogen, but with heavy traces of sulphur, carbon from the fires, the sweat of the villagers; all of this he took in without conscious effort.

'*Terrorsight,*' Boreas muttered, his armour's audio pick-up detecting the sub-vocal command. His view blurred and changed. The people of the village now stood out as stark outlines, and he could see their organs and their veins pulsing with life beneath their skin. It took a moment for Boreas's straining eyes to discern the over-lapping shapes and colours, until he could make sense of his surroundings again. To the villagers who stared open-mouthed at him, the eyes of his helmet turned from a dull red to a blaze of energy and an awed murmur rippled over the settlement.

Boreas calmly looked around the caldera, his enhanced vision passing through the rock to gaze at the people concealed within the caves, at their crude bedding and furniture all picked out as a maze of grey and green lines. There were few, infants mostly. Satisfied that all was as expected, and that no unseen threat lurked within the tribal settlement, he whispered another command that returned his sight to normal.

Boreas blinked inside his helmet to clear his vision. Even such a short spell of super-enhanced sight had left vague after-images dancing on the edges of his vision. When he had first been gifted with his armour, more finely crafted and filled with auxiliary systems than even standard power armour, he had thought the terrorsight a miracle. However, he had soon learned that to use it for too long could lead to severe disorientation and nausea, despite the many months of training and his centuries of experience.

'Area is secure, follow me,' he stated and his helm transmitted his words to the other Space Marines still within the gunship.

As he strode down the ramp, Boreas was followed by the other members of his small command. The first was

Hephaestus, his Techmarine and pilot of the Thunder-hawk. His armour was almost as ornate as Boreas's, his chest plate wrought with the design of a two-headed eagle with wings spread, a cog clasped in its claws, the severe green broken only by the red of his left shoulder pad to indicate his special rank. Next came the two battle-brothers, Thumiel and Zaul, who marched down the ramp side-by-side in unison, carrying their boltguns casually, but the constant movement of their helmeted heads betrayed their unflinching alertness. Last of the group was Nestor, the Apothecary and guardian of their physical well-being. His white armour bulged with fitted equipment, his forearms heavy with sprouting needles and half-concealed phials, and cables that swung heavily from his bulky backpack.

The eldest of the villagers stepped forward and bowed on one knee, followed by the rest of the tribe. He was thin and wiry, but despite his advanced years, his muscles were taut and he moved with fluid grace. He wore a short sarong of thick animal hide, dyed deep red and painted with the image of leaves. His body was covered in blue tattoos across his chest and arms, and over his bald head. Each was made up of small dots and depicted blazing stars, strange nebula swirls, and oddly drawn diagrams of orbital systems and moons. Across his shoulders he wore a long cloak woven from thin vines, studded with tiny barbs that worried at his flesh, leaving his shoulders and back raw and bleeding.

After a long pause of deference, he stood again, his head reaching only as far as Boreas's chest. Gazing up into the severe, stylised skull face, the chieftain smiled, his wrinkled face creasing deeper.

'We are honoured that you visit us again,' he said with a short nod of satisfaction. It took a moment for Boreas to understand the barbarians' dialect of Imperial Gothic, but after listening for a short while his mind translated the more archaic and parochial terms used. 'Twice now in my life the warriors of the stars have visited my people, and twice now they have taken the best of our sons to fight with them.'

'*External address*,' Boreas sub-vocalised, his helmet amplifying his voice so that it reached across the whole village. Reaching into his memory, Boreas recalled the name of the leader of this particular tribe. 'Yes, Hebris, the sons of your people now honour us with their skills and dedication. And now we have come again to choose new warriors for the Emperor beyond the cloud. I trust that you are prepared?'

'As ever, lords,' Hebris said solemnly. 'For long years we have awaited your return, and our best hunters and warriors have looked to the skies for a sign of your coming. A generation of our strongest have passed while your eyes were elsewhere, but the next worthy ascendants are ready to prove themselves to you.'

'That is good,' Boreas said, head tilted to look down at the tattooed scalp of the elder. 'We are ready for the trial to begin.'

'We are always ready, it is a good omen that you visit us today, the twentieth year since my father died and I was given the cloak of thorns,' Hebris said. 'This night shall be remembered by my people for many generations to come. Please, follow me.'

The group of warriors parted to form a path for their visitors. They were tall and lean, dressed in armour made from the hide of the fierce mutant beasts they hunted in the jungles. It was crudely shaped in imitation of the giant Space Marines who took their bravest young warriors every so often – bulging chestplates, rounded shoulder pads, flared greaves around their legs. Each held a spear tipped with sharpened bone and hung with tufts of fur, feathers and claws taken from their prey.

Their bodies, like their chief's, were heavily tattooed with stars and suns, symbols of crescent moons and long-tailed comets.

None of their people had seen these things for thousands of years; the night sky was a featureless sheet of cloud to them. The knowledge of their existence had been passed down from their ancestors who had first settled this world more than twenty thousand years before, ten millennia before the coming of the Emperor, in the time known as the Dark Age of Technology.

For hundreds of centuries, Piscina V had been plundered for its rich mineral deposits, the sky polluted with waste, the rivers sucked dry. When the Age of Strife had swept across the ancient galactic empire of mankind, Piscina V had been isolated for thousands of years and over this time the planet reclaimed itself from the human interlopers. The geothermal energy stations that had once leeched energy from the planet's core had fallen into disrepair and malfunctioned. The planet had been wracked by massive earthquakes that destroyed the mighty cities, killed the population by the million, plunging the world into a new age of barbarism.

Now Piscina V was dominated by immense volcanoes, the belching fumes from their fiery outbursts replacing the smog of a hundred thousand factories.

Hebris led Boreas and the other Space Marines between the two rows of his personal hunters and warriors, while the other villagers crowded close in behind them to get a good look at their otherworldly visitors. They followed the old chieftain as he led them up a shallow ramp that wound around the edge of the crater until it reached a flat platform to an opening some ten metres above the ground level of the caldera.

At the back of the platform was the largest cave opening in the village, flanked by two guards dressed in a similar manner to the warriors who had formed the honour guard, with the addition of helmets fashioned from animal skulls. Inside was a shrine, lit by hundreds of lamps made from the fat of the jungle creatures these people hunted for survival. On ornately carved tables, sacred artefacts from the prehistory of the tribesmen were kept on display, to be revered by those who would never understand their true origins or workings. They were almost as incomprehensible to Boreas as they were to the chieftain and his people, but he knew enough to recognise them as broken pieces of archeotech.

Most were almost unrecognisable under the thick layers of rust that had gathered despite the best efforts of Hebris's priests to keep them clean. The acidic, humid air of Piscina V was the bane of all metal. Here and there, though, was a shape that Boreas recognised, crafted from long-forgotten materials resistant to the planet's harsh environment – fan blades, gears and wheels, circuitry drawn with intricate crystal layers, ceramic bottles that glowed with their own light. Boreas glanced back to see Hephaestus bending over a particular object that looked like a mechanical spider with coils of wire sheath splayed from its rusted body.

'Don't touch anything,' warned Boreas as the Techmarine reached out a hand towards the device. He stopped instantly, his helmeted head turning towards the Interrogator-Chaplain.

'The Adeptus Mechanicus would be very pleased for these artefacts,' Hephaestus said over the inter-squad comm-link. 'They might prove useful for bargaining with them.'

'And you have no personal interest at all, of course,' joked Zaul from behind Hephaestus.

'I am a Space Marine first and foremost, a techpriest only after that,' Hephaestus replied in a disgruntled voice.

'We are here to attend other matters, conduct yourselves with decorum,' Boreas chided them both. 'These relics belong to Hebris and his people, do not dishonour our Chapter and yourself by treating them with disrespect.'

'I understand, Brother-Chaplain, I apologise for my error in judgment,' replied Hephaestus, straightening up.

'I too am sorry for any misdeed,' added Zaul with a nod to Boreas.

'Then all is well,' Boreas told them. He noticed that the village elder was looking at the giant warriors, his face a picture of wide-eyed awe. He was, of course, oblivious to the exchange going on between the Space Marines, but Boreas realised that their body language and gestures betrayed their communication.

'*External address.* We were just admiring the sacred relics of your people,' Boreas remarked to Hebris, turning away from the rest of the squad.

'We found another in the jungles seven summers ago,' Hebris said proudly, his face split with a grin as he pointed at a particular misshapen lump of debris.

'*External address.* Your diligence does you and your people credit,' Hephaestus said laying a massive gauntleted hand on Hebris's shoulder. The old man visibly sagged under the weight and the Techmarine quickly removed his hand and crossed his arms over his chest.

'I thank you for your kind words,' Hebris replied. 'But, enough of this! Bring out the bench for our lords.'

The elder clapped his hands and four muscular warriors ran to the back of the cave and emerged with a mighty seat hewn from a single tree trunk. Sweating and grunting under the weight, they manhandled it to the front of the platform outside the cave, where they set it down. Boreas and the others took their places and sat, the bench creaking under their combined weight but holding up under the strain.

'You may begin,' said Boreas with a nod towards Hebris. The chieftain scampered forward and called down to the villagers, who had gathered in a semi-circle below the shrine.

'My beloved sons and daughters,' Hebris cried out, his face beaming. 'Tonight is a night long-awaited! Our young braves shall fight in the trials before the eyes of the sky-warriors who serve the Emperor beyond the cloud.

Those that are worthy shall go into the stars, there to fight for glory, and great honour and fortune shall they bring to our people. Let the willing ascendants come forth!'

Out of a cave at the foot of the cliff filed a group of twenty youths, in their early teenage years. They were naked except for splashes of purple and red war paint daubed in handprints over their chests and faces. In their hands, they each carried a skull or large bone, trophies from the hunts they had participated in.

They solemnly marched into the semi-circle formed by the villagers and stood in a line facing the Space Marines. Raising their prizes above their heads they shouted out in unison.

'Great lords of the Emperor,' they cried. 'We shall shed our blood today to prove our worth to you!'

The furthest to the left stepped forward, bowed to one knee and reverentially laid a viciously-fanged skull the size of his torso in front of him. Straightening, he looked up at the Space Marines.

'I have hunted for six seasons of the storm,' he called to them. 'This past year I slew a dagger-tooth with my spear, and I offer its head in tribute.'

When he stepped back, the next in the line took his place, crossing a pair of bones each as long as his arm and placing them next to the dagger-tooth skull.

'I have hunted for seven seasons of the storm,' he intoned solemnly. 'My fellow hunters wounded this tree-jaw and I finished it with my knife.'

One by one, each of the aspirants stepped forward and proclaimed how they had come by their offerings, laying them on the ground beneath the platform. Boreas sat and nodded to each of them, but said nothing.

'And now we shall show our honoured visitors the strength of our people,' Hebris declared, clapping his hands again.

From one side of the caldera, a group of five warriors emerged carrying logs of different lengths and girths, and laid them out in front of the platform in ascending size. They then stepped back and the youths trotted forwards.

In the same order as before, each ran to the first log and grabbed it by the end. The warrior then stepped forward and placed his foot against the opposite end so that it would not slip and the youth hauled the log up and attempted to lever it above his head. As each stood there, arms quivering with the strain, the tribe gave out a great cheer and they gratefully dropped it back to the earth. All passed the first test with ease.

The trial was then repeated with the second tree trunk, and once more each of the aspirants was successful, though many wobbled dangerously and their legs threatened to buckle beneath the weight. At the third log, the first youth failed, throwing himself to one side as his straining arms faltered when it was at neck-height and the log tumbled from his grip. There was no cheer this time, but as he walked away from the group with his head hung with sadness into the arms of his family, they clapped him on the back reassuringly and ruffled his tousled hair affectionately.

Of the others, three more failed to lift the third log and were eliminated. It slipped from the grasp of one of them and he did not avoid its fall, catching a glancing blow to his leg which sent him sprawling. Shame-faced, he limped heavily from the contest, slapping away the hands of those who offered to support him.

After the fourth, two more had failed the task, but of those that remained, each managed to lift the fifth and final log, to resounding cheers from the gathered tribes people. As the fifteen remaining aspirants knelt in the earth and bowed their heads to the Space Marines, the logs were dragged away.

'And now we shall show our honoured visitors the speed of our people,' Hebris announced, once more clapping his hands together.

The crowd parted so that a path was formed from one edge of the village to the other, stretching out from the audience platform. At the far end, six warriors stood holding bright red cloths, and six more fell into line at the foot of the platform. The aspirants lined up ready for the race to begin.

As one, the warriors dropped the rags and the boys set off at a sprint. A small, red-haired lad soon streaked into the lead, gaining several metres on his competitors after only a dozen strides. The crowd clapped and roared as the boys ran between them, nudging and elbowing each other as they jostled for position.

The first boy reached the far end quickly and snatched up one of the rags and spun to begin the return leg. A few seconds later, the others were also halfway and those with the fastest hands managed to grab the five remaining rags. They all hurtled back towards the Space Marines, and it was here that some began to tire, lagging behind the others as the group slowly stretched out. Just fifty metres from the end, the youth in the lead slowed rapidly, his gait becoming awkward as cramp gripped his legs. Teeth gritted, he hobbled on as the others ran past him, clawing at each other to get in front and claim the remaining qualification places.

One tripped and fell and was stepped on by the boy behind him, eliciting a laugh from the onlookers. Dusting himself down, he rose to his feet and gamely sprinted on, one arm nursing his bruised back. In the final dash for the finish, a tall, long-limbed youth surged ahead. He had obviously been saving his strength and in the last ten metres hurled himself forward and made a dive for one of the remaining cloths. The others followed in his wake and there was a desperate mad scramble of those who had not yet claimed a cloth, but eventually the twelve winners emerged.

The three others turned to leave, but the red-headed youth hobbled after them and grabbed one by the shoulder. There was a brief exchange, while the boy tried to force the other aspirant to take the cloth, as he could not carry on himself, but the other youth refused, pushing him away. Hebris's guards stepped in and separated the two as they squared up to fight, banishing them both back to the crowd with angry cuffs round the back of their heads. Once things had settled again, the eleven remaining competitors returned to their places in front of Boreas, the red cloths now tied around their waists. Hebris raised his arms into the air and his people's chattering and shouting fell silent.

'And now we shall show our honoured visitors how we can leap through the air like the lash-monkey,' he proclaimed, clapping his hands together once.

This time, twenty warriors emerged from one of the caves, each carrying a bundle of thin sharpened stakes roughly waist-high in length. They formed a line from Boreas's left to his right at one pace intervals and crouched down, the spears held upright in front of them.

The first youth jogged to the end of the line and then turned and bowed to the Space Marines. After receiving a nod from Boreas, he ran towards the line of crouching warriors. Leaping into the air, he stepped onto the back of the first and jumped forwards onto the back of the next, over the spear tips. From one to the next to the next, he leapt nimbly along the line, using the warriors as stepping-stones over the jagged spear tips. On the twelfth he faltered and threw himself to the side and landed heavily in the dirt.

The villagers' cheer echoed off the caldera's walls as he pushed himself to his feet and stood up with arms raised.

The next youth fell after only eight jumps, scoring a bloody cut into his thigh on the spear tips as his balance failed him and he tumbled forward. He stood there on one leg, blood streaming down the other, and acknowledged the adulation of the crowd. The next aspirant almost made it to the end, falling only after seventeen jumps, and the roar of the appreciative tribesmen was deafening.

The other aspirants each took their turn to greater or lesser degrees of success until all had completed the trial. The tenth warrior in the row then stood up and with the hafts of the thin spears he carried, he whipped the four boys who had failed to reach him back into the mass of villagers. Now only seven remained.

They ran into one of the caves, out of sight of Boreas, and emerged again a few minutes later. Each carried a cudgel tipped with the long tooth of a giant predator, and a shield made from woven hide pulled taut in a wooden frame.

'And now that we have proven the worth of our bodies, let us prove the worth of our spirit!' shouted Hebris, and the crowd formed back into a semicircle facing the Space Marines, leaving the aspirants in an area roughly twenty metres across. 'Only in battle shall we know this!'

The boys began to drum their clubs onto their shields, and other drums from around the caldera took up the frantic beat. For several minutes they drummed louder and louder until the boys were sweating with the effort, their limbs trembling from exertion. Hebris looked over at Boreas, who nodded.

'Let the trial begin!' Boreas roared over the cacophony, standing up and raising his right fist above his head.

The boys broke rank and formed into a circle facing each other, their weapons and shields held ready. The other drums slowed pace, a low beat sounding out every couple of seconds as the young ascendants eyed each other warily, casting glances up at the Space Marines high above them. Without a word, Boreas dropped his hand and the ritual battle began.

A blond-haired youth to Boreas's right charged forwards across the open space, his weapon held high as he screamed a war cry. Brave, but rash, thought Boreas as he saw the boy quickly encircled by the others and cut down. The fight quickly broke down into a scattered set of duels, except for two of the warriors, who stood back-to-back towards one side, keeping a wary eye on the progress of the fighting.

Boreas paid particular attention to them, watching as they worked together when the survivors of the individual contests emerged and sought fresh enemies...

Soon only the pair remained and one other, the rest of the aspirants having thrown down their weapons and surrendered, lying unconscious from receiving a beating, or sitting in the mud bleeding heavily and unable to continue. All around them, the tribes people hooted and chanted, the ever-present rumbling of the drums echoing around the amphitheatre.

'Quick, strong and clever,' Thumiel remarked over the comm, obviously referring to the two who had banded together.

'Yes, they show signs of promise,' agreed Boreas, smiling inside his helmet. 'The other is brave, see how he continues to fight on, even though he has seen them beat everyone else.' He had seen enough, there was no point in allowing the bloodletting to continue. He raised his hand above his head, and after a moment, the fighting stopped.

'*External address.*' Boreas turned to Hebris. 'Bring those three to the testing chamber,' he said before turning away and walking back into the cave, followed by the other Space Marines.

He walked through the relic-strewn shrine to an opening at the back of the cave covered by a heavy curtain of woven leaves. Brushing aside the flimsy barrier, he stepped through the archway into the cavern beyond. It was a small chamber, dominated by a stone slab in the centre, waist high and stained with the reddish-brown of old blood. It reminded him of an interrogation cell back at the Tower of Angels.

It struck him as ironic that this place of recruitment – of hope for the future – should bear such a resemblance to a place dedicated to eradicating the shame of the past.

He was perturbed by the thought, and wondered why it was that he had been troubled so much lately by the memories of his first interrogation. For several weeks now during prayer and in quieter moments, his thoughts had strayed back to that encounter with Astelan. It had been nearly fifteen years ago, and he had performed two other interrogations since, but still that first battle of wills with one of the Fallen was etched into his mind.

He put it down to the isolation from his brethren. For several years he had been garrisoned here in the Piscina system with the others of his command, and in that time had not been in contact with any of his superiors or other members of the Inner Circle. The time preyed on his mind, and even his extended prayer sessions had done little to ease the doubts that had grown over recent months. Clenching his fists, Boreas exerted control over his wandering thoughts, bringing himself back to the matter in hand.

They waited for a few minutes until the curtain swayed and the three hopefuls entered, eyes wide with awe and fear. They saw the slab and stopped, darting nervous glances at the giant Space Marines who now surrounded them.

'Which of you shall be first?' asked Nestor, stepping towards the group.

They looked at each other and the eldest and tallest of them stepped forward. Boreas reckoned him to be little more than twelve or thirteen Terran years of age – perfect for the Dark Angels purposes. He was lean and wiry, with a thick shock of black hair that draped down over his deeply set eyes. He smiled wolfishly and took a pace towards the Apothecary.

'I am Varsin, I shall be the first,' the boy said proudly.

'Lie on the slab,' Nestor told him. The boy leapt onto the examining table and lay down, hands across his chest. Nestor loomed over him, a series of blades and needles extended from the narthecium built into his right forearm.

'Put your arms by your side, Varsin,' he said, placing a hand on the boy's forehead. The Apothecary's movements were deliberate and gentle, as fingers that could snap bones performed a cursory examination of the boy's body. 'This will cause you considerable pain,' he warned as he plunged the narthecium into the boy's stomach.

Varsin's shrieks rebounded shrilly off the walls as blades incised their way through skin and muscle and tendrils forced their way into his innards through the wound. Nestor placed a hand on the boy's chest and held him down as he scrabbled and yelled, his limbs waving wildly with agony. Blood bubbled up from the gash, spilling over the slab and splashing across Nestor's white armour in ruddy droplets.

The other two youths gave horrified gasps and began to back towards the curtained doorway, but their route was blocked by Thumiel, who carefully laid a hand on each of their heads and stopped them.

'You have seen worse when the hunt has gone wrong,' he said, and they nodded dumbly in answer, still aghast at the bloody scene in front of them.

As Varsin writhed, Nestor stood there calmly while the narthecium took what it needed. Automatic probes scored samples from the boy's stomach lining, extracted blood, bile and other fluids, measured blood pressure and pulse rate, injected anti-toxicants and cauterised wounds. The glowing amber light on the back of the device turned red and Nestor withdrew his fist. With a quick movement, a web of needles extended and stitched the wound shut in a matter of seconds. Varsin lay there covered with sweat, tears running down his face, his chest heaving under Nestor's palm.

'Do not move for a moment, or your wounds may reopen,' Nestor cautioned the youth, raising his hand and stepping away. The boy glanced at the others that had taken part in the trial by combat, who stood trembling with horrified stares. His gaze then passed to Boreas and the Chaplain gave a reassuring nod to the youth. Nestor fiddled with the displays of the narthecium, making readings of the samples he had taken. It was several minutes before a signal chimed and he approached Boreas.

'What are your findings?' Boreas asked.

'Ninety-eight per cent tissue match for suitability,' the Apothecary told him, consulting the green display on his arm. 'No endemic illnesses or inherited disorders. Acceptable tolerance levels of toxic influences, average life signals and pain response. The boy is perfect, physically speaking.'

'Good,' Boreas said, looking at the shivering boy. '*External address.* Come here, Varsin.'

Varsin swung his legs off the slab and lowered himself to the floor. Clutching his stomach, he padded across the stone and stood in front of Boreas, looking up nervously.

'Tell me of yourself,' Boreas asked him.

'I am the fifth son of Hebris, the chieftain, who was the second son of Geblin who took the cloak of thorns from Darsko in challenge,' the boy replied, his chest puffing up. 'My father's older brother was chosen to be a warrior for the Star Emperor.'

'Then the blood of your family is strong, you come from good stock,' said Boreas. 'What can you do to prove your loyalty to the Emperor beyond the cloud?'

'I don't understand, lord,' Varsin admitted.

'Would you kill your father if I commanded it?' Boreas asked.

'Kill my father?' the boy replied hesitantly. 'I would if you commanded it, though it would sadden me.'

'And why would it sadden you?' Boreas said, leaning down to look Varsin in the eye. The boy's face was reflected in the red lenses of his helmet.

'I would be saddened that my father had dishonoured our people by offending the Emperor beyond the cloud and his star warriors,' the boy replied immediately. 'I cannot imagine any other reason why you should wish him dead. He has served his people well.'

'And are you, a mere boy, to be the judge of that?' asked Boreas, the skull of his helm staring at Varsin.

'No, lord, I would follow your command to slay him because you are a better judge than I,' Varsin said with a slight shake of his head.

'Good,' said Boreas, straightening up. 'Go outside and tell your father you shall be leaving with us tonight,'

'I am?' The boy's eyes shone with pride and a grin split his face. He took a few hurried steps towards the door and then stopped and doubled up in pain.

'I said rest those wounds!' Nestor barked.

'I am sorry, my lord,' Varsin said through a grimace, before walking more slowly through the curtain.

Boreas turned to the two remaining aspirants and gestured towards the slab. They exchanged worried glances and then one of them took a faltering step forward.

'I… I am…' the lad was visibly shaking, staring at the fresh blood on the examination table. 'No! I can't do it!'

He fell to his knees weeping and buried his face in his hands. Boreas walked over and crouched beside him, the servos in his armour whining loudly as he did so. The boy looked up at him, tears streaming down his face, and shook his head.

'I am sorry,' he wailed. 'I have dishonoured you, and shamed my family, but I cannot do it.'

'What is your name?' Boreas's metal-edged voice echoed harshly around the chamber.

'Sanis, my lord,' the boy replied.

'It takes a brave man to know his limits, Sanis,' Boreas said. 'But a Space Marine of the Emperor must have no limits. You understand this?'

'I do,' said Sanis.

'Then follow me,' Boreas told the youth. He strode to the opposite side of the chamber and, delving his hand into well-concealed crack in the stone, activated a hidden switch. A section of the wall ground backwards out of sight, leaving a dark opening slightly taller than the Chaplain. Boreas motioned for Sanis to enter and the boy disappeared into the shadows, the Space Marine following him. He urged the boy further forward a few steps and transmitted a coded signal over his suit's comm unit. A dull red light flickered into life overhead.

They were in a chamber that stretched off into the darkness. The floor was littered with old bones, knee-deep in places. Eyeless skulls glowed ruddily in the gloom, staring at the aspirant.

'If you return to your family having failed this test, it will bring them dishonour,' Boreas told the boy, and the youth nodded in agreement. 'They would lose all status, most likely they would starve to death within the turning of a season. You will be beaten, bullied, scorned by your people.'

'It is true,' Sanis replied softly. 'I will take the test, I am sorry for being a coward.'

'It is too late to change your mind, you cannot refuse and then agree,' Boreas said. 'Your life, for what short time it will continue, will be full of misery and pain, and your return will doom your family. Though you have fallen at this hurdle, you were chosen to reach this far, and for that I give you credit and due honour. I will spare you and your family the wretchedness your refusal might incur.'

Boreas reached out and his gauntleted hand gripped the boy's neck. Even as the youth opened his mouth to speak, the Chaplain twisted his wrist, easily snapping Sanis's spine. Delicately, Boreas picked up the dead boy's limp form and carried him to the pile of bones and reverently laid him upon the top. He stepped back and bowed his head.

'May your soul be guarded from corruption and return again to serve the Emperor in a new life,' he intoned, kneeling and laying a hand upon the boy's chest. 'We will tell your people the truth – that you died during your trial and faced death bravely. They will be spared your shame.'

He turned on his heel and walked from the secret chamber, sending the signal to switch off the light as he did so. Stepping outside, he pressed the hidden switch again and the door ground back into place leaving no sign of the join.

The Interrogator-Chaplain turned to the last remaining youth and pointed at the slab. The aspirant had seen nothing that had happened in the other chamber, and his eyes showed more confidence than before.

'Do you submit yourself to the judgment of the Dark Angels?' he asked. The boy smiled and nodded.

VARSIN GAZED WITH wonder out of the armoured window of the Thunderhawk at the looming shape of the Dark Angels' starship hanging in orbit over Piscina V. Sharp-prowed and sleek, dominated by its massive engines, the *Blade of Caliban* looked like a space-borne predator. It was not so far from the truth; one of the fastest ships in the sector, the rapid strike vessel was built for extended patrols across dozens of explored and uncharted star systems, to respond with speed to any situation, and yet carried enough firepower to destroy anything of similar size.

Though considered small for a warp-capable vessel, it was nearly half a kilometre in length and could in theory carry half a company of Space Marines, although its primary function was to act as the Chapter's eyes and ears, the duty of transportation and war falling to the larger strike cruisers and immense battle barges.

Fully a third of the starship's length was taken up by its powerful plasma engines and the reactors to drive them, almost the entirety of the rest of the structure was pin-pricked with gun emplacements, scanning areas and launch bays. At the fore, the heavily armoured prow was pierced by the dark holes of its torpedo tubes. As they neared, the stars seemed to shimmer and there was a brief scattering of blue and purple light as they passed through the ship's void shields.

The other aspirant, Beyus, was strapped into one of the gunship's seats, heavily sedated. As he had been taken up into orbit above Piscina V, the shock had proven too much for him and he had begun sobbing and wailing, tearing at his eyes in disbelief.

It was not unusual for an aspirant from a feral world to suffer such catastrophic culture shock and Nestor had quietened him with a narcolepsia. If the boy did not recover his senses soon, he would be useless as a recruit and the techpriests would take him, scrub his mind of the traumas and turn him into a servitor so that he might still be of service to the Chapter.

The Thunderhawk passed into the shadow of the ship and powered its way to the landing bay. As darkness fell outside, Varsin turned away, eyes wide with excitement. The interior of the Thunderhawk was a mix of chapel and control deck, its arched alcoves filled with flickering screens and digital runepads, while an ornately embroidered banner covered the ceiling.

The Space Marines had discarded their helmets, and their backpacks were locked into stowage positions to recharge from the gunship's engines while their armour functioned on its own internal power source. Except for Hephaestus, who was in the cockpit piloting, they were all sitting with their heads bowed in prayer, each silently mouthing their own chosen catechisms to the Emperor and their primarch, Lion El'Jonson. Aware of the sub-dued mood, the boy quelled his excitement and seated himself at the rear end of the gunship, away from the intimidating presence of the Space Marines.

Soon light glared through the ports as the Thunder-hawk docked, accompanied by the clang of clamps sealing to the hull and bringing the craft safely inside the *Blade of Caliban*. Roused from their reverie, the Space Marines stood, and each backed onto his armour's power pack. With a hiss of hydraulics and the clank of locking mechanisms, automatic arms implanted the backpacks into their armour once more. They reached beneath the bench and picked up their helmets, uniformly carrying them under their left arm. As the assault ramp crashed down onto the decking, they filed out slowly into the docking bay. Techpriests and half-machine servitors moved to and fro, checking the Thunderhawk, giving praise to the Machine-God for its safe return and sprin-kling it with holy oils from heavy censers.

The Space Marines strode through the gathering crowd, Nestor carrying Beyus under his free arm, Varsin hurrying to keep up with his giant escort.

'Are not all of the star warriors like yourselves?' he asked. The boy's gaze was moving constantly, taking in every detail of the strange environment, alternating between surprise and dread. He pointed at the Chapter serfs who busied themselves around the flight bay – nor-mal humans who performed the hundreds of day-to-day functions of the Chapter on behalf of their Space Marine masters.

'There are very few of us,' Nestor replied as a group of robed functionaries scurried towards him. He passed the comatose Beyus to them and they carried him away. 'It is said that the Imperium of the Emperor holds more worlds than it does Space Marines. You have passed only the first tests, there are many more to come. Some do not survive, but those who fail and live to tell of it will serve the Chapter in other ways, as do these serfs.'

'More tests?' asked Varsin. 'When do they take place? How long before I can fight for the Emperor as a Space Marine?'

'Such impatience!' laughed Zaul. 'If, and it is only if, you become a Space Marine it takes years of training and surgery. I myself was twelve summers old when I was chosen, but I was eighteen before I received my black carapace.'

'What is that? Your armour?' asked Varsin.

'Yes and no,' said Nestor. 'Much of the years to come will be spent teaching you of the stars and worlds beyond the cloud, so that you might understand truly what is to become of you. My brethren in the apothecarion will change your body, making it grow strong like ours. You will be given new lungs to breathe poison, and a second heart so that your blood might continue to flow in the heat of battle despite grievous wounds. We will give you the precious gene-seed of the Lion, and his greatness will flow through your veins and be bound into your bones. You will feel no pain, you shall have the strength of ten men, you will see in the dark as clearly as day and you will hear an assassin's breath over the thunder of a storm. Lastly, you shall have the black carapace that melds your body to your armour so that you can wear it as you might a second skin.'

The boy was dumbstruck, incapable of even conceiving of the advanced gene-therapy and implantation process he would undergo. For him, such things were magical, the powers of the Emperor beyond the cloud, not for him to judge or understand.

'Not only shall your body be crafted into a living weapon of the Emperor's will,' added Boreas. 'Your mind must be trained also. You shall learn the Catechisms of Hate, the battle-prayers of the Chapter, the hymnals to the Lion. You must learn how to use the new organs that will grow inside your body, and control the rage you must feel when confronted with the alien, the traitor and the heretic. As your muscles grow, so shall your mental fortitude, so that like us you shall never know fear again, nor doubt nor compassion and mercy, for they are weaknesses a vile enemy will exploit.'

As he spoke the words, Boreas felt them ring hollow in his own heart. The legacy of Astelan's words still gnawed at him even now. Boreas knew himself guilty of all those things which he trained others to suppress – fear of himself and his own power, doubts of his own loyalty and motives, compassion and mercy for those his Chapter had sworn to destroy for ten thousand years. Like an open wound, his traitorous thoughts festered in his mind.

'Truly you are great. How blessed are we to have such lords!' gasped Varsin.

The Space Marines exchanged silent looks, for each knew of the pain and mental torture they had endured to become such superhumans. None of them could truly remember where they came from, or their family and friends. They were Space Marines of the Dark Angels Chapter; nothing less, nothing more. They lived only to serve the Emperor, honour their battle-brothers and protect mankind. Though they were the ultimate defenders of humanity, they themselves would never know true humanity again.

'Enough questions,' barked Boreas, annoyed at his own harmful introspection, causing Varsin to flinch and almost stumble. He glanced at the others but their faces betrayed no evidence that they sensed something was amiss. 'There will be questions enough when the Tower of Angels arrives in Piscina.'

IT TOOK SEVERAL days for the *Blade of Caliban* to return to Piscina IV. Unlike the feral fifth world, Piscina IV had maintained a veneer of civilisation through the Age of Strife, and when the Dark Angels had reclaimed the world during the Great Crusade, they had been welcomed with open arms by the humans living there. In many ways, Piscina was perfect for the Dark Angels' purposes. The barbaric warriors of the fifth planet provided excellent recruits – natural and hardy warriors that could only be found on such deathworlds, or in the savage depths of a hive-world. But the semi-cultured fourth world gave them a place for their outpost, a haven they could dwell in without interfering with the development of the tribesmen of Piscina V.

It was towards the capital, Kadillus Harbour, that the Thunderhawk gunship now descended. As the aircraft entered the upper atmosphere, Hephaestus called to Boreas to join him in the cockpit.

Through the armoured windshield, the Chaplain saw the massive oceans of the world and the thousands of scattered volcanic islands that ringed the planet in thousand kilometre-long chains. Almost all were still active and uninhabitable. The largest island, Kadillus itself, rose amongst those nearby, thousands of kilometres high and formed from five huge volcanoes. Long dormant, the same geo-thermal activity that had created such a world now provided the inhabitants with much of their power, and Boreas could see the thermal venting from the power stations hanging as a thick haze over the island, obscuring the ground below the tips of the volcanoes.

'Sergeant Damas at our keep has re-directed an emergency comms signal from Colonel Brade,' Hephaestus told the Interrogator-Chaplain. Brade was the commander of the Imperial Guard forces stationed on Piscina for the last few years, ever since an ork invasion had almost conquered the world. Pockets of orks still held out in the wilderness areas, and despite regular cleanse and burn operations to destroy the spores left by the greenskin aliens, never would Piscina be free from the threat of their wild attacks.

'Thunderhawk communication,' Boreas commanded the comms pick-up in his armour, which was then boosted by the gunship's longer ranged array. 'This is Interrogator-Chaplain Boreas, how may we be of assistance, colonel?'

'Lord Boreas, there is a serious ork attack under way at Vartoth,' Brade's crackling voice told him. Vartoth was one of the old mine heads, disused now, but for a warren of buildings and underground tunnels. Boreas realised immediately that if the orks were allowed to establish themselves there, it would take nothing short of a full-scale assault to drive them out.

'Please be more specific, colonel,' Boreas said, shaking his head slightly with unconscious disapproval.

'We estimate that nearly five hundred orks have broken through the perimeter walls of the complex, and have holed up in the mine buildings,' Brade explained. 'I have three infantry platoons already at the battle zone, and three armoured fist platoons en route, but the greenskins will be well and truly dug in by the time they arrive. The orks seem to be very well armed somehow. Please assist.'

Brade's men were currently outnumbered, Boreas calculated quickly, and despite the armoured personnel carriers and light support tanks of the armoured fist platoon, they would find it hard to establish any foothold with which to launch a concerted effort on the mine head.

'Of course, Colonel Brade,' said Boreas. He glanced at Hephaestus, who had been listening in on the exchange. The Techmarine manipulated the controls of one of the displays and brought up a tactical schematic.

'We will be with you inside ten minutes, colonel,' Hephaestus told the Imperial Guard commander, checking the digital map.

'Be ready to push forward when we arrive,' Boreas warned.

'I am a kilometre south of the mine head, I await your arrival,' Brade said. 'We shall discuss how best you can assist.'

'You misunderstand me, colonel,' replied Boreas. 'We will commence an immediate assault, please have your troops prepared to exploit any breakthrough.'

'Oh, I...' Brade stammered. 'Of course, we shall start our advance immediately and will be prepared to provide additional troops on your arrival.'

'Thank you, Colonel Brade,' Boreas replied before he cut the comm-link and looked at Hephaestus. 'Engage machine-spirit to take us in. Open the armoury and distribute jump packs.'

'Understood,' replied the Techmarine with a nod. His large hands danced quickly over the controls of the gunship before he stood up and made his way to the armoured section at the back of the Thunderhawk. Controlled by its own artificial mind, the gunship steered its way down through the clouds towards Vartoth.

The young aspirants huddled in the corner watching the Space Marines preparing for battle, plugging each other into their jump packs and tightening the grip-harnesses. The jump packs were even bulkier than a normal power plant backpack, most of their mass taken up with two flared engines designed to allow the wearer to bound through the air at high speed. They fixed their helmets and drew bolters from the weapons rack, while Boreas opened his small reliquary and brought forth his power sword.

He tested the activation stud and the long blade was enveloped by a shimmering blue haze of energy, capable of shattering armourplas and slicing though bone. Satisfied that all was in working order, he sheathed the sword and took out his rosarius, the symbol of his position. The ornate badge was wrought in the shape of a square set with a glinting ruby which doubled as projector for the compact force field generator contained within. Taking the winged-skull key from the reliquary, he fitted it to the rosarius and it hummed into life.

'Approaching drop zone,' warned Hephaestus from the cockpit and Boreas nodded to him.

'Check seals, clear for debarking,' the Interrogator-Chaplain told the squad and they assembled in single file in the belly of the gunship, facing towards the forward assault ramp. He walked over to Varsin and Sanis, who were dwarfed by the warriors around them, sitting silently in bewilderment near to the cockpit.

'Strap yourselves in tightly, we would rather you were not harmed before we get you to the keep,' he told them, pointing at the safety harnesses hanging from the inside of the hull. 'The Thunderhawk will take you to safety once we are gone. Do not attempt to rise from this position even when you have landed. The Thunderhawk may be recalled at any moment and it could prove unfortunate if you were not secure at that time.'

Both the aspirants nodded meekly. They had soon learned of the Dark Angels' discipline aboard the *Blade of Caliban*, and knew that they had to obey every order to the letter.

'Lowering ramp,' Hephaestus said, activating the gunship's hydraulics when he saw that the boys were safely secured in the crash harnesses.

'What will become of us?' asked Varsin shrilly. 'Can we not come with you when you land?'

'Land?' laughed Zaul. 'That would take too long. You'll not be following us anywhere, just stay in the Thunderhawk and you'll be safe.'

The roar of the engines grew to deafening proportions as the ramp opened and revealed the grey-blue of the Piscinan sky. Wind whipped into the gunship's interior and the boys grabbed the straps tightly as it blew their hair and lashed at their faces. The ground could be seen screaming past some hundred metres below, and Boreas looked at the others from the front of the column.

'Weapons check complete?' he asked, and they responded in unison. Breaking into a run, Boreas threw himself down the ramp. 'For the Emperor! Glory to the Lion!'

The Interrogator-Chaplain hurled himself off the end of the assault ramp and into the sky, the others quickly

following. Above them the Thunderhawk banked sharply
away from the conflict zone, its semi-sentient machine-
spirit guiding it to a safe landing zone to await recall by
Hephaestus.

A burst of fire from his jump pack slowed Boreas's
decent for a couple of seconds and his lighting-fast mind
assessed the scene below. The Vartoth facility was a group
of five buildings clustered around the mine head itself. A
high curtain wall had been breached to the north, the
rubble strewn across the rockcrete apron within.

Muzzle flare and las-bolts flickered in the darkening
twilight as the orks within the buildings exchanged fire
with the Guardsmen desperately trying to force their way
through the gate and the gap in the wall. But the humans
were pinned down, there was little cover for them to
shelter behind once they got inside the wall and the
ground was dotted with dead and wounded.

Inside the compound, the buildings were mostly three
and four-storey rectangles of grey ferrocrete, pitted by
erosion and cracked in many places from subsidence in
the over-mined ground beneath them. There were orks at
every glassless window, firing wildly at the Imperial
Guard, spraying the courtyard with bullets and spent
shell casings. The greatest concentration of fire seemed to
be coming from a ten-storey tower to Boreas's left.

'Nestor, Zaul, with me to the left!' he commanded.
'Hephaestus, Thumiel, take the pump house to the right.'

The ground rushed up to meet the squad and they fired
their jump packs just before landing. Even with the retro-
thrust they all landed heavily, their boots cracking the
rockcrete ground with the impact.

Boreas drew his sword and thumbed the power blade
into life whilst drawing his bolt pistol from his belt with
his left hand. They had landed in the middle of the fire-
fight and bullets and lasfire whistled around their heads
as the squad split and headed off towards their objectives
at a pounding run.

A bullet zinged off Boreas's left shoulder plate and he turned slightly and returned fire at the fanged face of the ork who had shot him. Three bolts flared across the gap in a single burst of fire, and the wall of the building exploded into dust and shrapnel as their explosive tips detonated a moment after impact.

The ork was flung back with shards of ferrocrete in its face, its gun tumbling from dead fingers.

As Zaul and Nestor gave him covering fire, Boreas ran towards the door to the tower. More bullets zipped harmlessly off his armour as he sprinted forward, and his bolt pistol barked continuously with his return fire.

The whole front of the tower was now pock-marked with bolt craters, and several of the brutish aliens hung dead out of the windows. Suddenly a rocket smoked across the courtyard from one of the other buildings and a tremendous explosion shook the ground close by. Zaul was hurled from his feet by the detonation and clattered loudly to the ground. Nestor spun and hurled a grenade across the open space through one of the windows, his aim rewarded with a billow of fire and smoke from the occupied building, and a scattering of dark blood and green flesh showered out of the opening.

Zaul pushed himself to his feet, firing his bolter one-handed at the tower's windows, his right shoulder pad ripped away. The twisted actuators sparked and whirred as they malfunctioned, and thick blood oozed from a crack in Zaul's upper arm. Nestor glanced at the injury but Zaul waved him away.

'Heal me later, Apothecary,' the battle-brother insisted, gripping his bolter in both hands and starting forward again.

'A scratch like that doesn't need my attention,' Nestor replied with a deep laugh.

The door to the tower was made of sturdy wood, but was no barrier for the power-armoured Boreas. A single kick from his booted foot splintered it in half and tore the hinges out, sending the door crashing onto the orks inside. The Interrogator-Chaplain's power sword blazed as he swung it left and right, lopping off heads and limbs with easy blows. The orks mobbed him, battered at his armour with the butts of their stolen guns, but were thrown back as his rosarius burst into life, blinding them with its white glare.

Boreas blew the head off another ork with a close range shot from his bolt pistol, while behind him Zaul and Nestor battered their way through the green-skinned aliens with their fists, smashing bones and tearing at flesh with their inhumanly strong hands. The orks were no weaklings, their slab-like muscles more than capable of viciously wounding a normal man, their tusks and claws capable of tearing flesh from the bone. But they were as children when matched against the armoured might of the Dark Angels.

The Space Marines cleared the ground floor quickly, stepping over the piled bodies of the dead aliens to blast at those behind. Zaul cleared the stairwell with a few well-placed bolter salvoes, and their hold was secured for the moment.

The other two Space Marines looked at Boreas and he nodded at Zaul. Ramming a fresh magazine into his bolter, the battle-brother started up the stairs. Almost instantly, volleys of fire rained down on him, scoring deep grooves into his armour and sending flecks of paint swirling in a cloud around him. Settling to one knee, he returned fire, the bodies of two orks plummeting down from the landing above to land at Boreas's feet. One shook its head dizzily before the blazing tip of Boreas's sword caved in its skull.

With covering fire from Zaul, Boreas and Nestor stormed up the steps, their bolt pistols roaring in the close confines of the stairwell. The orks fell back before the assault, retreating into the two rooms either side of the landing, and Boreas paused to pull a fragmentation grenade from his belt. Nestor followed suit, and they tossed them through the doorways simultaneously.

Even as the grenades detonated, the Space Marines rushed the landing, sprinting through the smoke and shrapnel, the flashes of their guns like blossoms of fire in the dusty haze. Reeling and coughing, the orks were stunned by the attack, as shots from Boreas's bolt pistol punched a hole through the skull of one and ripped through the thigh of another. Recovering, the green-skinned aliens hurled themselves at the Chaplain, smashing at him with their guns and trying to prise an opening in his armour with their knives. Four clung on to his armour, trying to drag him down.

The first was hurled back as a bolt exploded in its stomach, and the second stumbled away clutching its face as Boreas head-butted it squarely between the eyes. A short kick stove in the chest of the third, and the fourth was quickly despatched by a blow from Boreas's sword, which ripped its jaw clean off and threw the alien across the room. There were eight more orks in the room, but as they prepared to charge, Zaul appeared at Boreas's side and tossed a grenade forward. Two were shredded instantly in the blast, the others hurled to the ground. With bolter and pistol, the two Space Marines quickly despatched the survivors.

Floor by floor, the Space Marines waded bloodily through the orks. Boreas's armour was cracked and dented in dozens of places by the time they had cleared the top floor, and underneath it his thick blood had congealed over cuts and gashes to his arms and legs. After a few gory minutes, not a single ork was left alive within the tower.

Boreas glanced out of one of the windows to see the Imperial Guard swarming over the courtyard, firing up at the windows of the other buildings now that the deadly crossfire had been stopped.

'Progress report,' Boreas signalled the other two Space Marines who had attacked to the right on landing.

'Pump house clear, Imperial Guard have secured mine head, little resistance remaining,' Thumiel told him.

'Understood, withdraw to the courtyard and regroup,' Boreas transmitted to the squad.

Dust and smoke clogged the air inside the compound, but through his auto-senses Boreas could see Colonel Brade clearly, directing the extermination operation from just inside the gateway.

The Imperial commander looked up as the giant figures loomed out of the murk, his expression guarded. The Space Marines' armour was pitted and scarred, the paint scraped away in places, dents and cracks all over their bodies. One of Boreas's eye-lenses had been cracked by a point-blank shot from an autogun, and the colonel could see the mechanical probes from the helmet punched into the flesh around his eye. Breaking his stare, he offered a hand to Boreas.

'Many thanks for your help, Lord Boreas,' Brade said. The Interrogator-Chaplain's fist dwarfed the colonel's hand as he shook it.

'Your gratitude is welcome, but the death of the Emperor's enemies is reward enough,' Boreas replied, staring over the colonel's shoulder.

'Of course, of course it is,' agreed Brade, dropping his hand to his side and glancing backwards at the telltale jets of the approaching Thunderhawk closing in. He turned his gaze to the Techmarine who was guiding the craft back to its masters.

'I am confident that you and your men are capable of dealing with the current situation,' Boreas stated, looking at Brade once more.

'Yes, there's relatively few orks left now. We just need to burn the bodies to prevent them shedding more spores,' the colonel agreed. 'However, these attacks are becoming more frequent and more organised. Might I ask again when your esteemed Chapter will be able to spare more battle-brothers to aid us in our efforts?'

'When the Tower of Angels returns, Master Azrael will be notified of the situation here and will make his decision.' Boreas replied firmly. Though always respectful and well meaning, Brade's frequent requests for more Dark Angels to be stationed on Piscina were beginning to wear Boreas's patience. He had explained numerous times that Space Marines were not intended to garrison worlds en masse, and were it not for the recruiting world of Piscina V, the Imperial Guard would have been left to defend the planet on their own without even the aid of Boreas and his squad.

'I understand. I'll contact the Departmento Munitorium again with a request for more troops,' the colonel replied, looking away with disappointment.

'Good, then I will bid you goodbye.' Boreas turned and signalled for the others to leave as the roar of the approaching Thunderhawk's jets drowned out the crackle of flames and sporadic gunfire.

THE TALE OF ASTELAN
PART TWO

ASTELAN COULD NOT guess how long he had been chained to the slab in the cell. Boreas had visited him eleven times, that much he knew. Sometimes the psyker had been with him, at other times he had been alone.

His body was scarred with burns and cuts from the Interrogator-Chaplain's attentions. He had cut away parts of Astelan's black carapace to probe and bleed the exposed flesh beneath.

Hunger gnawed at Astelan, his throat was parched, his lips cracked, his mind dulled and fatigued. But he would not let himself sleep. He would show no weakness. In the moments of respite he was granted, he would fall into a meditative trance, allowing the pain to wash away from his body, leaving his mind clear. He was determined not to submit to them, for to do so would be the greatest betrayal of all.

Every ideal and principle Astelan believed in told him this was the true way, that it was his captors who were in the wrong. It was they who were ignorant and deluded, shackled by those who were scared of their power. It mattered not whether Astelan died or lived, he would stay true to the cause for which he had been created.

On his twelfth visit, the Interrogator-Chaplain was alone once more. He brought with him a goblet of water, which Astelan thirstily gulped down, ignoring the chilling spills across his face and throat. Next, he took the bread Boreas proffered him in torn chunks, mustering the strength to chew and swallow, though pain flared in the back of his dehydrated throat. When he finished, Boreas took a phial from inside his robe and sprinkled liquid on Astelan's wounds. The stinging wracked his body at first, but the pain subsided after several minutes.

'We must let the body recover, for it is weaker than the soul,' Boreas said, standing next to Astelan with his arms crossed. 'While the impure soul endures, the body must also endure.'

'Then you must preserve my physical shell for eternity,' replied Astelan. 'I will never submit to your misguided logic, your errant ways.'

'Tell me of Tharsis,' Boreas asked, ignoring Astelan's defiance.

'What of it?' Astelan replied with a shrug.

'I would know how a world could be so subverted from the service of the Emperor,' Boreas told him, walking to the shelves and picking up one of the blades that lay there.

'I did not subvert Tharsis, it was I who saved it,' protested Astelan.

'I do not believe you,' Boreas snorted, toying with the knife. 'You brought damnation upon that world.'

'No, that is not true, not true at all,' Astelan denied, shaking his head. 'I saved Tharsis from itself.'

'Tell me how such a feat could be accomplished,' Boreas said as he returned the knife to its place and walked to the interrogation slab, standing so that Astelan could only see his face.

'I arrived on Tharsis eighty years ago,' Astelan began. 'It was a beautiful world of high mountains and grassy plains, not unlike dozens of other worlds that I have seen in my long life. But that beauty hid a dark canker. The world was in turmoil, gripped by a vicious civil war.'

'A war that you began!' Boreas spat, crashing a fist down onto the stone table next to Astelan's head.

'No, I swear by the Emperor that it was not so!' Astelan argued, turning his head as far as possible to look up at his interrogator. 'We came for supplies. Tharsis is on the edge of wilderness space, self-sufficient and far from the claws of those who have turned the Imperium into a mockery of the Emperor's dream.'

'You said "we". Who else was with you?' Boreas's voice dripped with suspicion.

'I travelled for a century and a half before I came upon Tharsis and its woes,' explained Astelan. 'In that time, fate saw fit for my journey to cross with that of two others like myself. But we argued at Tharsis. They would not join me in my mission to deliver the planet from the tyrants who attempted to usurp the Emperor's rule.'

'They abandoned you there? Disloyalty even amongst your own kind, is there nothing so base?' Boreas scoffed.

'I let them go with goodwill,' Astelan replied with a slight shake of his head. 'Though they did not care to share the task I had set myself, I knew I had found a purpose again, a chance to do that for which I was created.'

'Which was?' Boreas asked.

'To fight for the Emperor, of course!' Astelan's hands subconsciously balled into fists and the chains creaked under the flexing of his muscles. 'The others left, but I remained on Tharsis. At first it was impossible to tell friend from foe, but I soon learned to mark them apart. Secessionism, heresy, rebellion, call it what you will, had taken hold. They had divided the population with grand, empty speeches of fraternity and equality. They defied the Imperial commander, and subverted members of his military. The war had waged for a year before I arrived.'

'A strange coincidence that such strife should herald your arrival.' Boreas made no attempt to hide his disbelief. His accusation was clear – Astelan had started the war.

'Not coincidence, fortuitous destiny,' the prisoner argued. 'Whatever it is that controls our fates had seen fit to bring me to Tharsis in its time of need. How could I not intervene? During the Great Crusade, eighty worlds fell to my Chapter for resisting the wisdom and rule of the Emperor. Eighty worlds! And here was another chance to prove myself.'

'What did you think you could do, a lone Space Marine in a worldwide conflict?' Boreas demanded, straightening again and pacing away from the slab. He glanced back at Astelan as he spoke. 'Such arrogance is unbecoming of a Space Marine.'

'No, not arrogance, it was a sense of purpose,' Astelan replied, his gaze following the pacing Chaplain. 'My heart told me that I would make a difference, and I did.'

'And how did you manage such a thing?' Boreas said, his back to Astelan so that his low voice echoed off the cell walls.

'At first I simply fought the rebels where I found them, but they were ill-trained and poorly equipped,' Astelan told him. 'It was more a just execution than a battle. But soon, I joined with others fighting for the Emperor. They welcomed me with cheers and cries of joy when I fought by their side at Kaltan Town, breaking through the enemy with bolter and fist.'

'Were they not surprised?' Boreas asked, turning to stare at his prisoner, arms crossed over his chest. 'Were their suspicions not aroused by a lone Space Marine?'

'They saw me for what I am, a warrior of the Emperor,' Astelan explained patiently. 'They took great heart from my presence. They were bolstered to know that I fought on their side, confirming the justice of their cause.'

'So you set yourself up as a symbol to be worshipped? You saw fit to replace the Emperor in their hearts and minds.' Disgust was written over Boreas's face as he considered this grievous sin.

'Must you twist everything I say?' growled Astelan, looking away with contempt. 'Have your own endeavours become so hollow that you now seek to belittle the achievements of those who still fight for the true cause?'

'Your cause was blatant megalomania!' snapped Boreas, striding forward. 'You sought nothing more than to achieve your own ambition. A former Chapter commander, stripped of everything, you lusted after that power again!'

'Power? I will tell you of power,' Astelan said in a terse whisper. 'My word is the word of the Emperor himself. My sword is his sword. Every battle I have fought has been in his name. He had a vision – to drive back the aliens and the mutants, to unite mankind under his rule and guidance. He strove for humanity, to take back the stars that had once been ours, a vision we had thrown away for petty-minded goals and the worship of technology. From the ashes of the Age of Strife, the Emperor arose to lead us back into the galaxy, to conquer the stars and to safeguard our future. He alone saw this, and it was the Emperor who created us to fulfil his vision. It was we, the Space Marines, who were to be the instrument of creation. It was our duty, our whole purpose, to forge the Emperor's dream into a reality.'

'And yet, at the end, you turned on him and threatened everything you had shed blood to build.' Boreas's voice was filled with sadness rather than anger.

'The first betrayal was not ours!' protested Astelan.

'And Tharsis?' Boreas stooped low and spoke quietly into Astelan's ear. 'What has this to do with your enslavement of a world? The Great Crusade was ten millennia ago.'

'And in that statement, you confirm your ignorance,' Astelan replied, staring into the Chaplain's eyes. 'The Great Crusade was not intended to be an event; it is a state of mind. The crusade never finishes, it is never complete while there is an alien alive to threaten our worlds, and while discord lingers in the heart of the Imperium.'

'And so you continued the fight on Tharsis?' Boreas's voice was now little more than a whisper from the darkness as he stepped back out of Astelan's sight.

'Yes, and as I did so, I rallied support around me,' Astelan exclaimed proudly. 'In time, I had an audience with Imperial Commander Dax himself. He had heard of the victories I had won in the Emperor's name, and he was overjoyed.'

'And so your ego was flattered and the sin of pride grew in you.' Boreas's haunting whisper seemed to come from every direction, resonating off the walls like a crowd of accusers.

'I never sought aggrandisement, but I admit I was glad of the praise,' Astelan said, moving his head from side to side, trying to catch a glimpse of Boreas. 'You cannot know what it is like to be abandoned, scorned by those who were once allies. I had been lost, I was searching for a way to regain my place, and on Tharsis I found it.'

'But there is still a long way from renowned warrior to despot.'

'Your insults deserve only contempt, they only prove your lack of character and woeful ignorance,' Astelan spat, tired of the Chaplain's attempts to disorientate and confuse him. 'Though we had won some battles, there was still much to be done if we were to prevail over the rebels. Though I was the greatest warrior on Tharsis, even I could not achieve victory by myself.'

'How modest of you, to accept such limitations.'

'If you listen, instead of poorly attempting to mock me at every instant, then you might gain understanding,' Astelan said slowly, resting his head back against the slab and staring at the ceiling. He cast his mind back to the first days he had spent on Tharsis. 'On my own I could not win the war purely by martial effort. But my skills, my knowledge, could still save Tharsis from the renegades. I handed my weapons over to the Imperial commander's tech-priests so that they might study them and turn the munitions factories over to production of superior arms. I had the hundred best soldiers sent to me at the capital. There I trained them in everything I knew. For half a year, I pushed and pushed them. Many did not survive, and at first there were doubts. The Imperial commander had full faith in me, but his aides expressed concerns over my methods. Their self-importance was galling – who were they, bureaucrats and priests, to argue with a Chapter commander of the Dark Angels on military matters? I ignored them, and the protests were silenced when I led my elite company into battle for the first time. They were not Space Marines – five of my battle-brothers could have achieved what those sixty men did – but they were better equipped and more deadly than anything the rebels had faced before. We stormed one of the strongholds in the Sezen-uan Mountains. For five hundred and seventeen days the Emperor's loyal forces had besieged the fortress; we took it in a single night.'

'Yes, I remember facing your so-called sacred bands when we retook Tharsis. Fanatical, courageous, they were worthy opponents.'

'Worthy indeed!' agreed Astelan. 'Fifty-one of the first sacred band survived the assault, and I sent them out to the other regiments to each train a hundred men, and those that survived to train a hundred more. As the number of sacred bands grew, the demand for bolters, ammunition, carapace armour, grenades and other weapons stretched the factories beyond capacity. The Imperial commander implemented my recommendation that we build more, for what use is farmland when the foe's hand is at your throat?'

There was silence in the cell for a moment before Boreas's disembodied voice replied.

'Perhaps to feed those you were protecting?' the Chaplain suggested. 'When we liberated Tharsis from your tyranny, you had turned it into a wasteland. The sprawling factory-cities you had built were rife with destitution and crime. Is that what you bring for humanity?'

'It was a means to an end, not the end itself,' Astelan explained. 'Do not judge me on this, I have seen the Imperium you protect. Hive-worlds covered in desolate ash wastes, the populace crammed into kilometre-high spires like insects, labouring every hour, leeching every last handful of resource from their dead worlds to supply other planets with metal ore, machine parts, chemicals. And, of course, weapons and warriors for the armies of the Emperor.'

'It is through mutual need that the Imperium is held together,' said Boreas. 'Each planet dependent upon another for food, or machines, or protection.'

'And that is its weakness, for it is a fragile structure,' declared Astelan, sitting up again as far as he could, filled with a resurgence of energy. 'Self-serving Imperial commanders compete with each other, risking the defence of the Emperor's domains to further their own ends. The most heavily guarded system can fall if its neighbours are overrun, its food or water supplies taken away. It is a teetering labyrinth supported by self-interest and mutual fear, no longer driven by the great ideal that drove us to create it.'

'And this was the new way you were showing on Tharsis?'

'No, I am a warrior when all is said and done, with a warrior's instincts,' confessed Astelan. 'Though we were winning battles, it was destroying Tharsis. Yes, the factories spread and we began to conscript the citizens into the army, but it was needed for the war. As our strength grew, so our enemies became more cunning. They did not seek open battle, they clawed at us from their hiding places, sowing terror and uncertainty. From fastnesses in the wilderness they struck at our supplies, bombed our factories and killed our people. No matter where our armies were, they were never big enough to root them all out, and the victories died away to be replaced by stale-mate. We would find a cadre of rebels and crush it, they would slink into the towns and attack the factories and barracks. The larger the army grew, the more guns were needed, the more ration distribution centres, recruitment bases and supply convoys. And as these grew, so we needed more troops to protect them.'

'Your own ambition had become its sole purpose, your desire to rule fuelling itself.'

Astelan ignored the Chaplain's statement. 'The war dragged on for eight more years,' he continued. 'The army leaders were vague, the Imperial commander and his aides became passionless. Though we killed thousands of rebels every year, there were always more foolish and misguided souls to replace them. They had lost faith in the cause we were fighting for, the glory of the Emperor mired in the tribulations of battle and survival. The war had become an end in itself, not the victory.'

'And so what happened?' asked Boreas. 'Your authority was absolute when we toppled you from power.'

'You deliberately misrepresent events,' said Astelan with a sigh. 'I grew sick of the slaughter of the people I had slaved to free from those terrible times.'

'Times you yourself created.' Boreas's low voice was now just behind Astelan, he could feel the Chaplain's breath on his scalp.

'Have you not listened to a word I have said?' Astelan snapped with growing exasperation. 'You must now see why we fought you when you attacked. A whole genera-tion of Tharsians died so that their descendants could fulfil their place in the Emperor's vision, they could not stand idle while you took it from them.'

'And so you took it upon yourself to take control, to usurp the Imperial commander and bring Tharsis your version of enlightenment,' Boreas said.

'No, not at first,' Astelan replied before stopping to cough, his throat dry. He heard movement behind him and Boreas's hand appeared with the goblet, filled with water. Astelan could not reach to take it, and the Chaplain dribbled the contents onto Astelan's parched lips. Gulping down the refreshing water, Astelan savoured the moment before continuing. 'Long had I advised the generals and colonels, but often they did not heed the wisdom of my experience. They continually doubted me, told me that what I asked of the army could only be expected of Space Marines. They were the old arguments, and though I spoke to them of striving towards greatness, of forging a new world in the crucible of battle, my impassioned pleas fell on deaf ears. It was after one of our regiments was ambushed and all but wiped out in the passes of Tharzox that Imperial Commander Dax appointed me commander of Tharsis's loyal armies. I swore an oath to him that under my leadership, I would bring him victory within a year.'

'A bold claim… Another sign of your conceit perhaps?' Boreas said, accompanied by the scrape of metal on stone as he placed the goblet on the floor.

'An achievable goal, now that I had been given supreme authority and direct control,' answered Astelan. 'My first act was to execute the existing army commanders. They were old planetary nobility, bred to hunt game and attend extravagant banquets, not to lead men in battle. I replaced them with the best leaders from my sacred bands, men who were strong and capable, men with keen minds and iron discipline. I knew that to win the war against the renegades, there would be hard fighting ahead, and the men I chose to lead in my name were utterly loyal to the Emperor, men who would command without doubt and follow without question.'

'And did you fulfil your oath?' asked Boreas from the shadows.

'I did, within two hundred and fifty days,' Astelan declared proudly. 'The old regime had been weak and short-sighted. Their narrow minds were unable to comprehend the final goal, to understand the necessity of hardship and sacrifice. They had baulked at some of my measures, never truly understanding the ultimate goal of victory. Those two hundred and fifty days were full of turmoil and trauma; blood flowed and there was much suffering. But it was necessary for the future of Tharsis. If I had acted as my predecessors, the war would still be continuing, the people of Tharsis forced to live a half-life in subservience and fear. It would have been a long, slow death for the world.'

'And so you found a harsh cure for this planetary malady?' Boreas's voice was now tinged with anger, Astelan could hear the Chaplain breathing more deeply. 'You, their self-appointed saviour, led them out of the darkness.'

'And dark it was,' agreed Astelan, choosing to ignore the accusation in the Chaplain's statement. 'My commanders were brutal in the execution of my orders. Misguided tolerance had bred weakness, and my command was to show no mercy. We razed the breeding grounds of the rebels, burnt down the holes where they hid, executed their kin and those who supported them with their inaction. Though I am not proud of what I was forced to do, and there was much opposition from Dax's court, the Imperial commander gave me his full support. At that time, he alone could see my intent and understood what was necessary. I will not deny the fact that it was a pogrom of fearsome scale, and many that might have been judged innocent were executed without recourse to considered judgment. But they were exceptional times, the people of Tharsis had to be shown the way, they had to understand that life under the rule of

the Emperor is not given freely, it is earned with sacrifice
– sacrifice of personal freedom, of labour and, when
needed, of blood. Tharsis burned for two hundred and
fifty days, as the cleansing continued. But on that last
day, as I personally led my sacred bands on the attack,
Tharsis's freedom was won!'

Astelan paused for breath, he was panting and sweating hard. While he had spoken, he had become more
animated, as much as the bonds around his limbs and
body allowed.

'You were not there,' he said to Boreas, interpreting the
Chaplain's silence as disbelief. 'How can you understand
our elation at the final victory, when you are so passionless, so devoid of life? We had driven them back for
month after month, until we had forced them to make a
last stand at the coast of the northern seas. Four thousand of them, that was all that remained. At my back
were fifty thousand warriors, with me at the fore were
twenty thousand of the sacred bands. There was nowhere
for them to escape this time, nowhere to run, no lair to
hide in. They were surrounded and we showed them no
mercy. They fought well, to their credit, and not one of
them attempted to surrender.'

'Would it have mattered?' Boreas asked.

'Not at all,' Astelan replied bluntly, his shrug making
the chains around him rattle dully. 'They knew they were
condemned to die, and they chose to die fighting. It took
less than an hour, as the shells rained down and the
sacred bands charged. I myself accounted for one hundred and eight of them. One hundred and seven I killed
in battle, and at the end, Vazturan, greatest of my commanders and worshipped by the troops, brought me the
last of the rebels, still alive. I remember, he was young,
no more than twenty years old. He was wounded, shot in
the arm, his face bloodied. His scalp was shaved and he
had been tattooed with the symbols of the rebellion –
the raven's head, the inverted aquila. I took him to the

edge of the cliffs, and my army gathered round in their tens of thousands, many of them standing on tanks to get a view, jostling and scuffling with each other in their attempts to see a glimpse of the death of the last Tharsian renegade. I tossed the youth off the cliff onto the jagged rocks below and a great cheer welled up from the army. Such a noise equalled the victory chants of my Chapter when we conquered Muapre Primus.'

'A cause for great celebration, I can see,' Boreas snarled, stepping out of the darkness, showing true emotion for the first time since he had arrived. The Interrogator-Chaplain unfolded his arms and took a step closer to Astelan. Without warning he lashed out, the back of his hand crashing across Astelan's face. The pain was momentary, but it was not supposed to hurt. It was an insult, a blow one would use to chastise an aspirant. The attack was filled with contempt, and conveyed Boreas's feelings more than any words could.

'I know what you did!' the Interrogator-Chaplain bellowed, his mouth right by Astelan's ear. 'There was an Administratum census-taker on Tharsis less than a decade before you arrived, before there was any war, before your bloodthirsty regime. The records we examined listed the population of Tharsis at just less than eight hundred million people. When you took power, you kept very good records. You listed your soldiers, the workers, the supervisors and their families. Your sacred bands controlled everything, and it was all noted down. I saw those records before I left. You were right to say a generation gave its life for you. Your own scribes estimated the population to be between two hundred and two hundred and fifty million, a quarter of the people you proclaim to have saved!'

'The war had its costs, sacrifices were made; do you not understand?' Astelan shouted back at him.

'You, an oath-breaker, a traitor to your own primarch, are guilty of genocide on a massive scale.' The Chaplain's voice had dropped to a venomous hiss.

'And you can say this with a clear conscience?' spat Astelan. 'The Dark Angels have no blood on their hands?'

'Oh, I agree that battle and sacrifice result in death,' Boreas replied with a grimace. 'I understand that we live in a brutal universe, and that amongst the unnumbered souls of the Imperium, a few million deaths are immeasurably minute. The Dark Angels have purged worlds that are beyond all attempts at redemption, and we have done it with joy for we know what we do is for the security of the future. Truly it is said that a moment of laxity spawns a lifetime of heresy.'

'Then you understand me!' Astelan felt a glimmer of joy. For the first time in two centuries, he thought that perhaps there were still those of enough mettle to forge an Imperium worthy of the Emperor. Perhaps the Dark Angels had not sunk so low as the others had taught him. 'You admit that you were wrong to attack me.'

'Never!' Boreas snapped, gripping Astelan's face in both hands, his mouth twisted in a feral snarl. 'Three hundred million Tharsians died after the war was declared over, when you usurped power. You had tasted blood, and you wanted more. You were depraved and vicious, delighting in the fear of those you ruled over! Those who did not serve in your sacred bands lived in terror, that was how you maintained rule. There was no shared vision of the great Imperium, no collective effort to serve the Emperor. There were two million hired killers and two hundred million terrified slaves! How could a Chapter commander have fallen so low? Or perhaps you have always been like this. Perhaps blood-hungry maniacs were needed during the Great Crusade.'

'They were right, ten thousand years without the Emperor has made you weak,' Astelan dismissed the Chaplain's accusations and turned his head away.

'Who?' Boreas demanded.

'The others of my kind who I met on my long journey, the ones who had been in your universe longer than myself. I learnt much from them,' explained Astelan.

'And was Horus weak when he led his Legions against the Emperor, or was he strong because he left slaughter and devastation in his wake?' said Boreas, releasing his hold and stepping away.

'You compare me to the cursed Warmaster?' Astelan turned his head back to glare at Boreas. 'You think that I wanted those deaths, that I craved the spilling of blood?'

'I think the guilt of what you have done, the sins you have committed, have driven you mad,' Boreas said. 'You have lost your judgment, you were never fit to command a Chapter, and when your failings were exposed, you sought to hide behind bloodshed and horror. Did their screams block out the voices that cursed you for a renegade? Did the blood of three hundred million lives you yourself claim you were protecting wash away the stain of treachery?'

'What we fought for so hard, I could not risk losing again,' Astelan explained, resting his head back against the slab, staring at the featureless rock of the ceiling. 'I could not countenance another betrayal such as we suffered on Caliban. I had to guard against doubt, against the rumours and whispers that eat away at men's hearts and erode their will to rise up and claim what is theirs.'

'And so you rose up and claimed what was yours, is that how it transpired?' Boreas asked.

'When the war was over, the celebrations continued for a long time, but as ever, the people's euphoria passed eventually,' Astelan said, saddened by the memory. Though he was aware of the weakness of normal men, he could not truly understand it. 'How soon the Tharsians forgot what bound them together, when there was no enemy left for them to fight. There were murmurings against what had happened, nothing that you could trace or prove, but a swell of discontent. They started doubting

the validity of keeping the sacred bands armed, igno-
rantly claiming that because the war with the rebels was
over, there was no need to maintain such an army. They
didn't understand that winning the war for Tharsis was
the first step on the road to greater glories. Forged in battle, the sacred bands were an army fit for the Emperor.
The spirit of the Great Crusade still burned inside me,
and here was a force that was worthy to take up the man-
tle that so many others had discarded.'

'You wanted to embark on a war of conquest, to further
your grip on the worlds around Tharsis?' snapped Boreas.

'I wanted to show the galaxy what I had achieved!'
argued Astelan, smashing his fist against the slab. 'I
wanted to cast aside the doubts of ancient history and
demonstrate to those with power that a way still existed
for the Imperium to grow stronger. But Imperial Commander Dax, after I had revealed my aspirations to him,
turned from me, just as El'Jonson had done a hundred
centuries ago.'

The memory pained Astelan, like a knife twisting in his
stomach. It had been a time of nightmare, his hopes suddenly dashed. Even now, the feeling of loss still haunted
him. For a while he thought he had purged his soul of
the regrets of the past, but to be discarded again had been
too much.

'He told me that I had done him and Tharsis a great
service, and I would be lauded for a hundred lifetimes.'
Astelan continued. 'His words meant nothing to me, and
suddenly his purpose became clear. Through me, he had
done what he had not considered possible, and had
allowed me to take the responsibility. Had my war with
the rebels failed, then he had lost nothing, but he had
everything to gain. Now he spoke of reducing the army,
of instating captains and colonels from the old families
again. I was horrified, but helpless. It was then, unbid-
den, that the sacred bands showed me the way. With no
command from me, I swear by the Emperor, they

besieged Dax's palaces. There was no one to resist them, all but a few soldiers in the whole army supported me as commander. Those few who spoke against the action were eliminated. Faced with such powerful opposition, the Imperial commander agreed to review his decision. But his cowardice got the better of him, and he was killed whilst trying to flee the palace.'

'How convenient for you,' the Chaplain retorted with a shake of his head. He crossed his arms and glowered at Astelan. 'The loyalty of your men must have been most gratifying, the death of the Imperial commander a timely incident.'

'I have no illusions that the soldiers had more than my great plans in mind,' admitted Astelan. 'During the rebellion, they had risked their homes and lives to fight off the enemy, but I had ensured that the rewards for them matched my expectations. I know that the hearts of normal men are weak, they will never be like the Space Marines. As well as leadership and direction, they require incentive to rise above their inherent selfishness. And so they had lands, and good food. Each soldier had been provided with servants to see to their needs, so that they might concentrate on the fighting. I did not want them distracted by petty concerns.'

'You created a warrior class to rule over Tharsis, with yourself at its head,' Boreas concluded.

'With your cynical eye, it may seem so, but consider this,' replied Astelan, meeting the Chaplain's contemptuous stare. 'Even now, your power leeched away, the Legions divided, how many of the people within the Tower of Angels are not Space Marines. Tens, hundreds, thousands?'

'The Chapter is maintained by roughly five hundred serfs, servitors and tech-priests,' Boreas answered cautiously.

'Five hundred people for a thousand Space Marines, that does not sound too much,' Astelan said with a wry look. 'But what about beyond the walls of this fortress, on ships and in distant garrisons? The same number again? Probably many more. And the food you eat, the ammunition in your weapons, even the paint for your armour, where does this come from? Thousands, tens of thousands, labour every day so that you stand ready to fight, to guard them from the perils of the galaxy.'

'But the Dark Angels are a Space Marine Chapter, the only purpose of our existence is to fight battles, to wage war on the enemies of the Emperor,' argued Boreas. 'Worlds do not exist for that purpose.'

'Why? Why not?' Astelan became animated again. This was the crux of his vision. It seemed so plain to him – why could Boreas not understand? 'Caliban once did! So you see, that was my dream, that was what I was trying to create. The weak men in power feared the Legions, broke them apart so that now they are thrown to the corners of the galaxy, strewn across the stars and rendered impotent. The regiments of the Imperial Guard are clumsy, unwieldy weapons. I learnt much about them during my time on Tharsis, and I came to despise what they represent. They rely on the ships of the Navy, which are controlled by a different organisation. A whole branch of the Administratum, the Departmento Munitorium, is dedicated to the sole matter of shipping regiments to war zones, and providing them with supplies. This you know, but you don't really understand what it means. Scribes and bookkeepers wage the wars of the Emperor now, not military officers. It is a shameful pile of politics and hierarchy, bogged down by its own complexity. Where has the vision gone? It was like my army on Tharsis had been, growing more unwieldy every passing day in an attempt to deal with its own unwieldiness. Who is there to carry on the Emperor's quest for a human galaxy free from danger? Clerks? Farmers? Miners?'

'And your way is better?' sneered Boreas. 'To place trust in someone like you, a man who unleashed unprecedented bloodshed upon a world you say you had adopted as your own?'

'You sound like the whining priests back on Tharsis!' snapped Boreas.

'The ones you murdered for speaking out against you?' said Boreas, stepping forward again, looming over Astelan.

'With the Imperial commander dead, it was the will of the people that I take his place.' Astelan was defiant, he would not let this interrogator bully him into admitting he was wrong when he knew in his heart that he was not. 'They recognised that really it had been I that had brought them success in the war. But the price of victory had been high, and soon the ruling class revealed themselves as the ingrates they were. While they had happily allowed the people of Tharsis to lay down their lives to protect them, the councillors, the cardinals and the aristocracy resisted my acceptance of authority. And the self-deluding hypocrites of the Ecclesiarchy were the worst of all. Since my awakening, I have seen first-hand the damage they have done. More than anything else it is their ridiculous mutterings and pompous sermons that have undermined the power of the Imperium.'

'And so you felt justified to eliminate them as well?' Boreas grabbed one of the chains and twisted it in his fist, tightening it across Astelan's muscled chest until it dug into his flesh. 'Perhaps you feared the power they had over your slaves. Were they the only true opposition your coup had, the only ones to rival your tenacious grip on the people of Tharsis? Was it jealousy of their privileged position and spiritual authority that incensed you?'

'Driven by meaningless dogma, they refused to endorse my claim as Imperial commander because I would not agree with them that the Emperor is a god,' argued Astelan, struggling against the tightening of the chains. 'Hah! I have walked alongside the Emperor, I have listened to Him speak, I have seen Him angry and sad. What do they know, with their carvings and paintings, their idolatry and superstitions? The Emperor is certainly more than a normal man, but a god? That was not his intent, and the fools who founded this Ecclesiarchy committed a grave error. The Emperor is not some distant figure to be worshipped, He is the will behind us all, the power that drives man to surmount the trials that face us. It was He who said that mankind must furnish itself with a destiny, and now that message has been thrown aside, so that the weak-willed can blame a god for their own shortcomings.'

'You profess a closeness to the Emperor?' Boreas asked, releasing the chain so that it slapped against Astelan's skin.

'No, I do not.' Astelan shook his head. 'I was one of several thousand Chapter Masters, proud of my achievements, but no more worthy of His attention then any other. I met the Emperor just once, on Sheridan's World, and then only briefly. Whenever I have doubts, I recall that meeting and the memory gives me purpose again. He spoke only a few words to me, praising the campaign, complimenting the fervour of my Chapter. It is the one true regret I have that I was not with him when they rediscovered Caliban. Perhaps if I had been there, things might have been different. But with the return of the primarchs everything changed, it was never the same as it had been when we followed the Emperor alone.'

'And so you ordered your death squads to murder the priests, the cardinals and even the deans and choir boys,' Boreas hissed between gritted teeth.

'You exaggerate,' Astelan said, trying to wave his hand in rejection of Boreas's accusation, the gesture stifled by his bonds. 'They presented me with an ultimatum – acknowledge the Emperor as a god, or face another revolt. Their own words and actions betrayed their treasonous intent. I presented them with an ultimatum of my own – retract their threat and abandon the trappings and advantages that their false teachings had gained them, or be tried as traitors. Some accepted, others refused. I had no part in their judgment, but they were all found guilty and executed. Choir boys indeed!'

'But you did not stop with the priestly orders,' continued Boreas. 'You waged a war upon all the agents of the Imperium who did not agree with you, and then you waged a war against your own populace when they voiced discontent.'

'They resented my successes,' Astelan snorted in derision. 'The judges, the arbitrators, the witch-cursed astropaths, the Munitorium quartermasters and the teeming hordes of the Adeptus Terra. I took back the power they had stolen over ten thousand years, subtly usurping the Imperium from those the Emperor had conceived to create it. In their petty-mindedness and internecine squabbles they had obscured the original vision, bastardised the Imperial ideal. I had vowed to restore it, and they stood against me. But not once did I ever kill out of hand. The people of the Imperium still know many of the great truths, but never truly think about the mottos and sayings they quote: *By the manner of their deaths, shall you know them,* is one that came to embody my rule. There were the loyal heroes who died in battle during the war, and there were the traitors who died on the gibbet afterwards. Tharsis shared my dream, they believed in me and the Emperor.'

'And so while you rebuilt your dreams of conquest, your sacred bands enforced curfew with boltguns, meted justice in the street with cudgels and blades and brutalised those who did not conform to that dream.' As he spoke, Boreas's fists clenched and unclenched slowly.

'I only wished harmony, of that I swear by my life,' protested Astelan. 'It was to banish the discord that has reigned since the Emperor defied Horus that I did what I felt was necessary.'

Boreas said nothing immediately. Instead, he turned away from Astelan and took a few paces towards the door, his head bowed in thought.

'But there was one dissenter who escaped your wrath,' the Chaplain said quietly.

'I do not understand,' replied Astelan. He was confused; who was this dissenter the Chaplain spoke of?

'Why do you think we came to Tharsis when we did?' asked Boreas, turning around, a look of triumph on his face. 'For seven decades you were there, isolating yourself from the rest of the Imperium. Who had ever heard of Tharsis? Certainly not the High Lords, and certainly not the Dark Angels. Your forces controlled the ships, so that none could leave without your permission, but you did not reckon on the faith and defiance of one man. He deserted your fleet, stealing a shuttle and flew it through an asteroid field to avoid pursuit. One deserter, though I suspect there were many others. He had no chance of survival, nowhere to go, but he felt the need to break free. And that was when coincidence, fate, destiny, or whatever you care to call it, paid interest in your affairs again. For fifty days he floated in space, on the verge of death, malnourished and severely dehydrated from drinking increasingly recycled water. Fifty days is not very far in the depths of space, but it was far enough for his transmissions for help to be intercepted by one of our ships that was patrolling the edges of the Tharsis system. His shuttle was recovered, and we learnt of the terrible events that had unfolded. And we learnt of you.'

'You attacked Tharsis because of the ravings of a madman?' Astelan said, his voice full of derision.

'No, Commander Astelan, we did not,' Boreas said slowly, taking measured paces towards him as he spoke, until he filled Astelan's vision, his eyes glittering in the dim light of the brazier. 'The memories of the Dark Angels go back a long time, back ten thousand years when those like you turned on their brethren and betrayed them. Little is now known about that time of anarchy, and few records of what transpired are left, but there is a list, a list kept by the Grand Master of Chaplains in a sacred box in the main chapel. For ten times a thousand years we have hunted the Fallen Angels that almost destroyed the Lion and his Legion, wherever they might be. We do not know how many of you there are, or where we might find you. But we have that list, and it contains the names of the hundred and thirty-six Space Marines who first swore allegiance to Luther when he rose against our primarch. Your name, Commander Astelan, is at the top of that list. We have been hunting you for a very long time, and now we shall learn the truth from you.'

Boreas turned and opened the door. There, swathed in robes, stood Samiel. The Librarian walked softly into the room and stood beside Astelan's head. He reached down and the former Chapter commander tried to move his head aside, but his restraints did not allow him room. The psyker's cold hands rested on his forehead, and Astelan felt a voice whispering at the back of his mind.

You have deluded yourself for too long, it sighed. *Now is the time when we strip away the lies. Now we strip away your delusions, until all that is left is the stark truth of your actions. You have hidden from the guilt at the core of your soul, but we will not allow you to hide any longer. You will know the shame and pain you have brought us, and you will repent of your evil ways.*

'I have done no wrong!' rasped Astelan, trying to shake his head free.

'Liar!' roared Boreas, and pain beyond anything he had ever endured before lanced through Astelan's head.

'Now we will begin again,' the Interrogator-Chaplain told his prisoner. 'Tell me of Tharsis.'

THE TALE OF BOREAS
PART TWO

IT WAS FOUR days after the clash with the orks, and Boreas knelt in silent meditation in the outpost chapel. He was clad only in his white robe, a mark of his position within the elite warriors of the Chapter – the Deathwing. What the others did not realise was that it was also a mark of his membership within the secretive Inner Circle of the Chapter. Lifting the robe slightly, he knelt before an altar of dark stone inlaid with gold and platinum. The altar was at one end of the chapel, which itself was situated at the top of the five-storey Dark Angels' keep in Kadillus Harbour, capital of Piscina IV. The chamber was not large, for space was at a premium in the small tower, big enough only for fifty people to attend the dawn and dusk masses that Boreas held every day.

Three of the keep's many non-Space Marine attendants were at work renewing the murals that covered the chapel's interior, failed aspirants who had nonetheless survived their trials. Two were busy reapplying gilding to a portrait of the Dark Angels' primarch, Lion El'Jonson, which towered some three metres in height above the altar.

Boreas tried to block out the occasional creak and squeak of the painters' wooden scaffolding. The other was renovating a scene added after the Dark Angels' last defence of Piscina, when the ork warlords Ghazghkull and Nazdreg had combined forces and fallen upon the planet like two thunderbolts of destruction. For Boreas, that particular picture brought both pride and a little consternation. It depicted the defence of the Dark Angels' basilica which had once served as their outpost in the capital. It was here that Boreas himself had led the fighting against the vicious alien horde on numerous occasions, as possession of the strategically vital strongpoint had changed hands back and forth for the whole campaign. It was during the battle for the basilica that Boreas had lost his right eye to an ork powerfist, which had nearly crushed his head. Though eventually the orks had been driven out of the basilica, and the planet saved by an epic battle at Koth Ridge, so intense had been the fighting at the blood-soaked chapter house that after the orks had been defeated, the Dark Angels had been forced to abandon the fortified administration building and construct a new keep. The ruins themselves still stood a kilometre or so from where Boreas now knelt, a testament to the protection the Dark Angels had provided for countless millennia.

Reminded of the valiant battle-brothers whose dying words he had heard in those shattered rooms and corridors, and mindful of the great sacrifices that his fellow Space Marines had made, both the Dark Angels and those of the Harbingers Chapter, Boreas felt a tightness in his chest. Had the basilica really been that important, he asked himself yet again? Perhaps it had just been pride that had driven Master Belial to command Boreas to defend the building at all costs? In the end, the fighting in the dark cathedral had been but a sideshow of the campaign, the relative merits of the engagement inconclusive compared to the slaughter at Koth Ridge.

With a terse command, Boreas dismissed the serfs, their presence breaking his concentration as he was trying to focus on the oath of fealty he had pledged when he had joined the Inner Circle. They did not give him a second glance as they quietly picked up their tools and left, for which he was thankful. Despite the doubts he felt, he still had a duty as the Dark Angels commander in Piscina to show strong leadership and set an example to the others. If he showed weakness for a moment, it could cause unknown damage, not only to himself but also to those who looked to his wisdom and guidance with absolute trust. If that trust were to be broken, then only Boreas truly knew what acts of anarchy and corruption might follow.

Realising that it was not the presence of the serfs that was disturbing his meditation, but his own dark thoughts, Boreas decided that he would not quiet his troubled soul in isolation. Perhaps he might find more solace in the company of the five Space Marines under his command, he thought, and resolved to leave. Glancing only briefly at the half-gilded primarch in front of him, he turned and strode from the chapel, his bare feet padding loudly on the flagstones. Passing through the double doors that opened out of the sanctum, he turned and closed them behind him, the boom of the heavy wooden doors loud in the stillness of the keep. Turning left in the corridor, he crossed the tower to the armoury, where he hoped to find Hephaestus.

BOREAS WAS PROVED correct as he stepped into the workshop of the Techmarine. Like most of the keep, the chamber was square and functional, the plain rockcrete of the walls unadorned. There, amongst the racks of weapons and worktables, accompanied by his five attendants, Hephaestus was seated at a workbench, working on Boreas's power armour. He had the chest plastron in a vice and was busily filing away at the scores cut into the breastplate during the battle against the orks. From beside him, one of his attendants occasionally dipped a ladle into a grail of sacred water and poured the contents over the mechanical file.

On Boreas's left were cases of bolters and crates of ammunition, all stacked neatly and marked with the brand of the Imperial eagle and the winged sword symbol of the Dark Angels. Next to them various swords and axes hung on the wall, amongst them chainswords, power swords and Boreas's crozius. They glistened in the light from the glowing strips in the ceiling, a tribute to the attention paid by Hephaestus, who lovingly cleaned them every night with blessed oils.

'And what brings you into my chamber, Brother-Chaplain?' Hephaestus asked, as Boreas realised he had been staring transfixed at the sheen on his crozius. The Techmarine was looking over his shoulder at Boreas.

'You were late for mass last night,' Boreas said, knowing he wasn't quite sure why he had come here.

'Come, come,' said Hephaestus, wiping his meaty hands on a white cloth and standing up from his bench. 'You know that I had to attend to my duties here, as I have every night since the fight at Vartoth.'

'Of course,' agreed Boreas, knowing full well that a Techmarine had dispensation from prayers if his attendance would interfere in the repair or upkeep of the Space Marines' wargear. 'I did not realise that our encounter had left you such a long task.'

'I would rather spend twenty hours repairing a bolter, than think for a moment that my battle-brothers had not committed fully to the fight in wayward consideration of my labours,' Hephaestus smiled. 'And I am paying particular attention to your armour, Interrogator-Chaplain, as it deserves.'

'Yes, I know of your love for the works of the artificer Mandeus,' Boreas said, allowing himself a rare smile. 'Did you not once say to me that you would die content if you could one day fashion a suit of armour half as great as the one that I inherited?'

'I might well have said that,' agreed Hephaestus, 'but in error. These days, having worked with your armour so much, I have learnt much of Mandeus's techniques, and now I will only be content if I make a suit as good as this one!'

'Would you not prefer to better Mandeus's work?' Boreas asked, walking to the bench and looking at the scattered pieces of servos and artificial muscle-fibres that Hephaestus had removed from the breastplate.

'If I can emulate his skill with the tools I have here and the time I have, then I will judge myself the better artisan,' Hephaestus said quietly. Boreas gave him a questioning look and the Techmarine continued. 'The great artificers Mandeus, Geneon, Aster and their like all worked in the Tower of Angels, amongst the brethren, with acolytes to perform many of the duties that fill my days. You have seen the great armorium of our Chapter. It dwarfs the entirety of this keep!'

'You feel burdened by your post here?' Boreas asked quietly, knowing that he too felt the same constriction on his soul, the same chafing to be free of Piscina and its confines. 'You feel you could better serve the Emperor in the armorium with your fellow Techmarines?'

Hephaestus hesitated, his eyes gauging Boreas's expression. After a momentary glance at the attendants in the room, who were busying themselves with their duties and paying little heed to their masters, or so it appeared, he answered thoughtfully.

'We all have fought here, shed our blood on these volcanic islands to protect Piscina from the orks,' he said, his voice low as he bent close to the Interrogator-Chaplain. 'I stand ready to do so again, and will labour in this place until such time as the Grand Master of the Armorium sees fit to send another in my stead.'

'Yet you have not answered the question,' Boreas persisted with a sad smile. 'I do not seek to judge you, for have you not been raised to glory by your works? I cannot hold you to account for longing to tread in the steps of your great predecessors. You are a magnificent artificer, and your patience is a tribute to our Chapter. I cannot speak the minds of the Grand Masters, but when the Tower of Angels returns to us again, they shall know of your dedication and skill.'

'I sought not for praise, Brother-Chaplain,' Hephaestus said quickly. 'You asked me the question and I answered as honestly as I can.'

'You are worthy of the praise, all the more so because you do not seek it,' Boreas replied, placing a hand on his comrade's shoulder. 'I ask the question not from suspicion, but out of trust. I would not have you burdened with your thoughts and ambition; you must feel free to speak of them freely, to me or to the others. Only in wishing to rise to greatness ourselves can we maintain the honour and pride of the Chapter.'

'In that case, might I ask you a question, Brother-Chaplain?' Hephaestus said, looking closely at the Chaplain's face.

'Yes, of course,' Boreas answered.

'It is your eye,' Hephaestus said. 'You seem troubled of late and I wondered whether it was functioning properly... Is it causing you pain?'

'It causes me constant pain, as you know, Hephaestus,' Boreas replied, removing his hand and stepping back. 'I would not have it any other way, for it serves as a reminder against complacency.'

'I would still like to examine it for a moment, to allay my own fears,' Hephaestus insisted.

'You did a fine job with my eye,' said Boreas. 'It is good to measure yourself against your deeds, but you judge yourself too harshly.'

Seeing the determined looked in the Techmarine's eye, Boreas gave a resigned nod and sat on the bench. Hephaestus bent over him, his fingers working deftly at the mechanism of the bionic organ, and with an audible click, the main part of its workings came free. Simultaneously, Boreas lost the sight in his right eye. It was not worrying for him – once a year Hephaestus would remove the eye to ensure it still worked smoothly. It was odd, however, that the Techmarine had asked to do so now, though, barely two months from his last check.

Taking a complex tool from his bench, Hephaestus unlocked the casing of the eye and slid the interior free. He delicately pulled free the lenses, polishing them on his cloth and setting them to one side, before delving inside the eye's innards with fine tweezers. Boreas studied Hephaestus with his good eye as the Techmarine continued his work, watching the intensity on the artisan's face as he examined his own construction. If Hephaestus was becoming overly concerned about Boreas's well-being, then perhaps the others had noticed his change of mood as well. The Interrogator-Chaplain resolved to speak to them when he was done here, to gauge their mood and ask them some pertinent questions. The inactivity and routine, though they had trained for it, had become monotonous. It had been two years since the Tower of Angels had last visited and the isolation from the rest of the Chapter might well have started taking its toll on them as it had done on Boreas.

'Everything appears to be functioning as it should be,' Hephaestus reported, fitting the bionic eye back together and slotting it back into its socket. There was a brief tingle in Boreas's right eye and then full vision returned to him. 'However, I did notice some additional scabbing on the implant, as if the wound had opened again recently. You might ask Nestor to have a look at it.'

'Thank you, I will,' Boreas said, glad of the excuse to go and talk to the Apothecary, not that he needed to justify visiting those whose morale and discipline he was responsible for preserving. 'Will I see you at mass this evening?'

Hephaestus paused and looked around the armoury, assessing his workload. He looked back at Boreas and nodded his head once before sitting down again at his workbench and picking up the mechanical file. The rasping teeth buzzed into life behind Boreas as he walked from the chamber.

THE INTERROGATOR-CHAPLAIN walked down the spiral stair at the centre of the keep to the level two storeys below. Here was the apothecarion, the domain of Nestor and medical centre for the outpost. When Boreas entered, there was no sign of the Apothecary. The harsh glowstrips in the ceiling reflected off shining steel surfaces, meticulously arranged surgical tools, phials of drugs and elixirs set in rows on long shelves. The room was dominated by three operating tables in its centre. Unsure where Nestor might be if not here, Boreas walked to the comm-unit by the door and pressed the rune for general address to the keep.

'This is Boreas, Apothecary Nestor to report,' he said and released the activation stud. It was a few seconds before the response came through, the display on the comm-unit signalling an incoming transmission from the vaults set deep into the tower's foundations.

'Nestor here, Brother-Chaplain,' the Apothecary answered.

'Please come up to the apothecarion, I have a matter I wish to discuss with you,' Boreas said.

'Affirmative. I will be there shortly,' Nestor replied.

Boreas walked over to the nearest operating table and looked at his reflection in its gleaming metal surface.

Many times he had been in such a place, either as a patient or to provide spiritual support for those undergoing surgery. He had also spent too many occasions in an apothecarion saying the rites of passing over a dying battle-brother, while an Apothecary had removed the progenoid glands so that the sacred gene-seed might be passed on to future warriors. It was the most important function any Apothecary could perform, and essential to the survival of the Chapter.

New gene-seed was all but impossible to create – certainly no Chapter Boreas knew of had ever achieved such a feat – and so future generations of Space Marines relied solely on the vital gene-seed storage organs that every Space Marine was implanted with. Every Marine had two progenoids, and in theory his death could help create two replacements. But despite the daring and brave efforts of the Apothecaries, too many progenoids were lost on the field of battle before they could be harvested to ever ensure the continued existence of a Chapter. It was the task of the Chaplains to teach every Space Marine of the legacy he held within himself, to educate them in their duty to the continued glory of the Chapter. A Space Marine was taught that although he may be asked to sacrifice his life at any moment, he should never sell his life in vain, for by doing so he betrayed those who would come after him.

There was a popular Imperial saying: *Only in death does duty end*. But for the Space Marines, even death did not bring an end to their duty to protect mankind and the Imperium the Emperor's servants had created. In death they lived on in newly created Space Marines. Some, those whose physical bodies could not be saved, might be interred in the mighty walking tanks called dreadnoughts, to live on for a thousand years as gigantic warriors encased in an unliving body of plasteel, adamantium and ceramite. In such a way, over ten thousand years of the Imperium, there was a bond of brotherhood from the very first Space Marines to those who had only just been ordained as Scouts of the Tenth Company. It was this very physical relationship that bound together every warrior of the Chapter. Not merely for tradition's sake were they called battle-brothers.

Or so the litanies taught, but Boreas knew different. He had learnt many things when he had become a member of the Deathwing, the elite Inner Circle of the Dark Angels. He had learnt yet more during his interrogation of the Fallen Angel, Astelan, things which even now still troubled him.

The hiss of the hermetically sealed doors opening heralded the arrival of Apothecary Nestor. Of the five Space Marines currently under Boreas's command, Nestor had been a Space Marine for the longest, and by quite some margin. Boreas had served as one of the Dark Angels for nearly three hundred years, but at over six hundred years old Nestor was one of the oldest members of the Chapter. Boreas did not know why the veteran had not risen higher, why he had never been admitted to the Deathwing. Nestor was one of the finest Apothecaries on the field of battle, and Boreas owed his life to him when he had been wounded in the battle for the basilica. Nestor had also been honoured for his heroic fighting during the first ork assault on Koth Ridge.

In looks, the Apothecary was even more grizzled than Boreas. His thick, waxy skin was pitted and scarred across his face, and six service studs were hammered into his forehead, one for every century of service. His eyes were dark and his head shaved bald, giving the medic a menacing appearance that was entirely at odds with the conscientious, caring man Boreas knew him to be. That care was not to be mistaken for weakness, though; in battle Nestor was as fierce as any warrior Boreas had fought alongside.

'How can I help you?' the Apothecary asked, walking past Boreas and leaning back against the operating table.

Boreas thought he caught a flicker of something in Nestor's eye, a momentary flash of nervousness.

'Hephaestus says my eye might have shifted in the wound, and he recommended that you examine it,' Boreas said quickly, looking directly at the Apothecary.

'Perhaps it became dislodged at Vartoth,' suggested Nestor, standing upright and indicating for Boreas to lie down on the table. The Interrogator-Chaplain did so, staring up at the bright lamp directly above the examination slab. Nestor disappeared for a moment before returning with one of his instruments, with which he gently probed at the cauterised flesh on the right side of Boreas's face. Most of it was in fact artificial flesh grafted on the metal plate that replaced much of Boreas's temple, cheek and brow. He could feel the point dully prodding at his face as the Apothecary examined the old wound. With a grunt, Nestor straightened up.

'There seems to be some tearing on the graft, nothing serious,' Nestor commented. 'Is it causing you discomfort?'

'No more than usual,' said Boreas, sitting up and swinging his legs off the table. 'Do you think it could worsen?'

'Over time, yes it will. Some of the capillaries have retracted, others have collapsed, and the flesh is dying off slowly. It would require a new graft to heal completely.' Nestor glanced around the apothecarion for a moment before continuing. 'I do not have the facilities here to perform such a procedure, I am afraid. I will provide you with a solution to bathe your face in each morning, which should hopefully slow the necrofication. There is no need to worry about infection, your body is already more than capable of cleansing itself of any kind of disease you might pick up on Piscina.'

'Hephaestus will be pleased,' said Boreas. 'He worries overmuch.'

'Does he?' Nestor asked quietly, placing his instrument in an auto-cleanser concealed within the wall of the apothecarion.

'Your meaning?' Boreas said, standing up and adjusting his heavy robe. 'You have just confirmed that there is no cause for concern.'

'With your eye, that is true,' Nestor said over his shoulder. He removed the probe and returned it carefully to its place amongst the scalpels, mirrors, needles and other tools of his craft. 'However, one cause for the loss of blood to your graft might be stress on the rest of your body.'

'You think I need a fuller examination?' Boreas asked, looking down at himself. 'I feel healthy.'

'That is not what I mean,' Nestor replied with a slight shake of his head.

'Then say what you mean,' snapped Boreas, tired of this subtle innuendo. 'What do you think is wrong?'

'Forgive me, Brother-Chaplain,' Nestor bowed his head in acquiescence. 'I was merely making an observation.'

'Well, make your observation clearer, by the Lion!' barked Boreas.

'Out of all of us, it must be hardest for you to be garrisoned here, away from our brethren,' Nestor stated, raising his gaze to meet Boreas's.

'What do you mean?' asked Boreas.

'When we are troubled, it is to you we turn to remind us of our sacred duties, to refresh the vows we have all pledged,' Nestor explained softly. 'When we lament the inactivity of our post, when we crave the companionship of the others, it is you who gives us guidance and wisdom. But to whom does the guide turn?'

'It is because of my faith and strength of mind that I was chosen to become a Chaplain,' Boreas pointed out. 'It is our role to pass on that inner strength to others.'

'Then forgive my error,' Nestor said quickly. 'One such as I, who on occasion has doubts, and who must be steered along the bloody path we walk, cannot understand what mind you must have to walk that path alone.'

'No more than I can understand the purposes of the machines in this chamber, or the secrets of the Caliban helix within our gene-seed, like you can,' Boreas answered after a moment's thought. 'No more than I can understand the workings of this fake eye which Hephaestus manufactured for me from cold metal and glass, and yet he gives it a semblance of life.'

'Yes, I suppose we each have our purpose here on this world,' agreed Nestor, slapping Boreas on the arm. 'Hephaestus for the machines, myself for the body. And you, Brother-Chaplain, for our mind and souls.'

'And so, I ask you in return what troubles you have,' Boreas said, seeing his opportunity to steer the conversation onto a track more to his liking. He was certain that Nestor was not questioning his thoughts or his loyalty, but the more he spoke about such things, the more Boreas heard the laughter of Astelan ringing in his ears.

'I am content,' Nestor replied. 'I have served the Emperor and the Lion for six centuries, and perhaps if I am fortunate I may serve him yet for two more. But I have done my duty. I have bathed in the white-hot fires of battle and created new generations of Dark Angels. The things I once strived to prove to myself and my brothers I have now done, and all that remains is to pass on what I know and retain the pride and dignity of our Chapter. If fate and the Supreme Grand Master see fit for me to end my days on Piscina IV, I shall not be the one to argue against it.'

'You are surely too experienced to be given such a mundane duty though,' said Boreas, crossing his arms tightly. 'With such experience as you have, do you not think your time would be better spent in the Tower of Angels teaching those who will follow after you? Acting as nursemaid to a Chaplain with a broken eye is hardly worthy of your talents.'

'Are you trying to provoke me, Brother-Chaplain?' Nestor said harshly. 'I follow the will of the Emperor and I say again that I am content. Piscina is a recruiting system, not just some watch post or augury. It is because of my skill and experience that I can judge those who might come after. I am entrusted in more ways than you can know with the Chapter's future.'

'I did not seek to belittle what you do here, my words were perhaps ill-judged and for that I apologise,' Boreas hastily replied, uncrossing his arms and taking a step towards Nestor. The Apothecary smiled and nodded in acceptance of Boreas's apology. With a last glance, Boreas turned away and walked towards the door.

'Brother-chaplain,' Nestor called after him, and he stopped and turned. 'Are you not forgetting something?'

'I can recite the three hundred verses of the Caliban Chronicles, I do not forget things,' Boreas pointed out.

'Then you don't want the elixir for soothing your face?' Nestor said.

'Bring it to me at this evening's meal,' Boreas replied with a smile.

BOREAS CONTINUED DOWN the stairwell to the next level in search of the other senior member of his squad. He paused at the landing and gazed out of the thick glass of the narrow window, collecting his thoughts. Thick smog obscured most of the view, so that the towers and factories in the distance were only vague silhouettes. A bird fluttered past close by, before disappearing into the brownish-grey clouds. As he watched it fade into the distance, he realised that the conversations with Hephaestus and Nestor had shown him that he needed to spend more time with the others, rather than dwell on his own misgivings. That they thought he somehow doubted them, that he was subtly testing them, proved to him that they had become unaccustomed to his company. Turning away from the window, he continued down the stairs to the first storey.

Here were the quarters for the aspirants, and Boreas knew he would find Veteran Sergeant Damas in the gymnasium with them, continuing the rigorous physical training they started as soon as they were brought to the keep. Although Boreas was in command of the outpost, the aspirants were Damas's responsibility. Having attained the rank of veteran sergeant, he had been moved to the Tenth Company as part of the recruiting force. Like the others on Piscina, Damas had received honours for his conduct during the ork invasion. He, along with his Scout squad and the now legendary Sergeant Naaman, had infiltrated the ork lines and, after gathering vital intelligence on the enemy, destroyed one of the relays the aliens had been using to power their massive orbital teleporter. It had been a huge setback to the ork advance, and though Damas was seriously wounded whilst the infiltrators retreated, he had held off the ork counter-attack long enough for his squad to get away.

Damas was amongst the fourteen youths under his tutelage. Nearly half as tall again as his charges, even without his armour, he was a giant even by the standards of the Space Marines. When Boreas entered, the aspirants were seated in a circle around the veteran sergeant. Boreas listened in for a moment, standing in the shadow of the doorway.

'Your first weapon is your body,' Damas was telling his attentive audience. 'Even before you are given bones and muscles like mine, I can teach you how to break a man's neck with a single blow. I can show you how to crush his internal organs with your fists, disable him with your fingers and cripple him with your elbows and knees.'

He bent down and placed his plate-sized hand on the head of one of the youths.

'With the strength given to me by the Apothecaries and my faith, I can pulp your brain in a second,' he told the boy, who laughed nervously, eliciting more laughter from the others. 'More than that, I can withstand any attack you might make on me.'

Damas instructed the youths to stand up, and pointed at one of them, telling him to hit him as hard as possible. Hesitantly, the boy approached.

'I will not strike back,' Damas assured the boy. 'But if you hesitate to follow my orders again, I will have you thrashed.'

Chastened, the boy charged with a shrill yell and flung his fist at Damas's abdomen. The blow would have merely winded an ordinary man, by Boreas's reckoning, and it failed to even rock Damas on his heels. The boy gave a squeal and clutched his bruised knuckles. Boreas chuckled, along with the aspirants. The only vital part of a Space Marine not protected by his black carapace was his head. Hearts, lungs, stomach, chest, all were impervious to any unarmed blow from even the strongest assailant.

Hearing the Chaplain's mirth, Damas looked over. Following their instructor's gaze, the aspirants caught sight of Boreas and fell instantly into a solemn silence, their heads bowed. Boreas walked in, and clapped a hand to the back of the lad who had attacked Damas, nearly knocking him from his feet.

'A brave attempt,' Boreas said, helping the boy to steady himself. He recognised him as Beyus, one of the two hopefuls he had brought in just before the battle at Vartoth. He had evidently recovered from his crippling shock. In just the few days that had passed since his arrival, the boy was already changed. His head was shaved bald, and all the puppy fat was gone from his strong torso. The boy stood straighter, and his gaze was fiercer than before. Damas was doing a good job.

'Run!' barked Damas, clapping his hands twice, and with no further words the boys began to jog around the wall of the gymnasium, which stretched across the whole floor of the tower. Their pounding bare feet on the wooden boards masked the two Space Marines' conversation.

'I see things are proceeding well,' Boreas started, look-ing at the running youths.

'They are a good selection. The last two in particular show a lot of potential,' agreed Damas with a nod. Then his look darkened slightly. 'But only fourteen this sea-son? The Tower of Angels will be here in less than half a year, and they will be expecting thirty recruits for second-stage testing.'

'Would you rather we fell short of our quota, than passed on boys who will fail within minutes?' asked Boreas. 'If the quality is not there, it is not there.'

'You know what I am talking about,' Damas insisted. 'I cannot understand your reluctance.'

'You are referring to the eastern tribes?' Boreas replied. 'You think we should take our recruits from those sav-ages?'

'They are all savages,' countered Damas with a shrug. 'I see no distinction.'

'And yet I do,' the Chaplain replied. 'I have told you before that they are too bloodthirsty, even for our pur-poses. If we still had a whole company stationed here I would exterminate them. Some of their practices are, well, bordering on the intolerable. They have stopped worshipping the Emperor, and have reverted to a bar-barism I fear even we cannot strip them of with a decade of training.'

'They remind me much of my own people of Slathe,' Damas commented pointedly. 'Perhaps your judgment of them is overly harsh.'

'Perhaps your continual persistence with this matter indicates other reservations,' suggested Boreas. 'It has been several months now since we have spoken about anything else.'

'I see the numbers of aspirants dwindling, and it causes me concern, that is all,' Damas replied calmly. 'I feel it is my duty to remind you of the options available to us. No disrespect of your position is intended, I understand that we each have our own duties and codes to which we must adhere.'

'Perhaps it is their similarity to the tribes of Slathe that burdens you,' Boreas said.

'You think I perhaps yearn for my homeworld?' asked Damas with a frown.

'Yearn is too strong a word, I do not for a moment doubt your loyalty to the Dark Angels,' Boreas replied. 'It is a wise tradition that we are not posted to our home-worlds, for fear of what that might bring. Perhaps it was an error for you to be here, near a world so similar to the one you came from.'

'I do not see it as an error,' argued Damas. 'My home-world is now the Tower of Angels and has been for two centuries. Slathe is just one of many worlds I have sworn to protect.'

'Then it is I who have erred,' conceded Boreas with a gracious nod. 'I do not wish you to think that I have any reservations about your performance. I am here as your guardian and advisor, I wish you to feel free to express any anxieties you may have.'

'Then I am anxious that we have so few recruits, and that is all,' Damas said quietly.

'Very well, I shall note your recommendations in my journal, so that if we fall below our quota, no blame shall be attached to you,' promised Boreas.

'It is not blame that concerns me, Brother-Chaplain, it is the future strength of our Chapter,' Damas corrected the Interrogator-Chaplain.

'Then I shall make my entry reflect that,' said Boreas. 'Their numbers notwithstanding, you are happy with this batch of aspirants?'

'All have improved their skills, and met my expecta-tions,' confirmed Damas, clapping his hands twice again. In a rush of feet, the aspirants gathered around the two Space Marines, attentive to their instructor.

'I shall leave you to your pupils,' said Boreas, and turned to leave. As he walked out of the door, he heard the veteran sergeant commanding his group to break into pairs for unarmed combat practice.

BOREAS'S THOUGHTS WERE disturbed. There was something amiss, he could feel it. On the face of it, everything was proceeding as normal, but he detected an undercurrent amongst his command. It was hard to pinpoint, but he could sense their slight reproach. Like him, they were frustrated, virtually marooned here in the Piscina system while their battle-brothers sought glorious battle hundreds, if not thousands, of light years away. Or perhaps it was only his own impotence that he was projecting on to them. The others chafed slightly perhaps at their posting, but maybe that was all. It was not entirely unexpected. Nestor, of all of them, seemed the most comfortable with their situation. But that in itself could be problematic. Had the old Apothecary resigned himself to his future? Had he lost his drive? Was he merely looking to his death now, perhaps jaded by his long service?

Before he checked on Battle-Brothers Thumiel and Zaul, the Chaplain decided he needed more time to think on this matter. He strode back up the stairwell to the very top of the tower, out onto the observation and gun platform on its roof. From here he could look out across Kadillus Harbour and up at the great volcano on the flanks of which it was built. The strengthening breeze gusted over his face and set his robe flapping, refreshing his mind. He frequently came up here when the confines of the chapel stifled his thoughts rather than letting them flow. He walked first to the south parapet, and looked down the slopes towards the sea.

Here was the industrial heart of Kadillus Harbour. Here were the massive docks where the enormous ocean-going harvesters came and went, and the high cranes and gantries that criss-crossed the bay to unload their cargoes of gas and minerals dredged from the sea floor. Factories spilt around the harbour like a stain, gouting smoke as they processed ore and smelted metals for transportation off-planet. Here were the hab-blocks, vast rockcrete structures crammed with the million-strong workforce of Kadillus Harbour. Night was closing in and soon the loud klaxons and sirens would signal the end of the day shift and the start of the night watch. When dark descended, the thousands of furnaces and smelting works would light the sky with red.

Boreas walked around the parapet and looked out eastwards. Here was the richer district, and close by the old ruins of the ancient basilica. Beyond the towering spires of the planetary nobles and the sprawling palaces of the Imperial commander, the Lady Sousan, lay Koth Ridge. It had been there that the Dark Angels and the Imperial Guard had made their stand against the orks. If that defence had failed, the two greenskin forces would have been able to unite and the planet would have surely fallen.

It was there, on that barren rocky stretch of ground, that thousands of Guardsmen and nearly one hundred Space Marines held off a seemingly endless alien horde. Boreas had not been there, for he had still been fighting in Kadillus itself. But he had heard the tales of victory and heroism with pride. The battle-brothers of the Dark Angels had fought hard and taken terrible losses, but their blood had secured victory and saved Piscina from being enslaved. Had Piscina IV fallen, then the orks would have met no resistance when they descended on Piscina V. The tribesmen would have been slaughtered or enslaved, and another world would have been lost to the Dark Angels forever.

Boreas couldn't help but reflect bitterly on the events of the past five years. Once, an entire company had been stationed here under the command of Master Belial. Now, only he and a handful of the campaign's veterans were left to defend the future of the Chapter. The Tower of Angels returned less and less frequently, and Boreas wondered how quickly those great deeds might be forgotten.

Continuing his circuit, Boreas looked to the north. The first thing he saw was the massive open apron of Northport, where starships landed and took off every week, bringing vital supplies and in return taking the mineral wealth of the planet away to distant systems. There was something amiss though. Concentrating, Boreas saw wisps of dark smoke snaking like tendrils from the streets that approached the starport. He could also make out the distant orange flicker of flames.

The Interrogator-Chaplain ran to the nearest gun turret and stepped inside. He flicked on the comm-unit and punched the stud for the command centre at the base of the tower. Zaul would be on duty at the moment.

'This is Boreas. Have you received any unusual communications from the north of the city?' asked Boreas.

'Negative, there have been no abnormal communications today,' Zaul replied after a moment. 'Is there a problem?'

'Connect me through to the headquarters of Colonel Brade,' commanded Boreas, activating the turret control systems. As the motors whirred into life, the comm crackled as Zaul fed it through the main aerial that towered from the centre of the keep. Manipulating the controls with one hand, he directed the emplaced gun to rotate towards the north, while he watched the long-range sensor screen. There on the screen, he could clearly see a number of fires blazing in the streets, the smoke filling the canyon-like roadways.

'Lord Boreas?' the comm spat into life.

'Colonel Brade. I am currently observing some form of disturbance near to Northport,' Boreas said. 'Please explain the situation.'

'There has been some rioting, my lord,' Brade replied. 'A few hundred individuals only, the Imperial commander's security forces are attempting to contain them as we speak.'

'Please inform whoever is in charge of the operation that I will be joining him shortly,' Boreas said, looking at the growing blazes on the monitor.

'I don't think that will be necessary, my lord,' Brade said, his voice terse. 'I am sure the Imperial commander's men are capable of handling the situation.'

'I wish to observe these events personally, please inform the ground commander to expect my arrival.' Boreas cut the link and powered down the turret. He strode quickly across the roof to the stairs and hurried down them, all the way to the first subterranean level. Jumping the last few steps, Boreas entered the fortress's garage. Here, two slab-sided Rhino armoured carriers sat in the gloom, and three combat bikes. It was to the bikes that he went. With huge reinforced tyres, armour plating and built-in bolters, each was closer in size to a small roadcar than a motorcycle, designed for Space Marines to make rapid hit-and-run strikes inside enemy-held territory. Boreas found them useful for travelling the winding city streets of Kadillus on the few occasions when he actually left the outpost, usually to attend traditional ceremonies with the Imperial commander.

Sitting astride the machine, he thumbed the engine into life, its mechanical growl echoing around the garage. Boreas opened up a comm-link to the command chamber.

'Monitor all local transmissions, I am heading to the Northport area to find out what is happening,' he told Zaul.

'I have your tracker on the oracle-screen,' confirmed the battle-brother. The transponder built into the bike's chassis would transmit its position every few seconds, allowing the other Space Marines to home in on its location rapidly should the rider encounter danger or fail to report on schedule.

'Open the gate,' ordered Boreas before gunning the engine and releasing the clutch. With a plume of blue smoke in his wake, he roared up the ramp and out into the twilight of the city.

Passing between the armoured bastions of the gate-house, Boreas moved rapidly up through the bike's gears until he was racing down the streets, his robes flapping in the wind. The occasional roadcars and heavy, slab-sided transporters on the road slowed to let him pass. It was at the height of the work-shift and the streets were almost deserted. Either side of him the grim buildings of Kadillus sped past, and he saw brief glimpses of the surprised faces of the few citizens on the streets. It was not often that they saw one of their mysterious, superhuman guardians, and some of the pedestrians began running along after him, shouting out blessings and praise.

It took only a few minutes of riding before the sky ahead of Boreas was thick with black smoke. There were crowds gathering, but they parted easily as he nosed the bike forward, more cautiously now the streets were beginning to fill with people. He spotted the dark red uniform of a Kadillus security enforcer, and swung the bike over next to her. The woman, her head and eyes concealed behind a reflective glass visor, gaped openly as he came to a stop just ahead of her. In her hands she held a lasgun, which began to tremble in her nervous grasp.

'Who is in charge, and where can I find them?' asked Boreas, leaning towards the enforcer. He dwarfed the woman and she was obviously intimidated by his presence.

'Lieutenant-at-arms Verusius,' the woman replied breathlessly. 'He's at the worst of the rioting. Head west at the next junction.'

'Stop any more people arriving in the area,' Boreas told her.

'We're trying to do that now,' she replied, taking a step back.

'Good,' Boreas said, revving the engine and riding off. More and more security personnel could be seen as he approached the junction, another kilometre along the road. The citizens were more numerous as well, being held back by the cordon. Their scrabbling and surging halted as the Space Marine pulled into view, and the crowds parted to let him pass, shouts spreading out to herald his progress.

Soon he saw the front line ahead. Smoke billowed overhead and dozens of enforcers were stood in a line across the road. He could see an armoured groundcar parked nearby, and a small group of officers standing next to it. They all turned in unison as the bike screeched to a halt behind the roadcar.

'Lord Boreas!' one of them exclaimed. In his hand, he gripped a comm-unit, which occasionally squawked bursts of incomprehensible noise. 'I'm honoured!'

'You are Lieutenant-at-arms Verusius?' Boreas asked the young man.

'No, I am,' said an older, shorter security man. He wore no helmet, and his uniform was a long red coat with gold piping. His face was broad and split by a dark moustache, his thinning hair cropped short. 'As I assured Colonel Brade when he offered assistance, everything is under control.'

'I have no doubt of that, I merely wish to find out what is occurring,' Boreas said.

'It's been building for months,' Verusius said gruffly. 'There's been unrest in the factories, people have started talking about the mysterious portents they've been seeing, like the freak storms in the middle of dry season, the mines all hitting dead seams in the space of a few weeks, strange mutated creatures attacking the ocean harvesters. Rumour went around that the astropaths were seeing whirls of blood in their dreams, and heard the screams of dying children. There's been more fights than usual, people even getting killed in brawls, and now this.'

'That still does not explain this outbreak of disobedience,' Boreas replied. 'Something, or someone, must have instigated this unrest.'

'A starship arrived this morning and docked at the orbital station,' explained Verusius. 'A story began to circulate that their Navigator had suffered some form of attack, that he'd been dragged out of his pilaster with blood streaming from his face, as if every blood vessel in his body had split. We tried to stop the rumours from spreading, ordered a security shutdown on the spaceport, but word got out anyway. People started flocking here for news, then it got ugly.'

'Why was none of this brought to my attention?' Boreas demanded. 'This information is pertinent to the security of our outpost.'

'That's nothing to do with me, you'll have to contact the Imperial commander's aides,' said Verusius with a shrug. 'If it gets any worse, we'll have to give the order to open fire.'

'No!' snapped Boreas with a glance at the security officers. 'There will be no unnecessary deaths. Allow me to assess the situation. I will inform you of further action to take.'

He walked further down the street, and saw that the rioters had built barricades of burning carts and tyres. They were throwing chunks of masonry at the enforcers, and hurling flaming brands into the buildings either side of the street. The security men and women had formed a rough line across the main boulevard leading to the starport, preventing the rioters access to the area, which was also close to the Imperial palaces. Boreas stepped up behind the line and gazed over the heads of the enforcers at the rabble further down the street. Those just in front of him glanced over their shoulders, startled.

There were some two hundred people in the mob, many carrying burning torches and improvised weapons of some kind. The street was filled with the cacophony of the riot, but Boreas's keen hearing could distinguish every sound. Their shrieks and shouts sounded over the crackling of the fires, the splintering of wood and the crash of breaking glass. He could smell the smoke from the fires, the sweat of bodies, the blood spilt in puddles across the street.

The red splashes of uniforms stood out against the black rock of the road where injured enforcers lay, their comrades unable to rescue them in the teeth of the rioters' fury. Boreas pushed his way through the line, one of the enforcers stumbling to his knees as the burly Space Marine eased past.

Boreas began to walk towards the rioting mob, as bricks and chunks of masonry splintered on the road around him. Within a few seconds, as the rioters caught sight of him, the rain of missiles faltered and then stopped; the shouting quietened and silenced. In a matter of moments, the Chaplain's sheer presence had quelled the violence, his appearance alone enough to drive thoughts of disobedience from the rioters' minds. Now it was replaced with fear and awe. Boreas was ten strides from the front of the mob, and continued his slow, purposeful walk. Just as the other citizens had done beforehand, the awed crowd split in front of him, forming into a circle as he stopped in the middle of the group. Only the crackling of flames and the odd chink of broken glass sliding under the feet of the protestors broke the silence that greeted him.

He gazed at those around him, their expressions of anger and hate now replaced by barely-contained terror. Many started crying, some fell to their knees and vomited from the shock. Others started gibbering prayers to the Emperor, bricks and clubs dropping from their grasp and clattering onto the rockcrete. Eventually silence fell, and all Boreas could hear was panicked panting and the hammering of hearts. None met the angered stare of the Interrogator-Chaplain as his eyes passed over the subdued crowd.

Boreas's own anger subsided as he looked at the people. These were not heretics to be killed; these were not malcontents intent on rebellion. They were citizens whose fear had turned to anger, who were crying out for guidance and help.

'Forgive us, my lord, forgive us!' begged one of the rioters, a scrawny man in the uniform of a Northport cargo loader, throwing himself at Boreas's feet. 'We did not seek to incur your wrath!'

'Be at peace!' Boreas declared, looming over the huddle of scared people. He reached down and pulled the prostrate man to his feet. 'Lay down your weapons, put aside your anger and fears. Look upon me and remember that the servants of the Emperor watch over you. Do not be afraid, for I am here as your guardian, not as your executioner.'

The crowd stood silently watching the Space Marine, casting glances at each other.

'But we are afraid, my lord,' the port worker told Boreas. 'A time of darkness is coming, we have seen the omens, we have heard the portents.'

'And I am here to protect you,' Boreas assured them. 'My brethren and I are here to watch over you, to guard you from danger. I stand here as a representative of the Dark Angels, a warrior of the Emperor, and I am here to remind you of the sacred oaths that bind our fate to yours. I renew that pledge here and now! I swear by the honour of my Chapter and my own life that I and my battle-brothers will lay down our lives in the defence of your world, whatever may beset us.'

'What is to become of us?' someone called out, a tall woman with blood in her blonde hair and a gash down the side of her face.

'I cannot blame you for your fears,' Boreas said. 'But I cannot pardon your actions. You cannot rise up against the servants of the Emperor and go unpunished. I shall request that the Imperial commander be lenient, but I ask you now to give yourselves to the mercy of your ruler, and subject yourself to the judgment of her judiciary. Who amongst you counts themselves leaders of this disturbance?'

There was some murmuring and three men stepped forward hesitantly, their heads bowed with shame. All three were similarly dressed in the overalls of port workers, supervisor badges stitched to their chests.

'There was another one!' somebody called out. 'He was the one who started it all!'

'An offworlder, he was there giving speeches,' another voice added.

'Tell me about this man,' Boreas demanded of the ringleaders. It was the oldest who replied, a man in his middle years with thick curly hair and a long beard.

'He worked on a ship that lies in orbit, it was his shuttle that brought the story of the mutilated Navigator,' the man said, gazing around the crowd. 'I cannot see him here.'

'Tell me about this ship,' Boreas asked, leaning over the man. 'From which ship did this man hail?'

'It was called the *Saint Carthen*,' another of the mob leaders answered. 'A rogue trader vessel, he said. He told us that he had come from other worlds, where there was revolt, where dark powers were at work in the minds of the governors. He accused Imperial Commander Sousan, said she was under the sway of alien influence.'

'The *Saint Carthen*? You are sure that was the name of the vessel?' Boreas demanded, gripping the front of the man's overalls and lifting him to his toes. The name had sent a shock through Boreas, as if he had been struck.

'Yes, yes, my lord,' he stuttered back, his eyes filling with fear. Boreas released him and turned away quickly, the gathered people stumbling and tripping to get out of his way. Boreas stopped after a few paces, seeing the enforcers walking cautiously forward. He turned to the crowd again.

'Subject yourselves to the judgment of the courts, and praise the Emperor that I am in a tolerant mood!' he warned them before striding off, his mind a whirlwind of dark thoughts.

Verusius stood beside Boreas's bike as the Interrogator-Chaplain walked quickly towards the gaggle of security officials,

'Many thanks for your intervention, my lord,' Verusius said with a quick bow. 'Your mercy does you credit.'

'Punish them as you see fit,' Boreas said, pushing Verusius aside and stepping over the bike. He had only a single concern now – to ascertain the truth regarding the *Saint Carthen's* presence. If it indeed was at Piscina, it heralded far more danger than a few rioting citizens and bursts of superstitious unrest.

'Remember that the weak of mind need a strong hand to guide them,' he told Verusius sharply. 'Benevolence is to be lauded, but weakness will only allow the cancer of heresy to fester unseen. It is not my judgment to make, that is for your lawmakers, but it is my suggestion to execute the ringleaders. They have betrayed their positions of trust, and this should not be tolerated. Chastise the others quickly and then return them to work, for inactivity will breed dissent. I must also demand that you find anyone who comes from the *Saint Carthen*, and execute them immediately.'

He did not explain that if Verusius did not heed the Chaplain's suggestion, it might well be that the Dark Angels would indeed have to become executioners. The fewer who knew about the *Saint Carthen*, the less likely that its unsavoury history would be discovered. Verusius began to speak again, but the throbbing roar of the bike's engine kicking into life drowned his voice out. Boreas slewed the bike around, the back wheel spitting dust and smoke, and raced off down the street. His heart was heavy as he powered his way back to the outpost, oblivious to the wandering citizens and patrolling enforcers he scattered in his wake.

THE TALE OF ASTELAN
PART THREE

THE ROOM SWAM and spun in Astelan's vision, swirling into
a vortex of grey above the slab. He had lost all concept of
time, his experiences reduced to alternating periods of
pain and emptiness. In some way, he had come to dread
the interludes of isolation more than the torture. When
Boreas was there, twisting everything he had done, turning
Astelan's own words into knives to stab him with, it made
it easier for him to focus. Despite the ache of his wounds
and the browbeating of the Interrogator-Chaplain, Astelan
could concentrate on defending himself against the
accusations. He realised that he was trying to get the Dark
Angels to understand why he had done the things they
were calling 'crimes'. That desire to strip them of their
ignorance, to get them to see the greater vision behind his
deeds, was a challenge he could hold on to, a tangible goal
to strive for.

But when they left him, for what seemed like days on
end, it was harder to continue the fight. Points that had

seemed so clear when he had explained them to Boreas became swathed in doubt.

The Chaplain's questions were etched into Astelan's mind, nagging at him, weakening his resolve. What if he had lost his way? What if he had gone insane, and everything he had done had been nothing but the vile acts of a tortured mind?

Astelan fought against these thoughts, because to pay any attention to them was to accept that everything he had done had been meaningless. And if that was true, then the greatest moment of his life, the time when he had voiced his support for Luther, was also meaningless. And if that were meaningless, Boreas was right and he had committed a grave sin.

But he had not sinned, Astelan was adamant of that in the precious moments when he could gather his thoughts. His interrogators had not been there; they did not know what it had been like. Now was the opportunity for them to discover that uncharted part of their history, the event that so obviously marked their souls. Astelan could teach them what he knew, lead them back to the true path of the Emperor. He would cast aside their suspicions and their doctrines, and turn the interrogation to his benefit. There was much he had to say, and the Dark Angels would hear it.

And yet he had also to contest with the psyker, the warlock Samiel. The memory of the man inside him, probing his thoughts and feelings, left Astelan feeling violated. This, most of all, was the most troubling thing to him. Along with the alien, the psychic mutant was the greatest threat to mankind. The Emperor had known that, he had told them of the dangers of possession and corruption. Had he not censured the Thousand Sons for their dabbling in magic? And now, ten thousand years of misrule had left the Imperium rife with witches. Entire organisations dedicated to their recruitment and training. They were an affront to everything the Emperor had wanted to achieve. The Adeptus Astra Telepathica with their soul-binding ritual to leech away the Emperor's magnificence for themselves; the Scholastika Psykana for inducting psykers into the military. It pained Astelan to think of it, the sheer negligence of allowing humanity's inner enemy to thrive, to be nurtured at mankind's expense. Had they forgotten the perils, or did they choose simply to ignore them, risking the future of the Imperium and humanity as a whole?

And the pinnacle of folly, they had allowed psykers to become Space Marines! Librarians they called them, a comforting euphemism so that they did not have to think too deeply of the consequences. It was a mask, a smokescreen, so that those in power could pretend that there was purpose in allowing these abominations to exist. Astelan feared for the Imperium that had grown from the calamity of the Horus Heresy, and he feared for mankind's chances of survival in a galaxy determined to extinguish it.

But what could he do? As a Chapter commander he had been at the forefront of the battle to protect mankind's future. Now he was surrounded by ignorance and hate for what he represented.

But what did he truly represent? Again, Boreas's questions teased at the edges of his thoughts, unravelling the arguments he had used to justify his actions. Was he truly any different from the primarchs, who had subverted the Emperor's cause to their own? Who was he, a warrior born, to judge the fate of mankind? It was his role to follow orders, to fight battles and command men, not to set the course of humanity's future. Was it really arrogance that had driven him to forsake Lion El'Jonson; did he really know the mind of the Emperor as well as he claimed?

'I see you have been ruminating on your life,' said Boreas. Astelan was panicked for a moment. He had not heard the Interrogator-Chaplain enter. How long had he been unaware of Boreas's presence, his attention locked inside his own head?

'I am trying to get that stinking warlock's voice out of my head, but he has poisoned me!' hissed Astelan, trying to wipe away the filth he felt on his face, but the chains were too tight and his hands waved mockingly in front of him. For a moment Astelan thought they were Samiel's hands, ready to blot out his mind again, to delve into the recesses of his memory, and he shuddered. Shaking his head, Astelan focussed on the cell and Boreas.

'You are doing well, Astelan,' the Chaplain told him. 'I see we are driving out the impurity and lies, and I hear your shouts as you cry out for forgiveness.'

'Never!' Astelan's resolve returned instantly, his mind suddenly clear again. He would never admit he had been wrong. It would be a condemnation of everything the Emperor taught, and would condone the travesty that now passed for the Imperium. 'I need no forgiveness. It is you who should beg for mercy, from the Emperor himself, for perverting his dream, his glorious ambition.'

'I have not come to listen to your ravings, I am here for information,' Boreas snapped.

'Ask what you will, I will only tell you the truth,' Astelan replied. 'Whether you welcome it, well that is something I doubt in my heart.'

'We shall see about that,' Boreas said, taking up his customary position, arms crossed, at the head of the slab. 'You claim you travelled to Tharsis on a ship, and there were other Fallen with you. Tell me how you came by this vessel and these companions.'

'First, I must tell you what befell me after the battles on Caliban,' Astelan told him. 'It was a time that began with great confusion and pain. For an eternity it felt as if I was shapeless, my form distorted and twisted inside out by seething power. I was at the centre of a storm, and part of the maelstrom itself. I had only an infinitely small awareness of myself, of who and what I was. And then I awoke, as if from a dream. It was as if Caliban, the fighting, the fire from the heavens, were all an imaginary memory at first.'

'Where? Where did you find yourself?' Boreas asked.

'That was most vexing of all,' Astelan said with a frown. He still felt dizzy and sick from his torture at Boreas's hands and the mental probing of Samiel, and he closed his eyes to aid his concentration. 'I was on a rock-strewn slope, a barren, lifeless wasteland stretching out before me. Gone were the thick forests of Caliban, the sky was yellow overhead and a bulging star hung above the horizon. At first I thought that perhaps I had not awakened, that I was still dreaming. The impossibility of it baffled me, made me doubt my sanity. But as that sun sank out of view and the night sky filled with stars I did not recognise, I realised that it was real. Uncomprehending of how I arrived, I determined to discover what manner of place I now found myself in. It was to be a long time before I discovered the truth.'

'And the truth was?' asked Boreas.

'I was far, far from Caliban,' sighed Astelan. 'When the next morning rose, I decided to walk eastwards. There was no real purpose behind it, but part of me said that I should go towards the sun. I hoped I would find a settlement, or failing that at least some indication as to where I was. I marched the whole day, across the scree-strewn slopes of a great dormant volcano, and I found nothing.'

'How did you survive?'

'The planet was not as lifeless as I first thought. There were scattered copses of spindly trees and thorny bushes. Here, I discovered, if you dug deep enough you could find trickling streams passing through the rock, small pools under the surface. There were rodents, serpents and insects all feeding upon each other, and they were not difficult to catch. In this manner I sustained myself. I fear that if it had not been for this wondrous body the Emperor has given me, I would have perished. Had not

Gav Thorpe

my stomach, my muscles and my bones been so efficient, I would have starved or been cursed with disease from infected water. But we were created to survive, were we not? The Emperor moulded us so that we could eke life out of death and continue the fight.'

'But what of the ship, how did you come by it?' Boreas asked impatiently.

'I counted the days as I wandered, always heading east, always towards the morning sun,' Astelan continued purposefully, glad of the Chaplain's frustration. 'At night I would hunt, for that was when most of the creatures sallied forth from their burrows and lairs for food. For two hundred and forty-two days and nights, I existed this way before I found any sign of intelligent habitation. I spent that time trying to make sense of what had happened, reliving the battles, trying to piece together the last moments of the fighting on Caliban. To this day I cannot say, I have not found the answers.'

'What happened after two hundred and forty-two days?' There was no anger in Boreas's voice, only a terseness born of irritation.

'I saw a light in the night sky,' Astelan said, smiling at the memory. 'At first I thought it a comet or meteor, but as I watched, it circled across the heavens to the north and then disappeared. No shooting star moves like it did and hope stirred within me again, as I realised that it was a ship or aircraft of some kind. At that point, I did not give too much thought to whether it was friend or foe, I took it simply as a sign of where to go. So for twelve more days I headed north, and on the fourth day I saw the ship leaving again and pressed towards its destination more directly.'

'And did you find where the ship had landed?'

'Like everything else on that forsaken world, humanity had chosen to live under the surface, to dig down into the rock for sanctuary,' explained Astelan. 'I saw armoured portals delved into the side of a great hill, atop which sat a great expanse lit with hundreds of lights to guide ships in. Having seen only sunlight and starlight for so long, that blaze of yellow and red was glorious in my eyes as it glowed on the horizon. I doubled my efforts, crossing the rocky plains at speed to reach the aurora of civilisation that lay ahead.'

'What then? What did you find there? Where was this place?' Boreas's questions were spat out like bolter fire.

'As I neared the end of my journey, uncertainty suddenly gripped me,' Astelan said languidly, enjoying the dissatisfaction of Boreas. 'The Imperium was being torn apart by the war unleashed by Horus. The dominions of the Emperor were divided, and I had no way of telling which side the inhabitants of that underground city belonged to. I could see no signs of war, and I spent a day watching, seeking some sign of their allegiance, but there was none.'

'But the Horus Heresy was over. For a long time the Emperor had been victorious,' Boreas pointed out.

'I had no inkling of the time that had passed, no way of knowing the great ages I had missed, or how such a thing might happen,' Astelan replied, opening his eyes and gazing at Boreas. 'In the end, I dared enter, reckoning that the risk of death at the hands of traitors was outweighed by the certain death that would eventually overtake even me in the wasteland. I presented myself at the nearest gate, a warrior of the Dark Angels. I had never seen such surprise as was written on the man's face when I appeared. But he did not try to attack me, and I realised my fears were misplaced. Overwhelmed, the guards brought me inside and called for their superiors.'

Astelan grinned, his cracked lips starting to bleed again, remembering the relief he had felt at being welcomed into the underground settlement. It had not been until that moment that he had realised how lost he had felt, how the tumultuous events of his recent life had so disorientated him.

'They called together their ruling council,' he continued. 'There was little I could tell them, for I knew nothing of how I had got there. The priests called it a miracle, saying that the Emperor had delivered me to them. But for all of the questions they asked me, I had so many more. What news of the Heresy had they learned? Where was I, and how might I rejoin my brethren? And I learned much in that initial meeting. To my horror, I was told that over nine thousand years had swept past me. It was impossible to grasp, it was too enormous, too vast to understand. I was shocked, struck dumb as I tried to assimilate this information.'

'But you eventually came to terms with what happened, I assume,' said Boreas.

'Never fully,' admitted Astelan. 'The scope of it is beyond imagining, beyond comprehension. I rested in the chambers they led me to, incapable of rational thought as I tried to unravel what had happened, but there were no answers. Unable to rationalise what I was experiencing, I instead resolved to discover as much as I could about what had happened in my extraordinary absence. I started with the obvious and explored this new place where I found myself. It was a mining colony, on a world called Scappe Delve. They had few accurate star charts, but I was able to estimate to my consternation that I was some twelve hundred light years from Caliban. Again, the isolation and fear struck me, so far from the world I had adopted as my home, but so strange had been the other revelations, it was easier to accept this horrifying fact.'

'And so you learned of what had come to pass since you rose up against the Lion and waged war on Caliban.' Boreas's voice was steadier now. He had evidently resolved to allow Astelan to tell his tale in whatever fashion he chose.

'Facts are hard to distinguish from hearsay and fabrication in these times,' sighed Astelan. 'Nearly ten thousand years have obscured the events of the Heresy, and the histories of Scappe Delve were not extensive. But I had been there at the time the Emperor still walked among us, I could sieve the grains of truth from the legends. The chronicles told of how Horus had struck against Terra, and battle had raged inside the Imperial Palace itself. The Warmaster had unleashed the bloodthirsty World Eaters, and the Imperial Fists had held the wall against relentless assaults. But the end, the end was so confused as to be unintelligible. All that I could extract was the Emperor's victory, his personal triumph over Horus in single combat, and the great wounds he had suffered to secure his triumph. It was then that the meddling of the Ministorum became more evident. The records spoke of the Emperor ascending to godhood from a golden throne, his magnificence spreading across the galaxy like a beacon.'

'Fanciful, to be sure, but inherently truthful,' Boreas confirmed. 'There are few who truly understand what transpired in those dark times, and even what I know, a member of the Inner Circle of the Dark Angels, is but a fraction of the whole truth.'

'It is unsurprising, when man has been taught to abhor knowledge, to venerate relics of the past over the living and the hopes of the future, and to confuse myth with reality.' It was a wonder to Astelan how much the Imperium had changed since the passing of the Emperor – a man dedicated to knowledge and understanding, of overcoming the superstition and ignorance of the Age of Strife. 'The Emperor embraced knowledge. It was this that allowed Him to create us, to know of the dire perils that awaited humanity and foresee the solution. You who have been born and raised in these unenlightened times, who became Space Marines and have fought wholly within the Imperium you know, cannot understand the way it looks to me. Your perspective is warped because you gaze at it from the outside. Even your histories have evolved over the millennia, reinterpreted, censored, rewritten so that they are worth little more than bedtime stories for children.'

'And so, with your wisdom from the ancient ages of man, you claim to know the way forward?' The scorn had returned to Boreas's voice and his face was twisted in a sneer. 'I have heard these delusions from you before, and they are no less arrogant now as when you implemented them in your tyranny over Tharsis.'

'This perspective has nothing to do with Tharsis, it goes far beyond that,' countered Astelan. 'It comes from before the Horus Heresy, back to when the change started, with the coming of the primarchs.'

'We shall deal with that later. First tell me more about your time on Scappe Delve.'

'At first it was impossible for my thoughts to encompass just how much the galaxy had changed, for it had remained the same in many ways,' Astelan said, struggling for the words to express how he felt. How could he explain what it was like to discover that the galaxy had aged ten millennia without his knowledge?

'Though no longer spearheaded by the Great Crusade of the Legions, mankind's expansion and reconquest had continued, and the Imperium now stretched beyond a million worlds.' Astelan paused, half expecting an interruption, but Boreas seemed content to let him continue without the usual sniping remarks. 'I had felt joy that the Emperor's vision was still alive, until I began to read more, and spoke to the priests, the tech-adepts and the councillors. I saw the great crumbling edifice that the Imperium had become, collapsing under its own size, lost amidst its own complexity. I saw the factions, the internecine conflicts, the ebb and flow of power from individuals to faceless, unaccountable organisations. After the passing of the Emperor, even the primarchs had failed to continue the very thing they had been originally created for. And when they died or disappeared, even less remained of that core ideal of the Emperor.'

'And so you have come to hate the Imperium you once built, jealous that the power now resides with others?' Boreas accused him.

'I do not hate the Imperium, I pity it,' Astelan explained, his pointed look telling Boreas that he pitied the Chaplain almost as much. 'The billions of adepts striving to make sense of it, their masters in their towers, to the High Lords of Terra who now claim to rule in the Emperor's name, they cannot control what they have created. Mankind no longer has leaders, it has weak men trying desperately to cling on to what they have. Oh, there have been a few enlightened individuals like Macharius, who have relit the torch and sought to push back the darkness, but the galaxy they lived in no longer tolerates heroes. It supports mediocrity, facelessness, suppression of man's right to endeavour to achieve glory.'

'And yet the greatest threat to the Imperium was Horus,' argued the Chaplain. 'He was imbued with the powers you speak of, who had the absolute authority of the Emperor, who was trusted to lead mankind forward into a new age. When you had just a small measure of that power, it corrupted you and you turned Tharsis into a charnel house. Admit that such power is not for a single man to wield!'

'It is the same woeful lack of courage that gripped Tharsis during the rebellion,' rasped Astelan. 'The fear of what might be strangles humanity, not daring to risk what they have in an effort to gain everything that it is their right to possess. Timidity and vacillation now rule the Imperium. You have become driven by a dread of the unknown, imprisoned by doubt, shackled by the desire for security and predictability. The vision has been clouded by a miasma of petty trials and tribulations.'

'And so you determined to alter this, to reforge the Imperium into what you saw as its original purpose,' snarled Boreas.

'My ambitions were never that grand, for only the Emperor could achieve such a thing,' Astelan said, shaking his head vigorously. 'But I thought I might light a signal fire, a beacon to others who strain at the bonds that keep them from the great fight, so the Imperium can become a thing of glory again, not just survival.'

'And so you had to get off Scappe Delve,' Boreas brought the questioning back to Astelan's account of events. 'There was nothing you could do on a distant mining world, no great triumphs to be had, no glorious battles to be won.'

'It was the need to know more, to find out all I could about the galaxy I now lived in, that drove me, almost consumed me,' Astelan explained. 'My existence had been turned inside out, and fate had cast me up on a dark, unknown shore. You are right, Scappe Delve became like a prison to me, confined to a narrow world of tunnels and artificial light. But the world was on the fringes of wilderness space, completely self-sufficient with its underground fungus cultivators and water recyclers, it had little contact with the rest of the Imperium. Even the ore they mined went nowhere, and they dug more and more halls and chambers just to store it. How ridiculous is that! It was a forgotten world, too unimportant, too small to warrant the attention of the wise and mighty of the Imperium.'

'But you had seen a ship before, so you knew that eventually another would come,' guessed Boreas. 'And so you waited and plotted patiently until an opportunity presented itself.'

'I indeed had to be patient,' agreed Astelan. 'For two and a half years, no ship even visited the star system. But then a vessel came. I learned that, by chance, it was the same one that had guided me to the mine all that time ago. It was called the *Saint Carthen*, captained by a merchant named Rosan Trialartes. A rogue trader, they called him, and I asked what it meant. You can imagine how I felt when they explained.'

'You saw the rogue traders as just another indication of the decline of the Space Marines,' Boreas stated flatly. 'Civilian explorers given charter to trade without restriction, to travel beyond the known borders of the Imperium to discover new worlds. I expect it vexed you greatly to know that when once it had been the Space Marine Chapters that had forged into the darkness of space, it was now the right of merchant families and dispossessed nobles.'

'Yes, it vexed me greatly, as you say, but I contained my ire,' admitted Astelan. 'The people of Scappe Delve were not responsible, they were victims. But the arrival of Trialartes was an opportunity to see what had become of the galaxy, to compare the dry words of the history scrolls with what really lay out beyond Scappe Delve.'

'And so you left with this rogue trader, Rosan Trialartes. What happened then?' asked Boreas. 'How did you come across the other Fallen? And what took you to Tharsis?'

'I did not leave immediately, Trialartes at first objected to my presence, for no other reason than selfish fear,' Astelan said, his jaw clenching angrily with the recollection.

'I would have thought that a rogue trader would be pleased to have a Space Marine aboard his ship,' argued Boreas.

'As did I,' agreed Astelan.

'So what were his objections?' asked Boreas, his face expressionless.

'They were vague generalisations,' muttered Astelan. 'He called it an affront to his Warrant of Trade, claiming that my presence would limit the freedoms his charter as a rogue trader gave him. He called me a symbol of the authority that he was free from. However, the council of

Scappe Delve argued in my favour, and eventually he relented and agreed to take me aboard. I think that the people of the mine were pleased to see me leave, for some unknown reason my being there caused them unfounded anxiety.'

'It is common enough,' said Boreas. 'For most of humanity, we Space Marines are a distant power, aloof defenders from history and legend. It is not surprising that sometimes they are perturbed to find out that we really exist and can still walk amongst them.'

'Trialartes's hesitation was far more understandable, as I discovered,' Astelan said with an abrupt, bitter laugh. 'We travelled from Scappe Delve to Orionis to offload the ore he had taken from the miners, in exchange for lasguns and power packs. But my suspicions were aroused. The exchange took place in the outer reaches of the system. No contact was made with the inhabited world there, and he made no attempt to dock with the orbital station.'

'He was a smuggler?' asked Boreas.

'It was unjust to use such a term for a rogue trader, he told me,' Astelan answered after a moment's thought. He was ashamed of what he had allowed the rogue trader to do without retribution. 'As he explained it to me, someone had to ship armaments from system to system. His conduct worried me, but I was unfamiliar with the customs and ways of this changed Imperium, and I felt an odd naïveté in my dealings with Trialartes, for he knew so much more about the galaxy than I did. So, in my ignorance, I did nothing and let the matter pass.'

'But what of the other Fallen?' Boreas's insistence had returned. 'Where did you meet them?'

'You wish to hear what befell me, then let me tell you in my own way!' snapped Astelan.

'I do not care for your endless tales, I am here to make you face your sinful actions and repent,' Boreas snarled back. 'Your dealings with the other Fallen, what of them?'

The two of them fell silent, their stares locked on each other as they both tried to exert their will. For several minutes, the only sound was their heavy breathing and the odd hiss or crackle from the brazier.

'I met them at a place that Trialartes jokingly referred to as Port Imperial,' Astelan said eventually. 'I had urged him to take me back to Caliban, so that I might rejoin my brethren, but he confessed ignorance of its location. I found this unbelievable, that the home of the first Legion should have fallen into obscurity. I showed him where it was on the charts and he vehemently denied that there was an inhabited world there. I demanded that he take me there, but he refused. In the end, I was forced to abandon the idea. We made several more journeys, travelling from system to system, unloading the arms in one place and taking on board plasma chambers, which we took somewhere else, and so it continued for many months. But none of the worlds we visited held what I sought. Trialartes plied his trade on the edges of the Imperium, travelling between the distant worlds on the borders of wilderness space. When I spoke to him of my desire to discover more, to go to a world with repositories of knowledge that I could study, he suggested I might find a more willing captain at Port Imperial. It was there that I met the other dispossessed brethren.'

'And where is this place?' demanded Boreas.

'Save yourself the labour of seeking it out, interrogator,' laughed Astelan. 'It does not exist any more.'

'You are lying!' roared Boreas, grabbing Astelan by the chin and thrusting his head back against the interrogation table.

'I have no need to lie,' spat Astelan between gritted teeth. 'Do you think I would seek to protect those renegades and outcasts who lived there? Do you think I hide my brethren from your attentions? No, I tell you the truth, Port Imperial is no more. I should know, I destroyed it.'

'More destruction to sate your appetite for carnage?' snarled Boreas.

'Certainly not!' Astelan wrenched his face from Boreas's grip, and the Chaplain stepped back. 'Port Imperial was a den of smugglers, pirates and heretics. I was horrified to find two Dark Angels there. Port Imperial was once an orbital dock and shipyard. The wondrous scribes of the Administratum had forgotten its existence over the centuries, after it had been abandoned after some ancient war. Once used as a staging post for Imperial fleets, it had been deserted for several centuries until the raiders moved in. On one of those ships, over one hundred years before my coming, had been Brothers Methelas and Anovel.'

'You knew them?' Boreas's voice betrayed his surprise.

'Not in the slightest,' Astelan replied with a dismissive shake of his head. 'They were not from my Chapter. They were not even from the old Legion, they were sons of Caliban. But they recognised me at once. At first they acted as if the Emperor himself had arrived, but I soon stopped their undignified behaviour.'

'Explain yourself,' Boreas snapped.

'They could not decide whether to be afraid or to rejoice,' Astelan told him. 'They had become undisciplined, they had lost their way. Oh, they had soon risen to control Port Imperial, none dared stand against them, but they were without purpose or resolve. Truly you might describe them as Fallen, for they had set themselves up as lords over pirates and scum.'

'Whereas you had greater ambitions, to set yourself up as a lord over a whole world of hundreds of millions of souls.'

'Still you persist with this innuendo and accusations, despite all that I have told you,' lamented Astelan. 'I find your fear of the truth utterly remarkable and inexcusable.'

'So what led to the destruction of the space station?' This time it was Boreas who ignored the jibe.

'With my coming, I took command, and they obeyed me without question,' Astelan said with pride. 'While they had been content to exist, to survive at the edge of civilisation, I told them what I had learned, of what I now dreamed I might achieve. It was not long before they shared my vision, for a return to an age of greatness. My vision inspired them, and together we devised a way for us to take a step closer towards that magnificent goal. For a start, we needed a ship. The *Saint Carthen* was the largest and best ship we could commandeer, but Trialartes turned down our offers. He resorted to violence to try to force us from his ship. It was a grave mistake on his part.'

'You killed him and took his ship?' Boreas was incredulous.

'A brutal but basically accurate summary of events,' admitted Astelan. 'Some of the crew took stand against us, and doomed themselves with their resistance. Some of the other ships' captains there also made the mistake of opposing us, and it was at that point we realised the shortcomings of our newly gained command. She lacked all but the most minimal weaponry, she had a few batteries of lasers to defend herself, but insufficient for the type of vessel we would need if we were to launch a new crusade. We boarded one of the other ships and offered her crew the same choice we had offered Trialartes. Foolishly, the captain could not see the sense of our offer and refused to support us. Again we were forced to fight, and had to kill all but a few of the crew before the others acquiesced to our needs. Once we had demonstrated our strength, there was no further resistance.'

'And so now you ruled a fleet of raiders and smugglers,' Boreas continued scornfully. 'It must have been hard for you, once a lauded Chapter commander, to be reduced to a pirate prince.'

'I had no intention of leading such a collection of scum,' snorted Astelan. 'We spent months refitting the

Saint Carthen to be more worthy of her role, taking weapons from the other vessels so that she was fit for command. The crews of the other ships co-operated out of fear, nothing more.'

'And so what did you plan to do with this warship you had created?' Boreas asked. 'Did you think you could single-handedly continue the Great Crusade?'

'It should never have ended!' Astelan rasped. 'The treachery of Horus was a great setback, but catastrophe had been averted, and it was the failure of the primarchs and humanity's leaders to launch mankind back into the stars. But I see that my arguments still fall on deaf ears.'

'You have no arguments, only delusional ravings,' said Boreas, turning away again as if to ignore his prisoner's words.

'My delusions, if that is what you wish to call them, are more powerful than anything else in the Imperium,' Astelan told the Chaplain's broad back. 'Can you not imagine what might be achieved if humanity were truly united again? There is not a force amongst the stars that could resist us!'

'United behind you, I suppose,' said Boreas, looking back at Astelan. 'You would set yourself up as a new Emperor and lead us into this fantastical golden age you dream of.'

'You do not comprehend the vileness of your accusations.' Astelan longed to be free of his chains, which were weighing ever more heavily on his tired body. 'I could never rival the Emperor, nobody can. Even Horus, favoured amongst the primarchs, could not match his greatness. No, it is not I alone that should lead mankind, it should be all Space Marines. They have taken away your true purpose, turned you into their slaves.'

'We exist to protect mankind, not to rule it!' Boreas turned on his heel and pointed an accusing finger at Astelan. 'Admit the heresies of what you preach! Accept that when you turned on Caliban, you broke every oath you had sworn, neglected every duty that was yours.'

'It was not we who were the oath-breakers!' protested Astelan.

'You abandoned everything for your own ambitions, from Caliban through to your reign on Tharsis!' Boreas's voice rose to a roar as he strode across the cell.

'That cannot be so, for I knew nothing of Tharsis when we set out from Port Imperial,' argued Astelan, managing to calm his voice.

'So what did you intend to do?' asked Boreas. 'Travel to Terra perhaps? Take your arguments to the Senatorum Imperialis so that the High Lords could see your great vision?'

'The High Lords are less than nothing to me.' Astelan would have spat if his mouth had not been so dry. 'They are puppets who pretend to hold power. No, it is the people of the Imperium, the untold billions who hold the key to mankind's destiny. The Imperium has grown stagnant, complacent over the centuries and millennia, with those holding the reins of power merely content to continue to rule. It is from those who toil every day, who fight aboard the starships and sacrifice their lives for the Emperor on distant battlefields, who will drive mankind forward into an age of supremacy.'

'And how did you think you could bring this about, with your crude warship and piratical crew?' Boreas asked, now composed again.

'To lead by example!' exclaimed Astelan, leaning towards the Chaplain, trying to urge him to understand. 'We turned our guns on the other ships, obliterated Port Imperial and chased down those who tried to flee. It was those raiders, those renegades, who were almost as guilty as the cowardly note-takers who hold power. They were parasites, feeding off the rotting carcass of the Imperium, draining it of its strength. How many ships are wasted chasing corsairs when they could be pushing back the boundaries of the Emperor's realm? How many lives are lost fighting these leeches – lives that could be spent exterminating aliens and settling new worlds to build our strength? Just as the Imperium has spiralled into decline, so too can one great act be a catalyst that can see the Emperor's vision complete. A world won is a world that can contribute to the greater cause. From that world, another can be rediscovered or conquered, and from that another and another. That is the Great Crusade: it is not about battles and war, it is about domination for mankind.'

'I still fail to see how you and a single ship could bring this about,' Boreas argued.

'The *Saint Carthen* was merely a means to an end, to take me to where I could enact my plans,' Astelan explained. 'As you have already learnt, I achieved that end on Tharsis until you destroyed my great army, blind-folded by those weaker than yourselves.'

'But you said you knew nothing of Tharsis. You must have had some plan, some objective in mind,' insisted Boreas.

'At first my goals were nebulous and unfocussed,' Astelan explained slowly. 'I learnt much from Anovel and Methelas. They told me of how the Legions had been broken down into Chapters following the Horus Heresy. Of how aliens continued to run rampant, and traitors rebelled against the Emperor unchecked. The plan, the return to the Great Crusade, was growing inside me, fuelling me. It did not reach such depth and scope until Tharsis, but it was subconsciously pushing me onwards. The star maps of Trialartes were woefully inadequate, and with no Navigator to pilot the ship any distance through the warp, we edged our way back into more populated star systems.

'It was then that the greatest tragedy of Horus's treachery was revealed to me. With their everlasting war against the Emperor, the traitors have sullied the name of the

Space Marines. As you said, others do not understand us, and when we encountered Imperial vessels, they took us to be renegades. They fled or attacked. Some we had to destroy to protect ourselves, salvaging what we could from the wreckage. We encountered resistance from the worlds we visited, and they drove us away. A ship cannot survive without supplies, and so eventually we had to take what we needed from other vessels, from outposts.'

'Piracy,' Boreas stated flatly. 'Your conscience reveals you as a pirate. The armour you wear, the cause you believe in, does not alter that. You had become the very thing you say you despised so much.'

'Is it piracy that you wield bolters from another world?' asked Astelan. 'Are you pirates because the food that sustains you is taken from others?'

'A poor comparison, for we are supplied by ancient treaties,' Boreas replied with a derisive shake of his head. 'As we fulfil our duty to protect mankind, so mankind has a duty to feed and arm us. There is no threat involved, no violence.'

'No threat, you say,' Astelan continued. 'What about the threat of angering the Dark Angels? What about the fear of retribution should your suppliers break their treaties? It is only different because you claim it is justifiable. What was I to do? My needs were no less legitimate, my goals no less worthy. But the impenetrable mass that the Imperium has become had no place for me. We did not fit into the warped scheme and so we were forced to take other measures.'

'And your brethren, Methelas and Anovel, what of them?' Boreas demanded.

'They never fully understood what it is that drives me,' Astelan told him. 'How could they, they were not old Legion? Yes, they had supported Luther, but I discovered that they were still driven by pettiness. I do not think they truly believed in my plans for the Greater Imperium. They sought merely to strike at those whom they believed had cast them out. It was vengeance they sought, not a higher purpose. When we finally came upon Tharsis they would not accompany me, and we parted company there.'

'They abandoned you,' Boreas suggested shrewdly.

'I do not know what their motives were, but they left without me,' Astelan confirmed.

'So just how did your rebuilding of the Imperium lead you to a world torn apart by civil war?' Boreas asked.

'Our ship was damaged, we sought a haven, but by chance we arrived in the Tharsis system first and my life was changed forever,' explained Astelan.

'How had your ship come to be damaged?' Boreas's tone was quiet, almost nonchalant, as if he was merely observing Astelan and had no genuine interest in his answers.

'We had been falsely marked as renegades and were hunted and hounded,' Astelan related the grim memories. 'The situation had become intolerable, my dreams were almost shattered. Circumstance had turned against me, engineered by those who did not want the servants of the Emperor to hear my message, for it threatened everything they had taught for ten thousand years. A fleet was despatched to destroy us, and we were almost caught at Giasameth. We had to flee, something I had never before done in my life.'

'So it is cowardice that has driven you for all these years?' Boreas asked sharply. 'Do you now accept that it was your fear of duty, your dread of the burden laid upon you, that caused you to turn upon your masters?'

'No, it was not as a coward that I fled, it was with the growing knowledge that my message, my vision, was crucial,' Astelan answered emphatically. 'It was more important than me, and I would willingly lay down my life if another was to continue the quest, but I found none that could do so. The trials of that time only strengthened my resolve to succeed. It reinforced my belief that the Imperium has become infested with corruption and self-servitude. They erect fanciful statues of the Emperor across the galaxy, pay homage to Him and plead for Him to answer their prayers, without any consideration of what the Emperor truly represents.'

'And what do you consider that to be?' Boreas was getting angrier and began pacing to and fro in front of the shelves of torture implements.

'Humanity, Boreas, He represents humanity,' Astelan said slowly, as if instructing a slow-witted child. 'Something that you or I could never do, for it has been a long time since either of us could consider ourselves normal humans. In creating the Space Marines He took mankind back to the stars. You still accuse me of selfish ambition, but you have not been listening to what I have said. It was not for my benefit alone that I fought in the bloody campaigns of the Great Crusade. It was not purely for myself that I waged war on dozens of worlds. The truth is, we did not create the Imperium for ourselves, we created it for those who were unable to. It was not for the Adeptus Terra, the techpriests, the Ministorum, or the merchant houses, it was for all of mankind. You must surely understand that the Imperium as it is now is not humanity, it has become simply a means to sustain itself.'

'I swore to protect the realm of the Emperor and defend mankind,' insisted Boreas.

'And I swore that same oath!' Astelan reminded him vehemently.

'You broke that oath when you betrayed the Lion!' bellowed Boreas, storming towards Astelan.

'And I tell you that it was not we who committed the first treachery!' Astelan was getting sick of protesting his innocence. 'It was the primarchs, your thrice-accursed Lion amongst them!'

'Your heresies are without limit!' Boreas roared, smashing a fist across Astelan's face, rupturing his puffy lips and spilling thick blood onto the slab. 'I see that you have not progressed at all. You are no closer to admitting your sins than before. Your deep-rooted hatred has tainted everything inside you, and you are blind to it. If you choose not to see it for yourself, then we will open your eyes for you.'

'No! You are not listening!' Astelan warned, ignoring the pain in his mouth and the taste of his own blood. 'Please, heed my words! Do not give in to the darkness they have wrapped around you. You can still be victorious, you can triumph over those who seek to destroy you.' Astelan's hands were outstretched towards the Interrogator-Chaplain as far as the chains would allow, and Boreas slapped them away.

'You and the other traitors destroyed us the moment you chose to side with Luther the Betrayer,' Boreas snarled. 'I see that there is yet more work for Brother Samiel.'

'Keep that warlock away from me!' Astelan could not keep the desperation from his voice. He had never been afraid in his life, but the thought of the witch's return filled him with unnatural dread. 'Keep him out of my head, his corruption is still inside me, I can feel it seeping into my soul.'

'Then repent your sins!' Boreas's voice dropped to a subtle whisper. 'It is an easy thing to save your soul. Just admit your sins, recant your heresies and it will end painlessly. You do not even have to speak, just nod your head.'

Astelan slumped back, his chains rattling and closed his eyes tightly. Sweat ran off him in rivulets that collected on the slab, and many of his wounds had reopened with his exertions, staining his body with blood.

'I do not acknowledge your right to judge me,' he said in a hoarse whisper. 'I do not accept your authority.'

'Then you leave me no other choice,' Boreas told him, striding to the cell door and wrenching it open.

THE TALE OF BOREAS
PART THREE

'THEY LEFT NO journey plans?' Boreas asked over the comm. He was standing on the bridge of the Dark Angels' ship, the *Blade of Caliban*, in orbit over Piscina IV. He had contacted the rapid strike vessel to prepare to seize the rogue trader's ship as he had ridden back to the keep, but it had left orbit. Now he and the other Space Marines were on board the *Blade of Caliban* to lead the search for the missing starship. Before they had left he had sent a coded astropathic message to the Tower of Angels telling of the presence of the Fallen at Piscina. It would be at least a dozen days before they received the message, and the same time again for a reply to return, and he hoped to be back on Piscina IV to receive it. But rather than wait idly for instructions, Boreas had decided to set off after the *Saint Carthen* in case the opportunity faded and the Fallen slipped away from his grasp.

'Intrasystem craft have already patrolled the designated exit passage, with no sign of the *Saint Carthen*, Lord

Boreas,' replied Commodore Kayle, head of the Piscina system defence ships. He had already pledged to assist Boreas in his pursuit of the suspicious ship, and was now directing the operation from the orbital docking station. 'I have four vessels quartering the outer reaches, two more in the biosphere and another headed to the inner system.'

'We shall also direct our ship to the core planets,' Boreas told him. 'It is possible they are aware they are being looked for. If they try to reach safe distance to jump into the warp, they know they will be detected.'

'Very well, Lord Boreas,' agreed Kayle. 'The inbound vessel is called the *Thor Fifteen*, under Captain Stehr. I shall inform him that you will be close to his position within a few days.'

'My thanks for your co-operation in this matter,' Boreas said. 'Please remind your captains that I merely wish them to locate the vessel. Under no circumstances is it to be boarded. If necessary, your ships may fire to cripple its progress but no other contact is to be made.'

'Your message has been passed on, Lord Boreas, though I do not fully understand such caution,' Kayle replied. 'My men are fully capable of dealing with pirates of this kind.'

'If we are just facing pirates, I shall be pleased, and my caution shall be proven unfounded,' Boreas told him. 'However, I fear a much worse enemy awaits anyone who attempts to board that ship. No one, absolutely no one, is to have any contact with members of the *Saint Carthen's* crew.'

'As you wish, Lord Boreas,' Kayle said. 'I will inform you if we make any contact, and I trust you will also keep me informed of any developments on your part.'

Kayle broke the contact and the comm buzzed for a moment until Boreas switched it off. He stood there for a moment glaring at the wide viewscreens that covered much of the bridge's dim interior, amongst the many dial-filled walls of readouts, gauges, speakers, display plates and monitoring positions. He silently willed the *Saint Carthen* to show herself on one of those screens, but he knew the search would not be so swift or so simple.

Like the keep on the planet below, the ship was staffed mainly with non-Space Marine serfs, mechanical servitors and a few tech-priests. He turned to Sen Neziel, the most senior of the ship's officers who served as captain when there were no Dark Angels aboard. He wore a simple robe of deep green over a black bodysuit, his thin face crossed with childhood scars suffered during his examination by the Apothecaries.

'Plot a course for the inner system, passing Piscina III inbound,' he told the man. 'I want the augurs to be fully manned at every minute. We must find the *Saint Carthen* before anyone else encounters it.'

'Very well, Interrogator-Chaplain, we shall proceed at full speed to Piscina III,' Neziel confirmed. 'I estimate our time to orbit at three and a half solar days.'

'Good, Neziel, good,' Boreas said absently before turning and striding out of the bridge. He made his way to the ascensor to take him down three levels to the Space Marine quarters. Here the others were waiting for him to give them a briefing. As he waited for the ascensor to clank and rattle its way up the shaft, he pondered exactly what he would tell them. None of them were members of the Deathwing, so they had not been made privy to the existence of the Fallen. In fact, they had only been given the scantest information, wreathed in legends and myths, concerning the whole of the Horus Heresy.

Boreas had taken sacred vows never to divulge his knowledge of those turbulent times, for it was only upon admission to the Deathwing that the first layer of the half-truths were peeled away. He agreed completely with the traditional secrecy of the Chapter. If it were common knowledge that the Dark Angels had once teetered on the brink of treason, then the Chapter itself would be doomed. None outside the Inner Circle knew the full truth, except perhaps a few of the Imperium's inquisitors who suspected much but could prove nothing. As an Interrogator-Chaplain, Boreas was a member of the third level of the Inner Circle, which itself was the seventh level of secrets within the elite Deathwing. He knew much about the treachery of the Primarch Horus, of how the Lutherites had sided against the Emperor, and the Dark Angels had quested for ten millennia to atone for their near-treason. But he had learnt much more in the interrogation cell with Astelan. Much, much more. Boreas had not believed it at the time, merely dismissing it as propaganda and blinded judgment, but over the last years, in particular the last few months, the Fallen's arguments had seemed to gather greater weight in his mind.

With a loud grinding, the ascensor arrived. The doors opened with a wisp of escaping steam and Boreas stepped inside. As they slid shut, he jabbed at the rune for the Space Marines' berths. It rattled slowly downwards, giving him more time to ponder what he would tell the others. When the ascensor arrived, he stepped out onto the metal decking and took a deep breath. Instead of going straight to the briefing chamber, he instead turned right and walked the short distance to the ship's chapel. It was sparsely decorated, with a simple embossed relief of the Chapter symbol and a small altar on which stood a golden cup and a ewer of red wine. Filling the cup, he knelt and bowed his head. He took a long draught of the wine, placed the cup beside himself on the floor, and clasped his hands to his chest.

'We live in a galaxy of darkness,' he whispered, his throat dry. 'The ancient enemies of the Chapter surround us. The alien surges forth from its hiding place. The heretic rises up within the domain of the Emperor. I fear that the vilest of evils stirs once more. The corrupt, the renegade, the traitor sworn to the Dark Powers reach out their claws to destroy what we have built. I have laboured to shield the galaxy from these woes, and to protect my warriors from the perverting truth of the universe in which we live. Now I risk my honour. I must break my oath of secrecy to fulfil the greater oath I swore to protect the Emperor and his subjects.

'Look kindly on me from beyond the veil, great Lion, mightiest warlord of Caliban. I ask for your wisdom that it may guide my words and my deeds from your place beside the Emperor. I ask you to give me the strength to root out this cancerous treachery. I ask your forgiveness for what I must do to protect your name and the honour of what you created. Though my oath as a warrior of the Deathwing will be annulled, I now swear a new oath to you that I will stop at nothing to expunge this darkness. I shall let no obstacle stand between me and protecting that which is most dear to me. Give us your blessing in this endeavour and we shall strive to serve you. Grant us victory in this crusade of ours.'

Standing, Boreas bent down and lifted the goblet to his lips again, draining the last of the wine. Placing it back on the altar, he turned and left, striding purposefully into the briefing room. His moment of reflection and prayer had reinforced his belief in what he had to do. Feeling fortified and ready, he looked at the others seated on the foremost of the ten rows of benches stretched across the room. A pulpit shaped into a stylised two-headed eagle spreading its wings faced the auditorium, and Boreas stepped up behind the lectern, his hands clasped behind his back.

'My brothers,' he began, looking at their intent faces. 'In these last few years, we have been called upon only briefly to do what it is that we were created for. Skirmishes, cleanses, patrols; these have been the closest we have come to the battles we were bred and raised for. But now that time of waiting has come to an end. Now those years of dormancy are over and it is time to unleash the Lion's angels of death, it is time for the fury of the Dark

Angels to be known again! A foe is close by, in this very
star system that we guard. They are the worst enemy we
can ever face, and we must exact terrible retribution for
their heinous crimes. Those crimes are made all the
worse for they were perpetrated against everything we
hold in our hearts. They are against the Emperor himself,
they are against our primarch, Lion El'Jonson, and they
are against the whole of our Chapter.'

Boreas paused, realising that he was now fiercely gripping the lectern, the metal of the eagle slowly buckling
under the pressure of his fingers. The others were staring
at his hands as well, alarm on their faces. Let them see my
anger, Boreas told himself, keeping his grip strong. Let
my example teach them the true meaning of a hated foe.

'There is something I must tell you all,' Boreas continued, meeting each of their gazes in turn. Zaul's eyes were
narrowed, his mouth pinched with apprehension.
Damas met the Interrogator-Chaplain's stare with equal
intensity. Thumiel rubbed at his chin, looking thought-
ful. Hephaestus crossed his arms, waiting patiently for
Boreas to continue with his speech. Boreas looked last at
Nestor. The Apothecary looked relaxed, his gaze alternating between Boreas and the others, his hands neatly
clasped in his lap.

A sudden moment of hesitation gripped Boreas as they
looked expectantly at him. As far as he knew, what he was
about to do was unprecedented in the Chapter's history. It
could be viewed as a terrible abuse of his position. Was he
about to exceed his authority, he wondered? Could he really
make such a decision on his own, with no guidance from
his superiors? He had no other choice, he resolved. It would
take weeks for a message to be sent to the Tower of Angels
and a reply to return, by which time whatever trail the *Saint
Carthen* had left could have disappeared altogether. The
threat of the Fallen, he decided, not only outweighed the
import of what he was about to tell his brethren, but also
the personal consequences for him.

'When you became Space Marines, you were taught many things,' Boreas began. 'Most importantly, you learnt of the great history of the Dark Angels, and of the founding of the Imperium of Mankind. Ten thousand years ago, darkness shrouded the galaxy, humanity was scattered across the stars. They were isolated, preyed upon by aliens, riven with discord. But then the Emperor revealed himself and brought about the end of the Age of Strife, and thus began this golden age of the Imperium. He gave birth to us, his Space Marines. We reconquered the galaxy in his name. We brought war to a thousand foes, we liberated humanity from the grip of evil. The Emperor created us as perfect warriors, and none could stand before us. We ourselves, the Dark Angels, were the first Legion, at the forefront of the Great Crusade. Lion El'Jonson, our true father and our primarch, led us to victory after victory and the name of the Dark Angels was renowned across the stars. The Emperor himself praised our bravery, our tenacity and our ferocity.'

Boreas could see the pride in the eyes of his assembled command. They had heard the grand tales, they knew the legends and could picture those glorious days as if they were there. The blood of the Lion pumped through their veins, the latest of ten thousand years of superhuman knights dedicated to the Emperor.

'But there was a darkness festering at the heart of what we built.' Boreas's voice dropped from a near-roar to a hushed whisper that would have been nearly inaudible to a normal human. 'You were told of how the weak amongst the Legions were corrupted. Of how the serpent Horus turned them from the path of glory laid down by the Emperor. They rose up and struck at the man who had created them, in an act of treachery so base it had never before been known or since repeated. Battle-brother fought against battle-brother and the Imperium wept at the destruction heaped upon it. But we triumphed over the darkness. The Emperor sacrificed himself to destroy Horus, his body crippled almost to death so that now he only can watch us through the strength of his mind and soul. They brought the Imperium to its knees, they shattered the empire that we had built and nearly took the Emperor from us. But we did not surrender, we prevailed. From the golden throne that sustains him, the Emperor has guided us for ten long millennia and we have striven to rebuild that which was almost torn asunder.'

Now the pride had gone, and hatred burned in the eyes of the Dark Angels listening intently to Boreas's words. For their whole lives they had been taught about the renegades who had followed Warmaster Horus and plunged the Imperium into catastrophic civil war. They had been taught that there was no foe to be more loathed, no enemy more deserving of death than the Traitor Marines. It was they who had turned to the Dark Gods and even now sallied forth from their lairs to bring misery and devastation.

The Dark Angels were ready for what Boreas had to tell them.

'But there is an even darker tale you must now hear.' Boreas paused again and took another deep breath. This was the point of no return. What he was about to say would change them forever. 'You have been told the names of these traitors, the Legions who we hate and shall hunt whilst even one of them still draws breath: The Emperor's Children, the Thousand Sons, the World Eaters, the Alpha Legion, the Word Bearers, the Iron Warriors, the Death Guard, the Night Lords and the Sons of Horus; you remember these names with fury. But there is a Legion whose name is not recorded on that roll of abhorrence. It is the name of the Dark Angels.'

The others sat in shock; Boreas could see the confusion written on their faces. He knew well the thoughts and emotions that now swirled through their minds. The sudden emptiness, the doubt, the denial. It was Damas who spoke first.

'I do not understand, Brother-Chaplain,' the veteran sergeant said, his brow creased with thought. 'How can our Chapter be counted amongst the traitors?'

'I am as loyal to the Emperor as the Lion himself!' Zaul exclaimed, standing quickly, his fist clenched to his chest.

'We are all loyal warriors,' agreed Hephaestus. 'How can you accuse us of such a thing?'

'Your purity and loyalty is beyond question,' Boreas told them, stepping down from the pulpit to stand in front of them. 'But the seed of heresy resides within us all.'

'Is this a test?' Thumiel asked, looking at the others. 'It is a test, isn't it?'

'Our lives are a constant test, Brother Thumiel,' Nestor said calmly. 'I do not think that is the intention of the Interrogator-Chaplain.'

'Listen!' hissed Boreas, waving Zaul to seat himself. The Space Marine returned to the bench reluctantly, eying Boreas suspiciously. 'Listen, and you shall gain wisdom and knowledge. Why do you think it was that the Dark Angels did not fight at the battle of Terra? Why did we not stand at the walls of the Imperial Palace beside the Imperial Fists and the White Scars?'

'We were delayed fighting the forces of the Warmaster,' Hephaestus answered. 'We arrived after the battle was won. Or are you saying this is another lie?'

'It is not a lie, but a half-truth,' Boreas replied. 'We indeed fought those who had turned against the Emperor. We fought against our own battle-brothers who had sided against him. When the Lion returned to Caliban, it was his own Space Marines that attacked him.'

'But that does not make sense,' protested Zaul. 'We were the oldest and greatest of the Legions, why would any of us bow to Horus?'

'Who can say what went on in the depraved minds of those who turned upon their battle-brothers?' That was an outright lie, for Boreas knew full well what had turned the Dark Angels upon themselves. He had heard it from Astelan. But understanding was not required here, merely obedience. 'They were corrupted by a man possessed of a great skill with words, whose bitterness he hid behind a falsehood of friendship with the Lion. It was El'Jonson's own adopted kin who turned on him, Luther the Betrayer.'

'Luther was like a father to the Lion,' snorted Damas. 'How could our legends not mention such a grievous act?'

'Because we expunged them,' Boreas replied brutally. 'Because the truth is too dangerous to be left unfettered. Because the knowledge of it is a corruption in and of itself. Because you, my battle-brothers, must think with purity and clarity, and the times of the Horus Heresy are filled with doubt and ambiguity.'

'You lied to us, treated us like children.' Thumiel clutched his head in his hands, his gaze at the ground. 'You doubted us and kept this from us. '

'No!' snapped Boreas. 'It is because this legacy of shame was not yours to bear. Knowledge is a dangerous thing. It clouds the mind, it breeds laxity and heresy. Only the strongest-willed, only the most devout and pure can understand the guilt that lies upon us for this heinous deed at the time of our greatest glory. Only those with the courage to face the darkness within our own souls can strive to restore honour to our Chapter. I believe you are ready for that fight, and I tell you this not to cause you harm, but to give you the strength to prosecute your duties with zeal and vigour.'

'And why now, Interrogator-Chaplain, do you decide to reveal this information?' Nestor asked quietly. The others looked at him sharply and then turned their attention to Boreas, nodding in assent.

'Because the opportunity for our redemption is at hand!' Boreas declared, starting to pace up and down in front of them. 'This is the vile foe of which I speak. The Lutherites, the Fallen Angels, may be here, in the Piscina system itself.'

'The renegades are here?' gasped Zaul. 'How can you know that? How can we trust anything you say?'

'For centuries you have all trusted in the Chapter, heeded the words of myself and the other Chaplains,' Boreas pointed out. 'We never lied to you, not directly. We sought to protect you, guard you against the stain of our history. It has been this way for ten thousand years. Do you not think I felt this way when I learnt the truth? Do you think I took my vows of secrecy light of heart, gleeful of what I then knew, and what you now know? I asked myself the same questions that now plague your thoughts. I sought meaning in the anarchy of my mind. And I found it, through my brethren, as you shall find it through me. This is your greatest test as Dark Angels. But it is not a test that you can pass or fail, there are no set standards. It is a test for you to judge in your own hearts how you deal with the truth. The truth is hard to bear, and now you are amongst those who must share that burden. You must walk amongst your battle-brothers knowing that which drives us while they do not. That is what it means to be Deathwing.'

'The Deathwing?' Hephaestus asked. 'What connection do the Deathwing have with the Fallen?'

'All those who are or have been in the Deathwing know what you have been told,' Boreas explained. 'You are all now, by the very fact of what you know, warriors of the Deathwing. They are one and same, the honour of the Chapter and the shame of our past shared in a single soul.'

'I'm now in the Deathwing?' laughed Thumiel. 'Just like that, I become a member of the First Company, the elite of the Chapter?'

'There are ceremonies, there are oaths to swear, and your armour to be painted,' Boreas said, stopping in front of the battle-brother, laying a hand on his head. 'But yes, you are now Deathwing, there is no other way. An ordinary battle-brother cannot know what you have been told, and so I shall induct you into the Deathwing, and instruct you in the secret knowledge of our Chapter.'

'I ask this again, Interrogator-Chaplain, why now?' Nestor asked.

'The Fallen are in Piscina!' Boreas repeated. 'We hunt their ship as I speak. I declare crusade on this mission, this is a holy war against the most ancient enemy of our Chapter. We shall go from here and prepare for battle. We shall not rest, we shall don our armour and our weapons and they shall not be laid down until the enemy is destroyed. This is a reckoning that has waited a hundred centuries, and our vengeance is at hand. You see, this is the true purpose of the Dark Angels. This is the real mission of the Chapter. Whilst a Fallen still lives unrepentant of his sins, we can gain no true honour, we cannot truly serve the Emperor as his greatest warriors. All else we might do is ultimately in vain, but the hunt, the quest, these are what give us our meaning. Only when we have healed the grievous wounds of the Horus Heresy can we start to build again.'

'I feel the pain burning inside me!' Zaul declared, slapping a hand to his chest. His eyes were wide, his muscles taut. He fell to his knees at Boreas's feet. 'I understand, Interrogator-Chaplain! Forgive my doubts! Thank you for opening my eyes to this mystery. Thank you for giving my life purpose. I swear that I will follow you into the Eye of Terror itself to expunge this deed from our past.'

The others followed his lead, kneeling before the Interrogator-Chaplain. Nestor hesitated for a moment, glancing at the others, and then knelt at the end of the line. Pride swelled within Boreas's heart as he walked down the line, touching each of them on the scalp. His doubts seemed to dissipate like a mist as he looked at the row of kneeling warriors. Zaul was right. Here was purpose. Here was what he had been seeking these last two years. They were ready to fight to eradicate the shame of the Chapter.

Boreas was ready to fight, to eradicate the memory of Astelan and his own personal shame.

FOR THE NEXT few days, as the *Blade of Caliban* prowled into the inner Piscina system, the Dark Angels prepared themselves. They were not just preparing for war; they were readying themselves for a crusade, the most sacred undertaking a Space Marine could make. It was not just a mission, it was a sacred oath they had sworn, and they would not rest until it was complete or they were dead. It was more than a simple quest, it was a state of mind that the Space Marines entered, foregoing all other considerations in pursuit of their goal.

During a crusade, they did not rest or sleep, spending only an hour each day in the semi-conscious meditative state allowed by the catalepsean node implant. They spent the remainder of their time readying their battlegear and in prayer. Now that Boreas had made them members of the Deathwing, they repainted their armour in the bone-white colour of the Dark Angels First Company, and applied new markings. They were now entitled to personal heraldry, and spent hours with Boreas and the old texts he possessed, researching their crests and colours according to Chapter tradition. The Interrogator-Chaplain taught them new battle hymns – the secret Catechism of Hate reserved for the Fallen, the Opus Victorius in honour of the loyal Dark Angels' victory over the Lutherites, and the Verses of Condemnation that listed the uncovering of the Fallen and their misdeeds since the quest had begun.

All the while, the *Blade of Caliban* cut through the ether searching for the *Saint Carthen*. Sen Neziel was in regular contact with the *Thor Fifteen*, and after eight days had passed, they had proceeded beyond Piscina III and were heading further into the inner reaches of the system. There had been a few false alarms, when one or other of the ships had detected an anomalous reading. Most turned out to be system malfunctions, radioactive asteroids, and once they came across a merchant trader that had suffered damage dropping out of the warp and had drifted in system, their long range communications array out of operation. The *Blade of Caliban* had nearly passed them by when they encountered the distress call. Boreas had a short and explosive exchange with the trader's master, refusing to abandon his search to guide the stray vessel back to the trade routes. A message of concern from the captain of the *Thor Fifteen* and Commander Kayle followed, but Boreas ignored them. He was focussed on the crusade, and would countenance no distraction or deviation from the goal of their search.

Boreas spent much time with the others, helping them come to terms with the revelations they had heard. He guided their prayers until they came to some rough understanding. Zaul had responded with anger, his hatred of the renegades fanned into a barely-controllable fury as Boreas taught him more of their betrayal and the civil war that had riven the Chapter. Damas's ire was colder, more introverted. He took every moment he could to work on his weapons and armour, painstakingly writing out the Opus Victorius on his power armour in tiny script, the act itself giving him release and focussing his thoughts on vengeance. Hephaestus similarly laboured in the ship's forge and workshop, blessing every gun, every bolt shell, every energy pack and blade with the strength of the Machine God. Thumiel spent his time on the firing range, chanting breathlessly as he fired round after round into static and moving targets, cursing the Fallen with every shot. For him, the confrontation could not come soon enough.

And then there was Nestor. He seemed least changed by Boreas's unveiling of the Chapter's hidden past. He gave them all a thorough physical examination, the most rigorous he could devise, and declared them all to be in perfect fighting condition, ready for the holy war. He had perhaps changed in one way though – he seemed even quieter. He became even more closed and uncommunicative the longer the search dragged on, as if he wanted to be free of the ship itself. Whenever Boreas broached the subject, he would reply that he was intent on concluding their mission as soon as possible, for he feared for Piscina while the Fallen might be in the system.

This fact also troubled Boreas. In his urgency to pursue the *Saint Carthen*, he had brought all of his command with him. For the first time in millennia, there were no Space Marines on Piscina IV, only their attendants. Always, even on the short recruiting missions to Piscina V, Damas, Zaul or Thumiel had been left behind as commander of the keep. Boreas fretted that he had misjudged the situation, that perhaps he had been lured from Piscina by his foe. He dismissed the idea but it kept coming back to him, nagging at the back of his mind during prayer, teasing him as he practised battle drill with his brethren. But there was nothing he could do except follow to its conclusion the course of action he had chosen. It was his sacred duty as a member of the Deathwing to seek out the Fallen wherever they might be, and here was a golden opportunity to fulfil that duty. He had declared crusade and the future was now set, for good or ill. Piscina IV was still garrisoned by fifteen thousand Imperial Guard and the Imperial commander's own troops; even the Fallen would not be able to face such numbers if they attacked.

After nine days of searching, contact was made. The *Thor Fifteen* had detected a ship just outside the stellar orbit of Piscina II and was moving to investigate. Boreas ordered the *Blade of Caliban* to power with all speed to the area. Outwardly, there was nothing more significant about this contact than any of the others, but he felt inside that this time they were on to the foe, that the ultimate moment of confrontation was fast approaching. It was still two days' journey to intercept the rogue vessel, and he gathered the Dark Angels in the chapel. All was physically ready for the coming battle, now they were to make the last preparations of their minds and souls.

For the first day they fasted and meditated, each Space Marine alone with his own thoughts. Boreas spent this time on contemplation musing on the future. Unless the Chapter was engaged in a full-scale war, the Tower of Angels would be redirecting itself to Piscina, dropping into the warp in response to Boreas's warning. Part of him worried that his fears were unfounded, and that his actions would be deemed rash and selfish. There was also part of him that wished that were true, for it would mean there were no Lutherites at Piscina, and he would not have to conduct another interrogation. He had performed one other since his encounter with Astelan, but it had been more straightforward than the first. The Space Marine had ranted and raved, totally corrupted by the Ruinous Powers, and despite the agonising attentions of Boreas had refused right to the end to repent his sins. He had finally died screaming from his numerous injuries, cursing the name of Lion El'Jonson. There had been none of the innuendo and guile of Astelan, none of the supposed revelations about the Horus Heresy, which even now disturbed the Chaplain's thoughts.

But the greater part of him wished for another confrontation with the ancient enemy. Boreas wanted the chance to prove his loyalty again, after many months of doubt and introspection. As much as Zaul, he longed for the cleansing of holy battle to wash over him, to wash away his questions and fears with the blood of his foes. Truly, Boreas realised with a shock as he prayed through the night, *we live for battle and battle alone.* A Space

Marine never felt so strong of purpose, so alive and aware of his own potential, as when he was on the battlefield, and it was a feeling that Boreas had too long been denied. Even the clash with the orks had been perfunctory, clinical, a mere brawl compared to the battle of the basilica – a cold, precise engagement that had not tested him or distracted him from his problems.

On the second day, Boreas led the battle-brothers in final prayer.

Born in the darkness, a dream given life,
Holy warriors to bring forth the light.
Armed with zeal, armoured with faith,
Gods of battle at the fore of the fight.
Swords of the Emperor, shields of Mankind,
Destined for war, fated for death.
Protectors of the weak, slayers of evil,
We fight 'til we draw our last dying breath.
There is no retreat, there is no surrender,
Our hate of the foe drives us eternally on.
While aliens live, while heresy festers,
There can be no peace until the last war is won.
Strengthen your heart, harden your soul,
Launch yourself gladly into death's hungry maw.
There is no time for peace, no respite, no forgiveness,
There is only war.

PHYSICALLY READY, AND spiritually pure, the Dark Angels waited impatiently as the *Blade of Caliban* neared the interception point. The *Thor Fifteen* was approaching from the inner planets, having made the detection on a return pass. It was partway through the middle watch of the day when the attendants at the rapid strike vessel's own augurs reported an energy source close at hand.

The *Thor Fifteen* had encountered the *Saint Carthen* first and was engaged in a long-range duel. The *Thor Fifteen's* captain, Jahel Stehr, was calling for aid when

Boreas strode onto the bridge. He glanced at the main display screen and watched the battle for a moment. Flickering lasers rippled out from the gun decks of the renegade ship, strobing across the system ship's void shields in explosions of undulating blue waves. Missiles fired in return streaked across the starry backdrop but passed harmlessly beneath the *Saint Carthen*. The pirate vessel was closing on the Imperial ship, and within a few minutes would be able to pass her stern and fire into her engines. On all fronts, the *Thor Fifteen* looked outclassed.

'She's heavily armed for a merchantman,' Stehr's crackling voice reported. Boreas knew only too well what the enemy ship was capable of, having heard from Astelan how he had her fitted out as a pirate vessel that had laid waste to many convoys under his command.

The *Thor Fifteen* was ill-prepared and poorly commanded, Boreas assessed, and ordered maximum power from the plasma reactors in an attempt to close the distance as quickly as possible. He commanded the others to stand ready in the loading bays. His plan was to cripple the *Saint Carthen's* engines and then make a small strike at her command deck. Once under control, he would turn off the life support systems and kill everyone inside. He could take the vessel with minimal losses and, more importantly, if there were Fallen aboard, only he and the other Dark Angels would encounter them. As he had done a century ago, he and the others had sworn to protect the Chapter's dark secret with their lives. Like him, they would go to any lengths to prevent knowledge of the Fallen becoming widespread, for the shame was of the Dark Angels' making and it would be they alone who atoned for it.

'Whatever you do, ensure that you close off any escape route,' Boreas responded. He glanced at the tactical display that was illuminated on the main screen. 'We will be within attack range soon.'

'Very well, Lord Boreas, we shall engage her for as long as possible,' Stehr said. 'We shall target her engines when we are able and attempt to board her.'

'No!' Boreas bellowed, causing everyone on the bridge to stop in shock. 'My orders are clear, you are not to board the *Saint Carthen*.'

'We risk getting cut to pieces here,' Stehr protested. 'Closing the range and boarding is the only chance we have.'

Boreas started to signal back, before realising that the *Thor Fifteen* had broken contact.

'Keep signalling Captain Stehr to stand off the *Saint Carthen*,' Boreas ordered the comms officer. 'Tell him that if he attempts to do so, we shall be forced to intervene.'

Sen Neziel walked from the weapons command position with a data-slate in his hand and gave it to Boreas. He shared a smile with the old officer as he looked at the tactical information it contained. Readings from the *Blade of Caliban's* sensor arrays, combined with a steady stream of technical reports from the *Thor Fifteen* indicated that the *Saint Carthen's* weapons systems were broadside only. She had yet to fire to the fore during the engagement. It was perfect for Boreas's purposes – they could attack from the front, launch an assault boat and fly in without facing a hail of fire. Of course, it was an assumption, and would be very dangerous if it proved wrong, but Boreas could see no other course of action if he wanted to take the enemy vessel without a protracted fight.

'Capturing the vessel is our primary goal,' Boreas told Neziel. 'She must not escape, ram her if you have to.'

The weapons officer reported that they were nearly within firing range.

'Sound full battle alert!' shouted Boreas and the klaxons began to beat the crew to quarters as they prepared to open fire. The bridge buzzed into frantic activity as the orders were relayed to the stations across the ship.

'Drop to combat speed, divert power to void shields,' Neziel ordered after a nod from Boreas. 'Load torpedo tubes two and four, plot firing solution to target.'

'Torpedoes targeted.'

'Shields at ninety per cent power.'

'Engines at fifty per cent thrust, manoeuvring transferred from navigational to helm position.'

'Gun batteries powered, crews mustering.'

'Blast doors sealed, fires extinguished.'

'Switch display to enhanced visual,' Neziel concluded and the tactical display blinked out and reappeared on a sub screen, replaced by a view of the *Saint Carthen*. She was an elegant ship, with a raked cross-section and two clusters of plasma engines flanking her hull. Her metallic skin glinted with hundreds of yellow flashes as pulses of laser fire erupted from the cannons concealed within her belly. A flicker of blue and violet shimmered around her aft section as her shields absorbed a blast from the *Thor Fifteen*.

'Lord Boreas, the *Thor Fifteen* is closing fast with the target, it looks as if she's going to board,' one of the surveyor officers reported. Boreas strode to the comms console and jabbed at the transmit rune.

'*Thor Fifteen*,' he demanded. 'Abort your attempt to board or I will be forced to fire upon you.'

It took a few seconds for the reply to come through.

'Emperor's teeth, man!' Stehr cursed over the speakers. 'We're on the same side! You can't be serious.'

'Torpedo controls, retarget trajectory on vector one-five-six,' Boreas called to the weapons officer.

'Confirm, new trajectory one-five-six,' The officer replied after a moment at his panel.

'Launch torpedoes,' Boreas ordered, glancing at Neziel.

'Are you sure, my lord?' Neziel asked, checking his own tactical display. 'At that course, we would be firing on the *Thor Fifteen*.'

'Launch torpedoes!' roared Boreas, causing Neziel and the other officers to flinch. 'Question my orders again and I'll have the tech-priests render you into servitors!'

'Aye, my lord,' Neziel said uncertainly. 'Launch torpedoes, target vector one-five-six.'

'Torpedoes away!' the weapons officer called out.

Boreas activated the comms rune once more.

'*Thor Fifteen*, cut speed by thirty per cent and alter course forty degrees to port,' he said, darting an angry look at Neziel. 'Failure to do so will result in impact with our torpedoes.'

'You launched torpedoes at us?' Stehr's voice sounded hoarse over the link. 'Whose side are you on, Emperor damn you!'

'I repeat, alter course by forty degrees to port and reduce speed by thirty per cent,' Boreas replied. 'Break off your closing course and you will be safe.'

The Interrogator-Chaplain looked over at the surveyor officer's station. He was watching his reticule intently.

'*Thor Fifteen* reducing speed,' he said, confirming what Boreas was reading on his own tac-panel. 'She's veering to port and rising.'

'Good,' Boreas grunted. 'Prepare for assault boat launch, and power up the starboard batteries. I want the target's prow raked as we close.'

'Confirm target, please,' Neziel said pointedly.

'The *Saint Carthen*,' Boreas said with a scowl. 'Another remark like that, Neziel, and I will have you executed for insubordination. Am I understood?

'Forgive me, Lord Boreas,' Neziel said, hanging his head. 'I have never fired upon an allied vessel before.'

'Neither have I,' Boreas replied heavily. 'Signal the docking bay to prepare for my arrival. Neziel, I trust you will follow any subsequent orders to keep the *Thor Fifteen* from boarding. If she puts troops onto that vessel, they will be killed along with the enemy crew.'

'I am sorry, my lord,' Neziel said, wiping the sweat from his eyes. 'I understand now. The *Thor Fifteen* will be prevented from closing.'

'Good,' Boreas said, striding towards the doorway. He lifted his helmet from a stand next to the door and hooked it onto his belt.

'One other thing, my lord,' Neziel called after him. Boreas turned, a questioning look on his face. 'May the Emperor watch over you and guide your hand.'

'Thank you, Neziel,' Boreas said after a moment. 'The Emperor's blessing on you and our other subjects while we are gone. Keep the ship safe for me, Neziel.'

'I will, Lord Boreas, I will,' Neziel said with a smile and a nod.

WITH A ROAR and a judder, the assault boat launched explosively from the *Blade of Caliban's* hull. A modified drop pod, the assault boat was much like an armoured teardrop, with claw-like grappling clamps at its base and a ring of melta-burners set into the hull to cut through even the thickest armour of an enemy ship. Small manoeuvring thrusters burned sporadically along its length as Hephaestus steered the craft on an intercept course with the *Saint Carthen*. Satisfied that their trajectory was correct, he unlatched his harness and stood, his magnetic boots clamping him to the hull in the zero gravity. As he thudded down the hull towards Boreas, the Chaplain signalled for the others to rise.

'Time to impact?' The Interrogator-Chaplain asked, checking the chronometer display in his auto-senses.

'Approximately twenty-seven Terran minutes, Brother Boreas,' Hephaestus told him.

'Display chronometer countdown, twenty-seven minutes,' Boreas told his suit, and a readout flickered into life in the lower left of his field of vision, reeling down through the minutes and seconds. Though much could happen in half an hour in a space battle, Boreas trusted to the speed and small size of the assault boat to see them through to their objective. The augurs and scanners of a large vessel were immensely powerful, built to peer into the vast depths of space. However, an object as small as the assault boat was unlikely to register at all until within close range of the enemy's low level scanners, and even if they were picked up, they would most likely appear as an errant asteroid or piece of debris.

'Weapons check,' he ordered, testing the activation stud of his crozius and clicking off the safety of his bolt pistol with his other hand. He made a count of the equipment on his belt, though they had all done so three times already in their pre-combat checks. Along with the powerfield-enclosed crozius and his bolt pistol, Boreas had five spare magazines, each carrying fifteen rounds; four fragmentation grenades; two blind grenades; two meltabombs; five proximity-triggered anti-personnel mines; an auspex scanning array; a monomolecular-edged combat knife; a spare power cell for his crozius, and another for his rosarius conversion field generator.

Battle-brothers Zaul and Thumiel had their standard-issue boltguns and combat knives, as well as the same quantity of grenades and mines. Damas wore a massive powerfist on his right hand to complement his bolt pistol, and a chainsword hung at his belt next to his knife. Hephaestus carried a hefty power axe and a plasma pistol, both of them crafted by his own hand. Nestor also had a bolt pistol and chainsword, and the cabin filled with the throaty whirring of the spinning blades as he tested the motor. Satisfied that the weapons check was complete, Boreas bowed his head and the others followed suit.

'What is it that gives us purpose?' he intoned.

'*War*,' the others replied.

'What is it that gives war purpose?'

'*To vanquish the foes of the Emperor.*'

'What is the foe of the Emperor?'

'The heretic, the alien and the mutant.'

'What is it to be an enemy of the Emperor?'

'It is to be damned.'

'What is the instrument of the Emperor's damnation?'

'We, the Space Marines, the angels of death.'

'What is it to be a Space Marine?'

'It is to be pure, to be strong, to show no pity, nor mercy, nor remorse.'

'What is it to be pure?'

'To never know fear, to never waver in the fight.'

'What is it to be strong?'

'To fight on when others flee; To stand and die in the knowledge that death brings ultimate reward.'

'What is the ultimate reward?'

'To serve the Emperor.'

'Who do we serve?'

'We serve the Emperor and the Lion, and through them we serve mankind.'

'What is it to be Dark Angels?'

'It is to be the first, the honoured, the sons of the Lion.'

'What is our quest?'

'To purge our shame through the death of those who turned from the Lion.'

'What is our victory?'

'To remake that which was broken, to earn the trust of the Emperor once more.'

'And what is the fate of the Fallen we hunt?'

'Retribution and death!'

The last intonation was roared across the comm-link, a vocal thunder filled with anger and hatred.

Silence followed for a moment, and then Boreas took a small phial from a pouch at his belt. He walked along the line of Space Marines and dripped a little of the fluid within the phial onto the bowed helmet of each warrior.

'With the blessed waters of Caliban, I sanctify your souls to the Emperor and the Lion,' chanted Boreas as he performed the ritual. 'Be pure in mind, body and spirit. As the water flows over you, let your hate flow through you. As the lost water is spilt, let us spill the blood of our foes. As the water dries, let us harden our hearts to fear. We are the Dark Angels, the chosen of the Emperor, the holy knights of Caliban. The blood of the Lion flows through our veins. His strength beats in our hearts. His spirit resides within us.'

'Praise to the Lion,' the Dark Angels chorused, straightening up.

Boreas led them down the craft to stand at the exit port. Glancing at the countdown display, he saw that they were a little under ten minutes from impact.

Looking through the viewing plate, he could clearly see the *Saint Carthen*. The ship had haunted his nightmares for years, and now he looked upon it for real for the first time. Barrages of high-powered laser blasts from the *Blade of Caliban* lanced overhead into the enemy ship. An explosion of purple and green waves of energy signalled a void shield being overloaded, and the next salvo crashed into the hull of the ship itself, spewing gouts of igniting air and tangles of wreckage.

'Lord Boreas!' suddenly the comm crackled into life with the urgent voice of Sen Neziel. 'We have detected power build-ups in the lower prow of the *Saint Carthen*. I believe she possesses forward batteries and is about to open fire.'

'Close in, brace for impact and draw her fire!' Boreas spat back. 'Launch torpedoes to mask our signal!'

Despite the perilous situation of the assault boat, Boreas couldn't help but admire the cunning of the *Saint Carthen's* captain. During the fight with the *Thor Fifteen* he had been presented with plenty of opportunities to conclude the fight if he had launched an attack with his prow batteries, but instead he had prolonged the duel to tempt the *Blade of Caliban* into a vulnerable position. His assumption might yet prove dangerous, but he was still confident that they would reach their target. The chances of a main gun being able to lock on to something as small and fast as the assault boat were slim, but there was also a chance that the Dark Angels would unintentionally get caught in the fire from the enemy.

'Hephaestus, get back to the piloting chair and steer us upwards, I want to get above the battery's elevation of fire,' he ordered, staring intently through the armoured port. His augmented eyes picked out the flaring trails of a missile salvo, disappearing below the assault boat as the Techmarine clambered back to the controls and set the boosters to push the craft out of the *Saint Carthen's* line of fire.

It was then that the pirate vessel's anti-boarding turrets opened fire. A lattice of laser beams erupted from six point-defence emplacements scattered across her prow. Far too small to worry a starship, they were still more than powerful enough to blast the assault boat into shrapnel with a direct hit. Flickering beams of blue energy enclosed the assault boat, and Boreas's helmet automatically dropped a filter over his eye-lenses to stop him being blinded by the glare.

He checked the countdown again. Two minutes until impact.

'Scan for possible location of command chamber,' Boreas told Hephaestus. From here, the forecastle of the *Saint Carthen* was a mass of turrets, armoured plating and observation galleries. One of them had to be the bridge though, and Boreas wanted to punch into the ship as close as possible to the nerve centre. His plan was hinged on a swift, decisive strike. Even in close confines and with far superior armour and armaments, they would not be able to hold out against an entire ship's crew. They had to take the bridge and cut the life support within minutes, or else they would be trapped and killed. Or worse, Boreas realised with a start, they might be captured. The thought repelled him, and he resolved that he would take his own life rather than fall into the hands of the Lutherites.

'I've located a communications array,' Hephaestus reported, breaking Boreas's morbid thoughts. 'Guidance systems locked on.'

The hull shook as a las-beam scored along the outside, melting partway through the armoured shielding of the assault boat. An instant later, they took another hit, which caused the lights to short out and explode.

'*Terrorsight*,' Boreas barked to his armour and his vision instantly cleared as the sophisticated lens array creating an artificial view from powerful emitted radiation waves rather than ordinary light.

'Stand-by for impact,' Boreas warned as the hull of the *Saint Carthen* rushed towards him through the window. Retro-jets fired at the last moment, slowing their pace slightly.

It was still a tremendous impact when the assault boat hit home. The servos and muscle bundles in Boreas's armour whined and creaked to keep him upright as the ablative nosecone of the craft was crushed and the docking clamps lashed out, tearing into metal and pulling the assault boat tight against the enemy ship. With a white-hot flare, the melta-cutters burst into life, searing through ceramite and metal in a few seconds, before pneumatic rams punched out, hurling the severed section into the enemy vessel and leaving a serrated circular opening into the metres-thick armour plates. Boreas hit the button for the assault ramp and it swung down with a clang.

Instantly, a storm of las-fire filled the opening. A beam struck Boreas's helmet, knocking his head back. The roar of Zaul's bolter filled his ears and drowned out the zip of lasguns. Recovering quickly, Boreas leapt down the ramp, taking in the four bloody bodies strewn across the metal mesh of the passageway they had cut into, great holes ripped into them by the explosive bolts. More of the

enemy crouched behind pillars and buttresses, firing
wildly at the attacking Space Marines.

Zaul and Hephaestus flanked Boreas as he levelled his
bolt pistol at the nearest target, a man with a visored helmet who had paused to change the energy cell on his
lasgun. An aiming reticule sprang up in Boreas's sight as
the bolt pistol's targeter linked into his helmet. He
squeezed the trigger softly as it changed to red, and a
moment later a flickering trail of fire marked the bolt's
passage. It tore through the man's padded vest without
slowing before its mass-reactive warhead detonated, ripping his chest open from the inside. Boreas and the
others advanced steadily down the corridor, each step
punctuated by the bark of a bolter or pistol and the
scream of a dying man.

'Forward for the Emperor!' Boreas bellowed.

'Retribution and death!' answered Zaul as his bolter
ejected its empty magazine and he smoothly took
another from his belt and slammed it home, las-shots
pattering harmlessly off his power armour.

Las-shots also struck Boreas repeatedly, searing the
paint from his left shoulder pad, scorching a mark
across his left gauntlet, glancing harmlessly from the
shaped armour plates protecting his thighs and groin.
A ball of flickering blue plasma erupted from Hephaestus's pistol to his left, punching through a
stanchion and incinerating the man cowering behind
it, his steaming arm and head flung messily to the
deck. Twenty metres ahead, the corridor met an inter-
section, with passages continuing ahead and to the
left. Three dozen bodies left in their wake, the Space
Marines continued their relentless assault to the junction and took up covering positions. Boreas shot away
the leg of a crewman as he attempted to run away, his
scream echoing in the Interrogator-Chaplain's audio
pick-ups. Suddenly quiet descended, as the last enemies fled out of sight.

'Status check,' Boreas demanded, his pistol aiming down the corridor to the left. Zaul and Thumiel had the forward approach covered.

'Entry point cleared,' confirmed Zaul. 'Praise the Lion!'

'We need to orientate with the bridge,' said Boreas, holstering his pistol and passing his auspex to Hephaestus. The Techmarine activated the scanner and swung it in a slow arc to the left and right and then up and down. Swirling static on its screen coalesced into an image of their surroundings, extending out some fifty metres.

'I have numerous life-signs ahead and to the right,' Hephaestus reported, holding out the auspex. 'I'm detecting the power grid, there seems to be a terminal thirty metres ahead, in a chamber to the right. Detecting communications nexus as well, same position.'

'Zaul, Nestor, secure this point,' Boreas ordered, taking the proffered auspex from the Techmarine. There were between thirty and forty crewman nearby, waiting around a corner ahead, and within side rooms to the left. 'Prepare for counter-attack. The rest of you with me. Take and hold the terminal chamber.'

The Space Marines stalked quickly ahead, and just as they approached the sealed door to the chamber, the crash of bolters sounded out behind them.

'Enemy attacking, heavy casualties inflicted,' Nestor reported. 'No assistance required.'

Hephaestus bent to examine the keypad next to the chamber door. At that moment, more than twenty of the *Saint Carthen's* crew charged from around the corner ahead. Bullets clattered off the bulkheads and lasfire flashed brightly down the corridor. Thumiel returned fire immediately, his bolter firing on semi-automatic, carving a path of bloody craters across the chests of the first line of attackers, hurling them from their feet into those that followed behind. By the time they had clambered over the dead, Boreas had his bolt pistol in his left hand and was firing, the bolts punching fist-sized holes into the poorly protected men. The last few realised their mistake too late and were cut down as they tried to turn and run, their lifeless bodies falling upon the heap of those already dead.

'They've engaged security rites, the area is locked-down,' Hephaestus reported.

'If I may?' Damas said, holding up his powerfist, which erupted with a sheen of shimmering blue energy.

'Affirmative,' Boreas agreed with a nod, turning his attention back to the auspex. There were no life signs within fifty metres.

Damas squared up to the armoured door and placed his left hand against it. Clenching his powerfist, he swung. A thunderous detonation boomed down the corridor as his fist smashed through the metal. Opening his hand, he peeled away the torn metal as if it were paper-thin, ripping a hole large enough for them to duck through.

'Thumiel, sentry point. Zaul and Nestor, remote secure area and advance to this position.' After receiving their affirmative replies, the Interrogator-Chaplain pushed his way into the power chamber, followed by Hephaestus and Damas. It was not large, barely five metres square, and filled with thrumming power conduits and coils of finger-thick communications cables.

'Relay interface,' Hephaestus said, pointing at a screen and terminal to their left. Boreas gave him a nod, and stepped over to the machine. Pulling an assortment of wires from his backpack, Hephaestus tried a couple until he found one that could connect with the interface. 'Assimilating schematics,' the Techmarine announced.

Boreas checked his chronometer. Just short of two minutes had passed since they had initiated the boarding action. Another fifteen seconds went by before Hephaestus declared that he had the information he needed.

'We're four levels down from the main control bridge, and about sixty metres to the starboard,' he told them.

He paused for a moment as he consulted with the three-dimensional layout plan he had taken from the communications grid. 'There's an ascensor shaft twenty metres further on, which will give us access to the bridge entryway.'

Boreas's comm buzzed as it received an external transmission and decoded it.

'Lord Boreas,' he heard Sen Neziel say. '*Saint Carthen* has reduced her fire considerably. I believe she is mustering her crew to repel boarders.'

'Acknowledged,' Boreas answered, before he turned to Hephaestus. 'How secure is this area?'

'One access point by the stairwell within one hundred metres, three ascensors within the same distance,' he replied after a brief pause.

'Can you shut down the ascensors from here?' Boreas asked.

'Not quickly, rites of command have been initiated,' the Techmarine said with a shake of his head. 'However, from here we can cut the power grid to the whole section, which will slow down reinforcements.'

'Agreed,' Boreas said with a nod. 'Set melta-bombs.'

As Hephaestus began placing the charges, helped by Damas, who was following the Techmarine's directions for the best sites, Boreas ducked back into the corridor where Zaul, Thumiel and Nestor were waiting for him.

'Zaul, Thumiel, advance around the corner and secure the ascensor,' he ordered. They headed off up the corridor, bolters held ready. Hephaestus and Damas hurried back out of the relay chamber, a moment before the interior was lit by white-hot light. Sparks cascaded from the severed energy lines and instantly the lights died. Boreas's artificial sight bathed everything in a red haze.

'Quick advance, that will only slow them down for a short while,' Boreas said, leading the others after Zaul and Thumiel. Passing the corner, he saw the two battle-brothers flanking the double doors that gave access to the ascensor shaft. With his power armour-enhanced strength, it only took a moment for Boreas to force the doors open. The shaft stretched several levels above and below their position. The ascensor itself was on the next level down.

'Thumiel, Zaul, covering positions on the shaft. Nestor hold this point. Hephaestus and Damas with me,' he said before holstering his pistol and jumping out into the shaft to cling onto the ascensor's cables. The threaded metal creaked under the additional weight. Certain that it would not hold up to the strain of three fully armoured Space Marines, Boreas leant across the shaft and drove his fingers through the comparatively thin metal walls, securing himself a hand hold. Releasing the grip of his other hand, he swung over the gap, the toe of his boot driving into the wall. Steadying himself, he set about climbing up the shaft, punching hand and footholds as he went.

Suddenly light filled the shaft as doors opened above. Zaul fired immediately, the traces of the bolts screaming up past Boreas to explode three levels above his head. Something bloody and ragged fell past him and landed on the top of the ascensor with a wet thud. He ignored the intermittent gunfire coming from above and below as he climbed, concentrating on maintaining his balance as he clambered up through the erratic lasfire and the whirring of bullets.

One level down from the open doorway, which was also the floor on which the bridge was located, Boreas stopped and glanced down. Hephaestus was just a couple of metres below him, and Damas a similar distance further down. He signalled for them to stop climbing and pulled a fragmentation grenade from his belt. With his free hand, he primed the timer for a one-second delay then flipped the firing pin and lobbed the grenade up. It arced slightly towards the open door and exploded in mid-flight, shrapnel clattering noisily off his armour and shredding anything stood in the open portal. With a grunt, he pulled himself up a couple more handholds and then leapt for the opening, his fingers digging into the mesh of the floor.

Hauling himself up, he pulled out his crozius and looked around. Four dismembered bodies littered the hallway he found himself in. He stared face-to-face with a group of more than a dozen crewmen, armed with lasguns and shotguns, who staggered back, terrified.

'*External address.* No mercy, no respite, no retreat!' Boreas bellowed, his exterior speakers turning his battle-cry into a deafening roar that stunned the traitors even more.

He was on them before they could react, his crozius smashing the jaw from one and crushing the chest of another with his return swing. Hephaestus sprinted past him, his glowing axe cleaving another in two through the midriff and lopping the arm off another. They broke and fled, but couldn't outrun the Space Marines as they bounded forward with long, powered strides, hacking them down from behind, their power weapons leaving a trail of steaming blood and cauterised flesh.

'Exit point secured,' barked Boreas. 'Reform at my position.'

As he waited for Nestor, Zaul and Thumiel to catch up, Boreas checked the chronometer again. Five and a half minutes since the operation had begun. He unslung the auspex and activated it, pointing it in the direction of the bridge. The flickering screen was almost completely white with pulsing life signals.

'Full charge, close assault,' he announced when the others were all present. 'Covering fire Zaul and Thumiel, rearguard Nestor.'

They nodded in understanding and readied their weapons for the final push. Hephaestus jabbed the button to open the chamber's portal.

'For the Lion!' cried Boreas, launching himself out into the entryway that led to the bridge.

The passageway was deserted and Boreas halted just a few steps down, momentarily puzzled. It stretched ahead for twenty metres before opening out onto a hallway. Right in front of him stood the doors to the bridge, a heavily armoured portal with hydraulic bars dropped into place. He checked the auspex again; it still read overwhelming life signals. He thumped it with the butt of his pistol and it gave a plaintive electronic whine and the display faded.

'Brother-chaplain, I am detecting an interference signal emanating from the bridge,' Hephaestus announced. 'They are jamming our scanners.'

Boreas hooked the auspex back onto his belt and looked back at the others.

'They have taken refuge inside the bridge itself,' he said, advancing cautiously along the corridor, the others following him. 'Impossible to know how many of them there are, we must assume it will be heavily guarded.'

'We do not have breaching equipment to cut through the portal,' Hephaestus told them.

'Are there any other access points?' Boreas asked as they reached the hallway. It too was empty of life. Boreas spotted a scanning lens set into the wall above the door and shot it with his bolt pistol, sending sparks cascading down onto his armour.'

'There are several weak points in the bulkhead itself,' Hephaestus replied, his head turning left and right as he surveyed the wall.

'*Augment terrorsight,*' Boreas muttered and his constructed vision faded to a wireframe schematic. He could see the wall, the banks of machinery and consoles beyond, the enemy crew standing out as red blobs amongst the overlapping lines. There were at least three dozen waiting inside, probably more, many of them clustered around the doorway. He saw the outline of

Hephaestus moving forward as he indicated a section of the bulkhead that was thinner than the rest. '*Cease augmentation*,' Boreas told his armour and a hazy approximation of normal sight returned.

'If we use the rest of our melta-bombs, we can blast a hole through here,' the Techmarine said, activating his power axe and scoring a rough outline into the metal of the wall about five metres right of the doorway. He marked six points to indicate where to attach the melta-bombs. Damas collected the charges and set to work, de-activating their timers so that they would only explode by remote detonation. When it was done, they gathered in a semi-circle a couple of metres back from the breaching point, readying their frag grenades.

'Zaul, Damas, first in and break to the right. Hephaestus and Nestor next in to cover forward. Thumiel follow with me to the left,' Boreas snapped out the plan. 'Prime grenades with three-second fuse.'

Damas took a step forward, his powerfist glowing, with Zaul slightly crouched behind him. Hephaestus glanced over at Boreas and the Interrogator-Chaplain gave a small nod. With a hiss and then a loud crack, the melta-bombs detonated, melting through the metal bulkhead in an instant. Damas jumped forward, his powerfist smashing through the weakened wall and clattered into the bridge, his bolt pistol firing. Zaul followed quickly, bolter held in one hand, combat knife gripped in the other. His chanting sounded over the comm-link as Nestor and Hephaestus followed up, their pistols spewing fire. Boreas charged in next and rounded to the left towards the door, Thumiel close behind him, his bolter roaring.

There were twenty or so officers and crewmen by the entry portal, armed with a mixture of lasguns, stub pistols and shotguns. They were turning in reaction to the attack but Boreas opened fire first. The first bolt tore into the face of a man with a red bandana, a moment before his head was vapourised. The second round ripped into the butt of a shotgun and flung the man back as his firearm exploded in his hands.

Boreas launched himself across the gap, still firing, his crozius held above his head. Flares of light reflected off the gleaming surfaces of control panels and displays as his conversion field burst into life as shotgun rounds, las-bolts and bullets pelted into him. He took a heavy hit to his right knee and stumbled. A lucky shot had pierced the bendium seal between the armour plates on his leg but the pain passed in an instant as his armour stimulated his pain-suppressing glands to kick into action. Thumiel loomed over the Interrogator-Chaplain, spent bolt casings showering around him as he fired semi-automatic bursts into the enemy.

With a grunt, Boreas pushed himself upright, dropping his pistol and gripping his crozius in two hands. The first swing threw a man five metres across the bridge to land heavily in a crash of splintering dials and exploding wires. His next blow crushed the chest of an officer in a long blue coat decorated with gold braiding. He slumped to the floor, blood bubbling from his lips from his collapsed lungs. Another man had drawn his sword and chopped wildly at Boreas's head. The blade crashed off his helmet and threw his head back. The Interrogator-Chaplain let go of his crozius with his right hand and as the next attack swung in, he warded it away with his arm, his gauntleted fist closing around the blade. Exerting his strength, the blade buckled and twisted between Boreas's fingers until it snapped. He rammed the point into the man's throat and let go, leaving his body to fall to the floor drenched in arterial blood.

Only three men were left alive and they threw down their weapons and raised their hands above their heads. Zaul fired into the chest of the first, ripping apart his spine and internal organs. Boreas grabbed the head of the next in his hand and snapped his neck, tossing the body aside with ease. The third man collapsed to his knees, tears streaming down his cheeks, his white trousers stained as he soiled himself. The man gibbered some unholy prayer before Boreas's booted foot crashed into the back of his head, stamping his life out on the hard deck.

'Damas, Nestor, secure entry point,' the Chaplain barked, turning from the sprawl of bodies and pointing to the smoking breach in the bulkhead. 'Hephaestus, locate and shut down artificial gravity and life support systems.'

The bridge was theirs.

THE TALE OF ASTELAN
PART FOUR

VOICES CALLED TO Astelan from the dark shadows of the cell. He thrashed feverishly within his chains, his once mighty frame now wasted and haggard. Not a scrap of flesh had been left unmarked by the Interrogator-Chaplain's cruel ministrations.

Astelan's mind felt as equally ravaged by the psychic intrusions of Samiel. His body battered, his thoughts in tatters, he struggled to maintain a fragile grip on reality.

Unable to move his head very far, his world had constricted to a space only a few metres across. He knew every crack and crevice above him, he could picture them in his head as clearly as a map. He knew there were thirteen blades, three drills, five augurs, eight clamps, nine brands and two barbed hooks on the shelf. He could remember the feel of every one on his flesh, each a little different. Even when Boreas was not there wielding his vicious implements, so confused was Astelan's mind that sometimes he would wake feeling their savage touch upon him.

With creeping fingers, he had counted the links on his chains hundreds of times to keep his thoughts occupied. Every moment that he did not concentrate on something, the voices returned.

He had long given up his refusal to sleep. It mattered not that he cried out when the nightmares assailed him. Awake, he was barely more lucid, the barriers between what was a dream and what was real had blurred for some time.

All this he knew, from a detached, coherent part of his mind that sometimes fought through to take control. He knew the voices were simply echoes in his head of Boreas's questioning and the psychic probing of Samiel. He knew that it was merely an illusion of his tortured senses when the shadows grew hands that reached out towards him. But those times were few, and his moments of lucidity were growing rarer and shorter.

Astelan had lost count of the number of visits he'd had from his captors. Perhaps it had been fifty, perhaps five hundred. Sometimes he argued, other times he shut himself away, ignoring the slice of the scalpel in his flesh, the boring of the drill through his bones, the searing of his skin on the tip of a brand. Boreas came and went, Samiel came and went, and there was no pattern that Astelan could fathom. Sometimes he awoke to see Boreas standing there watching him, listening to his nightmare-induced screams. Other times the Chaplain plied him with questions, examining every aspect of his answers, but did not inflict any more pain on him. Sometimes there was only pain and no questions, or the insidious whispering of the psyker inside his head, calling him a liar and an oath-breaker.

As he lay there, tormented and delirious, he dreaded the sound of the large brass key in the lock. And then there were the times when he longed for Boreas to return, when his strained mind could no longer be contained and he had to communicate his raging thoughts. He struggled to remember why he was here, and then recollection would surge back, washing away the pain. Though it was a constant struggle, somehow he managed to retain a small piece of what he had been.

In his mind he pictured it as a glowing star hidden away in the centre of his brain. Shadows snatched at it, the burning red eyes of the warlock studied it, but it was safe and secure. It was his dream, his ambition. The return to the glory of the Great Crusade, the casting aside of the meaningless institutions and arrangements that had brought mankind low. As he concentrated on it, the glowing star would grow, fuelled by his memories, fanned into greater life by his desire.

Astelan knew that he would never see the Greater Imperium, would never again lead the armies of the Emperor across war zones amidst the crash of bolters and the crackling of flames. That was beyond him now; they had taken that from him when he had given himself up on Tharsis. If he had known, if he had truly realised what they had intended, he would have fought harder than he had ever fought before.

Regret turned to grief as he saw his plan lying in shattered pieces, the golden star just a hazy glow that bobbed and weaved, eluding him. For centuries he had been a protector, a leader, a warrior bred for conquest. He looked at the wreck he had become and cursed the Dark Angels, and cursed Lion El'Jonson who had set them on this path. Grief turned to anger and he raged feebly at the chains that bound him to the stone table, barely able to lift himself.

Astelan felt a familiar breeze on his check and looked at the open door, his head lolling weakly onto the slab. Through bruised and bloodshot eyes he saw Boreas enter. Inwardly, Astelan was grateful that Boreas had come alone. The Interrogator-Chaplain walked quickly to the slab, and Astelan heard the clanking of chains and the metallic scratching of a key in a lock. One by one, the chains fell away, their great weight lifting off his limbs and chest. Unencumbered by the heavy iron, Astelan tried to sit up, but found he had not the strength to do so.

'Try harder,' Boreas said softly in his ear. 'Your muscles need reminding what they are for. Try again and they will start to remember.'

Astelan croaked wordlessly, focusing every fibre of his being, summoning all the strength he had. His spine felt like it was on fire, every joint in his body ached and his muscles screamed with the exertion, but after what seemed like hours, Astelan managed to pull and push himself upright.

'Very good,' the Interrogator-Chaplain said, pacing back and forth in front of him. Boreas pointed towards the door. 'You can leave now.'

Astelan turned his head slowly between the door and Boreas, not really understanding what the Chaplain was saying. He frowned, unable for the moment to recall the words to communicate his dulled thoughts.

'Do you have a question?'

Astelan closed his eyes and concentrated. With a supreme effort of will, he stopped his mind from spinning. He pointed feebly at his throat.

'You require some water?'

Astelan nodded, his head flopping uselessly from side to side as he did so.

'Very well,' Boreas agreed, walking out of the door. Astelan sat there, staring at the light from the guttering torches beyond. It burnt his eyes after so long in the dull shadows. All he had to do was stand and walk five paces and he would be out of the cell, but he was exhausted. He would gather his strength, and then he would walk free.

The Chaplain returned holding a jug of water and goblet.

'You wish to leave, yes?' he said, and Astelan noticed for the first time that his hands were stretched out towards the door. He dropped them back to his side.

Boreas stepped forward and poured water into the goblet before placing the jug on the ground. He took one of Astelan's hands and wrapped the fingers around the goblet, and then did the same with the other hand. As the Chaplain took his hands away, the cup slipped from Astelan's grasp and clattered to the ground, splashing him with water as it fell. The cold sharpened his senses immediately.

'Try again,' Boreas urged him, refilling the goblet and holding it out towards him, within easy reach. 'You managed to sit up, now you can manage to drink by yourself.'

Astelan's fingers clawed at the cup, but Boreas's grip was firm until he had it safely in his hands. He raised the goblet shaking to his lips and dribbled a few drops onto his tongue. Savouring the sensation, he let a few more drips into his mouth, before he could resist the urge no longer and gulped down the contents. The water refreshed him immediately, washing away some of the confusion and pain.

'I can leave?' he asked, his voice wavering.

'The door is there, all you have to do is stand up and walk out.'

'No trickery?'

'I am above trickery, I am following my sacred calling.'

'You will not close the door before I reach it?'

'No, you have my oath as a Space Marine that I will not close the door before you reach it. In fact, that door is never going to be closed again while you are in this cell. You are free to leave at any time you wish.'

Astelan sat there and pondered Boreas's words for a while, his thoughts slow at first but gathering pace and clarity. Nodding to himself as he reached his decision, Astelan pushed himself forward onto the floor, his legs buckling, but he held himself up against the slab. Boreas stepped back out of his way and waved him towards the door.

'Very good, commander,' Boreas said with a nod. 'Just a few steps and you will be out of this cell.'

Astelan looked at him, but the Chaplain's expression was noncommital and told him nothing. Summoning his strength, he took a step forward, still leaning against the stone table. His legs barely held his weight and he cautiously pulled back his hand until he was standing free, swaying from side to side. He took a step forward, shuffling his foot along the ground, feeling his mal-treated joints grinding as he did so. Pain lanced through his knees, hips and spine, and he gritted his teeth against the agony. In front, the rectangle of light beyond the door swam in and out of focus.

'You do understand what leaving means?' Boreas said to him. Astelan ignored his taunts and took another fal-tering step forward. 'If you leave this cell, it is because you are afraid. It is because you know your convictions to be false.'

Astelan turned to look at the Chaplain.

'I do not understand,' he said.

'Your great vision, the mighty plan,' Boreas explained. 'I do not believe you. I think you are a liar and a tyrant who has never acted out of anything other than selfish desires.'

'That is not true,' Astelan argued. 'I did it for the Emperor, it was for mankind.'

'I am not convinced. But, you are leaving, are you not? It is immaterial whether I believe you or not. Of course, you are dying, even a Space Marine cannot endure what I have subjected you to. For all your superhuman organs and unnatural strength, they have failed you now and without medical assistance you will soon die. You have lasted long, your gene-seed is very strong. Perhaps the Apothecaries will study it after you have passed on. But you will die peacefully.'

'I do not live for a peaceful death!' Astelan's voice was little more than a rasp.

'What do you live for then?' asked Boreas.

'Death in battle, to build the Imperium of Man, to serve the Emperor,' croaked Astelan weakly.

'And you do that by walking out of that door and lying down to die in some forgotten chamber, do you?' Boreas's mocking tone lashed at Astelan, sending his thoughts spinning into turmoil again. 'Are you running from the fight, Chapter commander? Are you afraid that perhaps your convictions are not as strong as you thought, that perhaps your lies are beginning to unravel? But, leave! Leave and die with the knowledge that you did not have to face that ultimate test, that you abandoned the chance to tell me more of your vision, to convince me of your worth. Leave and you will save yourself much misery and pain, and I will know that you die as a heretic because it will prove to me that you are weak. That you are the type of man that could break his oaths, that could turn and attack his masters, and wage bloody war against those he once served. Leave!'

'No!' Astelan took a step towards Boreas, a sudden surge of strength welled up within him, fuelled by his anger. 'I am right! I tread the true path, it is you who have wandered.'

'Then stay and prove it,' offered Boreas. 'How much pain is the Emperor's true will worth? The pain you feel now? The same amount again? Thrice as much? How much pain will you endure to stay true to the Emperor?'

'All the pain in the galaxy, if it proves to you that what I say is true,' Astelan replied.

'Do you believe me now that I could keep you alive for a hundred days?' Boreas asked.

'Yes, yes I believe it,' Astelan said, his head nodding against his chest.

'And yet you have only endured my attention for fifteen days,' the Chaplain told him with a grim smile.

'Fifteen days? That is not possible.' The strength that Astelan had felt leeched from his body. Could it possibly be true? Had he undergone only fifteen days of this torment?

'I do not lie, what would be the purpose?' Boreas said, crossing his arms. 'You were brought here only fifteen days ago. That torment, that pain, is the work of a mere fifteen days. You can end it all. Just three steps and you will have left this cell, left the agony behind.'

Astelan looked at the glow beyond the door, which beckoned and taunted him with equal strength. He took two steps forward, up to the door itself, and stopped there to ease his protesting body.

'A single step, just a single step from peace,' Boreas goaded him.

Astelan leant on the door, and turned his head to look at the Interrogator-Chaplain over his shoulder. Swinging his arm, he slammed the door shut, the clang reverberating around the cell. For an instant, just a fraction of a moment, Boreas's studied expression changed, a glimmer of approval that quickly faded back to the Chaplain's normal blank demeanour.

Astelan straightened himself and walked purposefully back to the slab and lay down upon it, and stared at Boreas. The Interrogator-Chaplain walked over and leaned over his prisoner.

'Very well, you have made your choice,' he said. 'But there is still another way. A way without chains, without pain, without Brother Samiel.'

'I wish to hear no more of your tricks,' Astelan replied, turning his head away.

'There is no need for this. I can put away the blades and hooks, and we will just speak, as one Space Marine to another,' Boreas said, his voice quiet and soothing. 'All I ask is that you open your mind and your heart. Examine your feelings, probe your motives. Look with eyes untainted by centuries of hate, years of isolation and misunderstanding. Scrutinise your ambitions and see if they are pure.'

'I know that they are,' Astelan said defiantly.

'For now,' Boreas argued, leaning forward on the slab. 'But we will just talk, and you will listen to me as I will listen to you, and you will learn that your arguments have no weight.'

'I think not,' snorted Astelan.

'Then if you have nothing to hide from, speak freely, tell me your story, open your thoughts to me and we shall see,' Boreas said insistently.

Astelan sat up and looked directly at Boreas, but he could read nothing in the Interrogator-Chaplain's expression.

'What do you wish to know?' Astelan asked.

'Tell me of Caliban, your homeworld,' Boreas said.

'You talk of speaking openly and with truth, and yet your first question is based upon ignorance,' Astelan started to laugh but it turned to a choke that made him retch.

'What do you mean?' Boreas's brow was creased with a frown of confusion.

'Caliban is not my homeworld, it never was,' Astelan told him, lying back against the slab and pausing until his ragged breathing had eased. 'I was of the old Legion, of the Dark Angels before the coming of Lion El'Jonson. I was born on Terra, from a family whose forefathers had freed the ancient birthplace of humanity from the evil grip of the Age of Strife. Since the Emperor revealed himself and his purpose, my people have fought alongside him. When first he began to breed a new type of superhuman warrior, it was from my people that he took his first test subjects. With their aid, the Emperor reconquered Terra and humanity was on the brink of launching into a golden age, the Age of the Imperium. So it is not strange that when he perfected his techniques for the creation of the Space Marines, many of my people were chosen to lead the Great Crusade, myself amongst them. That is why you speak in lies, because Terra was the world of my birth.'

'So you cared nothing for Caliban?' suggested Boreas.

'That is not true either,' Astelan said, closing his eyes, feeling the sweat from his exertions rolling down his face. 'As the Legions conquered the galaxy, rediscovered human worlds and freed them from aliens and their own self-destructive ignorance, we came across the primarchs. It had been a version of the gene-seed that the Emperor had used to create us, so each of the primogenitors, the Legions, in part were bound to the fate of their primarch. When the Emperor found Lion El'Jonson on Caliban, we all celebrated. The Emperor told us that the Dark Angels had a new home and we were filled with joy, for we were now far from Terra.'

'So what happened next? What started you on that dark path to treachery?' Boreas's voice was flat, emotionless.

'We adopted Caliban as our own, and when El'Jonson was given the command of the Legion, we thought it fitting,' Astelan answered slowly, having to gather his thoughts before every sentence, ignoring the accusations of treachery. He no longer had the strength to argue every barbed comment made by Boreas. 'It was good that new Chapters of Dark Angels would be raised from Caliban's people, for it gave them identity and focus, something that was precious in those tumultuous times. I did not know then that our new primarch would betray us, would destroy everything that we had created.'

'Tell me of the fighting on Caliban. How did it begin?' asked Boreas.

'Our glorious primarch, in his supposed wisdom, had abandoned us there. He had turned from those who had come before him, who had welcomed him as a lost father and taken his homeworld as their own.' A chill swept over Astelan's body as he thought of the events that had led to his defiance of the primarch. He looked at Boreas. 'It had been a grave mistake, but we had sworn oaths of loyalty and we would not break them. We hoped that our primarch would see the error he had made. I sent deputations to him to reconsider his decision, but they were all returned without a reply. Not even a reply! From afar, El'Jonson was pouring scorn on us with his silence.'

'And that is how Luther bent you to his evil ways?' Boreas asked, his voice now becoming more insistent.

'Luther? Ha!' Astelan's exclamation dissolved into another painful cough and it was several seconds before he could speak again. 'Your histories demonise him, blame him for all that has befallen the Dark Angels, and yet you know so little of the truth. It is convenient for your legends to show him as the arch-villain, the viper within the nest while the great Lion conquered the galaxy, but El'Jonson's betrayal of Luther was the greatest of all! Without me, Luther would have been left ranting and shouting from his tower to no avail.'

'Are you saying that it was *you* who was responsible for the schism of our Legion, and not Luther?' Boreas gasped, unable to mask his disbelief. 'That is a grand and dire claim to make!'

'I did not say that,' Astelan said quietly. 'Rarely are the facts of history as convenient as written words pretend. Luther had the most to be aggrieved about, that is for certain. He had been like a father to the primarch, his closest friend and ally. He had saved El'Jonson from death in the woods. And what did El'Jonson do to repay him? He banished him to Caliban, like the rest of us. He left him to rot while he sought glory for himself.'

'Luther was the Lion's guardian of Caliban,' Boreas said, starting to pace back and forth across the chamber. 'He had been honoured by the primarch, in showing such faith and trust in him to leave the protection of his homeworld in Luther's hands.'

'Luther was almost as great a commander of men as Lion El'Jonson,' argued Astelan. 'Though our primarch was gifted beyond compare as a planner and strategist, Luther knew the hearts and minds of men well, better than El'Jonson ever did. When the Emperor had first arrived, and the Dark Angels were given to El'Jonson to lead, Luther had wept that he was too old to become a Space Marine.'

'As did many of the knights of Caliban,' replied Boreas, stopping his pacing and looking directly at Astelan. 'That is why the Emperor sent his best chirurgeons and apothetechs, so that those who were too old for the primarch's gene-seed might still be given many of the benefits of our altered bodies, living long past their natural deaths and capable of great feats of arms.'

'And so is it not even stranger that Luther should be left on Caliban, rather than leading those warriors on the field of battle?' asked Astelan, shifting his weight so that he could look at the Chaplain more easily. 'I think it is. I think that El'Jonson grew to be afraid of Luther, of his popularity amongst the troops, and so left him on Caliban where his star would rise no more.'

'These are the lies of Luther. They have polluted your mind, as they polluted the others who turned on their brethren.' Boreas's denial was absolute, his face set.

'For all his skills at fiery speeches and impassioned whispers, Luther was never and could never be a Space Marine,' Astelan pointed out. 'There were a few who listened to him, most of them of the new Legion. My Space Marines, while having the deepest respect for Luther and his great achievements, had served under the Emperor himself and owed their loyalty to him alone.'

'And so how did it come to pass that those supposedly loyal Dark Angels turned on their primarch and betrayed the Emperor, if they did not care for Luther's oratory?' Boreas asked, stalking forward.

'Because I stood up beside him and offered him my support,' Astelan replied in a hushed whisper. Doubt filled his mind for a moment. Had he not done that, would things have occurred differently? He dismissed the thought; the future of the Dark Angels had been set long before that moment.

'And why did you do that?' Boreas's voice cut through his thoughts.

'So that we could do what we were always meant to do – fight the Emperor's enemies and force back the darkness that surrounded mankind,' Astelan said.

'Explain.'

'The primarch was far away, continuing the Great Crusade, when we were brought word of terrible news,' Astelan told the Chaplain. 'Horus, greatest of the primarchs, the Emperor's own Warmaster, had turned traitor. Accounts were fragmentary, and infrequent, but slowly we pieced together what had happened. We heard of his virus bombing at Istvaan, and the dropsite massacre. Primarchs and their Legions were turning against the Emperor, and against themselves. It became impossible to tell friend from foe. We heard on more than one occasion that the Dark Angels had turned on the Emperor, or that Lion El'Jonson had been killed. There was talk of the Space Wolves fighting against the Thousand Sons, and of battle-brother killing battle-brother across the galaxy.'

'And so you saw the opportunity to turn traitor as well, to side with Horus,' Boreas accused him.

'We wanted to leave, to go and fight Horus!' Astelan's defiance was weak, his body failing the strength of his spirit. 'We could be sure of nothing except that which was in our own hearts. It was Luther who first spoke of us leaving Caliban and joining the fight to defend the Emperor.'

'Luther would have led you to Horus!' snapped Boreas. 'And what of the Lion's commands? Did the stewardship of Caliban mean nothing to Luther and you?'

'It meant much to Luther, less to me as you might understand,' admitted Boreas. 'But how did we know what our primarch wanted us to do? Communication was shattered, and the intent of the Lion obscured by hundreds of light years and conflicting stories. He could have been embattled on some distant planet, or have sided with Horus, or leading the Emperor's defence, we did not know. And so we took it upon ourselves to divine our own path, for it was the only thing that we could do.'

'So what happened then? What caused the fighting?' Boreas stood close again, his robes and skin bathed in the red light of the brazier, giving him a half-daemonic appearance.

'There were some among our number, newly raised battle-brothers who perhaps slightly lacked the faith and zeal of the old Legion, who opposed our leaving,' Astelan replied.

'And so you attacked them, wiped out the dissenters.' Boreas's face twisted into a snarl as his anger grew again.

'It was they who attacked first, and revealed their treacherous intent with the death of hundreds,' Astelan corrected him. 'We had prepared everything to leave, and were embarking onto the transports to take us into orbit where the battle barges and strike cruisers of the Chapter awaited us. As the ships began to leave, the traitors struck. Their orbiting ships opened fire on ours, they stormed the planetary defence batteries and opened fire on the transports. Defence lasers blew the transports out of the sky and they rained down in pieces onto us. Some tried to continue into orbit, and they were destroyed by the enemy, while others were blasted into shrapnel as they attempted to land. Their strike was short-lived, however, as we counter-attacked in force. Their ships fled, and those who had taken the batteries were driven out or killed.'

'So they acted to stop you disobeying the primarch's orders,' Boreas suggested.

'They had no right to!' rasped Astelan. 'I have already told you that the primarch's wishes were as unknown to us as the state of the war against Horus. Theirs was the sinful act, firing on us.'

'But you did not leave, did you?' Boreas pointed out.

'We could not,' Astelan said with a sorrowful shake of his head. 'We were afraid of what might happen if we left Caliban in the hands of the treacherous brethren. We could not leave until we were sure that Caliban was safe.'

'And how did you hope to ensure that?' demanded Boreas.

'We hunted them down, of course,' Astelan told him. 'They hid in the deep woods, and struck with hit-and-run attacks, but eventually our numbers took their toll and we thought them exterminated. For three months, our guns were silent and it was then that perhaps we committed the only sin – that of complacency. Thinking our foe destroyed we relaxed our guard as we began to make preparations to leave once more. That was when they struck. They had hidden themselves away more thoroughly than we could have ever imagined, in the most inhospitable places on Caliban. Without warning, they gathered their might and launched an attack on the starport, taking several transports. Stunned, we did not react quickly enough and by the time the defence lasers were active, they were already amongst our fleet and we could not target them for fear of hitting our own ships. They concentrated their attacks on the largest craft in the fleet, my own battle barge, the *Wrath of Terra*. They stormed her, took control, and turned her immense guns and torpedoes on the rest of the fleet. The battle was short-lived, for the *Wrath of Terra* outclassed any vessel in orbit, and soon my Chapter's fleet was reduced to smoking wrecks.'

'And so you were stranded on Caliban, and those who had stayed true to their primarch had finally succeeded in preventing you from joining the Warmaster,' Boreas said, sharing some pride in the desperate act.

'It was not their final act,' Astelan said bitterly. 'They piloted the *Wrath of Terra* into Caliban's atmosphere, where she burned up and exploded into fiery fragments that rained down onto the surface. Plasma reactors trailing infernos exploded in the forests leaving craters kilometres across and sending dust and rock into the sky to obscure the sun. Fragments crashed into the cities and castles, destroying them, and the largest portion of the ship plunged into the southern ocean, creating a tidal wave that wiped out everything within twenty kilometres of the southern coast. Not only had they marooned us on Caliban, they wrought untold destruction upon the planet that had now become our prison.'

'If what you say is true, then how was it that you fired upon our primarch when he returned?' Boreas said accusingly.

'Caliban was then a ravaged, desolate place,' Astelan continued, his voice dropping to a barely audible murmur. 'The forests died, the life-giving energies of the sun blotted out by the clouds of dirt and ash that hung in the air. The world was slowly destroying itself, because we had failed to protect it from our own battle-brothers. You speak of shame, but it is nothing compared to the guilt we felt at that time, as the trees burned, and the light of the stars was taken from us.'

'But why the attack on the Lion?'

'Luther had taken up residence in Angelicasta, the Tower of Angels, largest citadel on Caliban and greatest fortress of the Dark Angels. I had taken personal command of the outer defences and the laser batteries, from a command centre hundreds of kilometres away. When we received a signal that spaceships had entered orbit, we thought at first that the traitor ships had returned – the ones that we had driven off in the first battle.'

'And that is why you opened fire?' asked Boreas.

'No, it is not,' Astelan replied with defiance. 'It soon became clear that our primarch had returned. Luther contacted me to ask for my advice. He was troubled because he had intercepted a communication that claimed El'Jonson himself led the approaching ships. He did not know what to do, fearing the wrath of the Lion for what had befallen Caliban.'

'And what did you tell him?'

'I told him nothing,' Astelan said grimly. 'I gave the order for the batteries to open fire on the approaching ships.'

'*You* gave the command?' spat Boreas, gripping Astelan's throat and pressing him back against the slab. 'It was *you* who precipitated the destruction of our homeworld? And you say that you have no sins to repent!'

'I stand by my decision,' Astelan replied hoarsely, ineffectually trying to prise away the Chaplain's vice-like grip. 'There was nothing else I could do. El'Jonson was going to wipe us out, for I suspected that the traitor ships had met him, and their version of events would have damned us all. Our beneficent primarch would have had us all killed for what had happened to his homeworld. I also feared that our primarch was no longer loyal to the Emperor. We had heard little of the exploits of the Dark Angels during the Horus Heresy, and I did not discount the thought that this was due to El'Jonson having sided with Horus.'

'So you fired because you were scared of retribution?' Boreas snarled, raising Astelan's head and cracking it back against the stone table.

'I fired because I wanted El'Jonson killed!' spat Astelan, pushing weakly at Boreas to free himself. 'My loyalty was first and foremost to the Emperor, and to El'Jonson a long way second behind that. It was my duty to the Emperor to protect the Space Marines under my command – Space Marines that the Emperor himself had picked and raised, and who were now threatened by this primarch. Do you understand?'

'Not at all, I cannot comprehend the treachery that pulses within your heart,' Boreas said, letting go of

Astelan in disgust and stalking away. He did not look at his prisoner as he spoke. 'To turn on your primarch, to wish him dead, is the gravest sin that you could have committed.'

'It was the primarchs who turned on the Emperor. Before their coming there had been no dissent, no civil war,' argued Astelan, pushing himself into a sitting position. 'It was the primarchs who turned the Legions against their true master, who furthered their own ambitions with the thousands of Space Marines under their command. It was the primarchs who nearly destroyed the Imperium, and it was Lion El'Jonson who had doomed Caliban with his own actions.'

'Your arrogance was fuelled by jealousy, lubricated by the dark lures promised by Luther!' Boreas roared at Astelan. 'You turned on your primarch in return for power and domination by the Dark Powers!'

'I defended myself from a madman who had already tried to destroy my Chapter and would not hesitate to do so again!' Astelan snarled back. 'I never swore to any Dark Powers, I was nothing but loyal to the Emperor! But I was also wrong.'

'So you admit it!' Triumph was written across Boreas's face as he swept across the cell towards Astelan.

'I admit nothing.' Astelan's words stopped Boreas in his stride, his elation turning to fury. 'I was wrong in believing that Lion El'Jonson sought a reckoning with me. It was his mentor and friend, Luther, that he was intent on destroying. It was Luther, steward of Caliban, his saviour, that El'Jonson had grown to hate, to envy. His actions prove my point! Did he not personally lead the attack on the Tower of Angels, while his ships bombarded Caliban from orbit? Was he not seeking to destroy all evidence of his own weakness, striking out at those who had seen him for what he truly was?'

'The Lion had indeed heard of Luther's treachery and knew that to cure the malady, he had to act decisively and swiftly,' explained Boreas. 'He hoped that by striking at Luther, he could save Caliban from his evil influence.'

'When the missiles and plasma came screaming down from orbit, it was all too plain to see the primarch's intent,' Astelan argued. 'The seas boiled, the land cracked and the fortresses tumbled into ruins. I remember the ground lurching beneath my feet, and then tumbling into what seemed like a bottomless pit, before I lost consciousness.'

'And there lies the heart of the evidence against you, the overwhelming proof of your guilt!' Boreas bellowed. 'At the end, as tortured Caliban tore itself apart, your dark masters reached out to snatch you from death. As the world shattered, a great warpstorm erupted over Caliban and spirited you away, along with all those who had turned on the Lion. That is why you are guilty, that is why no amount of justification and argument can convince me of another intent behind your actions. The Ruinous Powers saved you and your kind, and scattered you across time and space so that we might not have our vengeance against you. Luther was as corrupt as Horus, as you all were! Admit this and repent!'

'I shall not!' growled Astelan. 'I renounce every charge you have laid against me! I have been loyal to the Emperor from the day I was first chosen to become a Space Marine, and I will stay loyal to the Emperor until my dying breath! Torture me, probe my mind with witch-powers! I refute your accusations! I see now what has become of the so-called pure gene-seed of Lion El'Jonson! You have become creatures of shadow and darkness, and I do not recognise you as Dark Angels!'

'So be it!' Boreas declared, shoving Astelan back against the slab. 'I shall return, and I shall take up my blades, and my brands, and I shall call for Brother Samiel. Your soul shall know justice, whether you choose it or not. You have chosen the path of suffering, when you could have walked the path of peace and enlightenment.'

Boreas stalked towards the door and wrenched it open.

'Wait!' Astelan called out.

'No more of your lies!' the Chaplain snapped back, stepping through the door.

'I still have more to tell!' Astelan shouted after him.

The Chaplain stopped and turned around.

'You have nothing more I wish to hear,' he said.

'But you have not heard the full story,' Astelan told him, his voice dropping to a cracked whisper. 'You have not learned the truth.'

'I will find out the truth in my own way.' Boreas turned to leave again.

'You will not,' Astelan told him. 'Now it is your turn to decide, as must we all, which path your life will follow. Go now and return with your warlock and take up your implements of pain, and I will never divulge the secrets I keep within me. Not even your psyker will be able to probe them free from my soul. But if you stay, if you listen, I will freely tell them to you.'

'And why would you do such a thing?' Boreas asked, not looking back.

'Because I wish to save you as much as you wish to save me,' Astelan said, pushing himself to his feet, gasping as pain flooded his body. 'Through pain and suffering, you will not hear my words, you will be blinded to the truth. But if you listen, as you asked me to listen, then you will learn many things you would not otherwise unearth.'

'What inner secrets?' Boreas turned. 'What more could you tell me?'

'An interesting thought, a concern of mine,' Astelan said, meeting the Chaplain's gaze.

'And what is that?' Boreas asked, stepping back through the door.

'Though we heard little at the time, and accounts of it afterwards are hard to uncover, I have learned as much as I can about the siege of the Emperor's Palace and the battle for Terra at the end of the Horus Heresy,' Astelan explained as hurriedly as his ravaged lungs allowed. 'It is a stirring tale, I am sure you agree. There are stories of the exploits of the Imperial Fists holding the wall against the frenzied assaults of the World Eaters. There is praise running into hundreds of pages for the White Scars and their daring attacks on the landing sites. There are even accounts, most false I suspect, of how the Emperor teleported onto Horus's battle barge and the two fought in titanic conflict.'

'What of it?' Boreas asked suspiciously.

'Where in all these tales of battle and heroism are the Dark Angels?' Astelan replied.

'The Lion was leading the Legion to Terra's defence, but faced many battles and arrived too late,' Boreas said.

'So, Lion El'Jonson, greatest strategist of the Imperium, who was never once defeated in battle, was delayed? I find that hard to believe.' Astelan's strength failed him again and he slumped back against the interrogation slab, his legs buckling under him.

'And what would you believe, heretic?' Boreas demanded.

'There is a very simple reason why Lion El'Jonson did not take part in the final battles of the Horus Heresy.' Astelan let himself drop to the floor, his back against the stone table, his eyes closed. 'It is beautifully simple, when you consider it. He was waiting.'

'Waiting? For what?' Boreas asked quietly.

Astelan looked into Boreas's eyes, seeing the curiosity that was now there.

'He was waiting to see which side won, of course.'

Boreas stepped into the cell, and closed the door behind him.

THE TALE OF BOREAS
PART FOUR

IT TOOK SIX hours for the crew of the *Saint Carthen* to die. In that time, the desperate heretics launched fourteen counter-attacks on the bridge in an attempt to recapture the control chamber and reactivate the environmental systems. Each assault was met with controlled, deadly salvoes of bolter fire. The chances of the bridge falling would have been slim in the best of situations – as implacable as they were on the advance, the Dark Angels excelled at ruthless defence, stubbornly refusing to give a centimetre of ground to wave after wave of wild-eyed crewmen. With their atmosphere leeching out of opened airlocks and deactivated vents, and contending with the lack of gravity, their assaults failed miserably and over two hundred corpses floated in the vacuum as a testament to their increasingly reckless attacks.

Only when the ship's internal scanners register zero life signs outside the bridge did Boreas consider their position secure. Even then, there was much work to do. For over an hour, the Space Marines swept through the corpse-littered corridors and chambers searching for survivors, or evidence of the Fallen, but they returned empty-handed to the bridge. When they had mustered again, it was Nestor who raised the point that had been nagging at Boreas ever since they had stormed the bridge.

'If this ship belongs to the Fallen, where are they?' the Apothecary asked, turning from a view screen to look at Boreas. 'What makes this ship different from any number of other pirate ships in the sector? Perhaps your information was incorrect, perhaps this slaughter was unnecessary?'

Boreas did not answer immediately. He paced heavily across the bridge to the command chair, the black leather now spattered with blood and shredded with shrapnel and bullet holes. He gazed over the sparking consoles, looked at the floating corpses and globules of blood rising and falling in the thin atmosphere left in the ship. Was Nestor right? Did the presence of the *Saint Carthen* mean the Fallen were in Piscina after all, or had he over-reacted?

'This ship was once captained by one of the Fallen,' Boreas told the others. 'For nearly a century he waged war against the Imperium from this bridge.'

'But he is not here now,' Nestor said, pushing aside a body and stepping towards the Interrogator-Chaplain. He pointed at the uniform of one of the officers. 'Look at this one. He does not look like a traitor to me. Look at their clothes, the badges and insignia. Imperial badges, Imperial merchant insignia.'

'Of course they have civilian insignia,' interrupted Damas. 'They docked with the orbital station, they sent a shuttle down to Piscina IV. They were hardly likely to be bearing placards proclaiming their traitorous ways.'

'Questions will be asked,' Nestor said solemnly. 'Doubts will be raised.'

'Let them be asked!' growled Zaul from where he was standing next to the breach in the wall, a cloud of bolter casings suspended in the air around him. 'You speak as if we acted wrongly.'

'We fired on an Imperial vessel,' Nestor pointed out. 'We boarded and wiped out the crew of another ship, with no evidence to support our claim.'

'Evidence is inconsequential,' Boreas said, turning from the tattered chair.

'The Inquisition will hear of this, Commodore Kayle will make sure of that,' Nestor sighed.

'No!' snapped Boreas. 'It is their claim against ours. We swore to keep the secret of the Fallen, nobody must learn of it. Nobody! It matters not if we can prove it, because to do so will only declare our shame to the galaxy. We will be crushed, hunted down as heretics, and the Chapter will be destroyed.'

'They were here,' Hephaestus said quietly. He had been busying himself at one of the data consoles for some time. The rest of the command squad turned and looked at him.

'You have found something?' Damas asked, crossing the bridge and looking past the Techmarine at the flickering screens.

'Yes, brother-sergeant, I have,' replied Hephaestus. 'I have found their navigational records. They have been in the system for several months, and have made frequent journeys to Piscina II. One of its moons, to be more precise.'

'Aside from planets three and four, the system is uninhabited,' Thumiel said. 'A secret outpost of some kind?'

'That would be my conclusion,' Hephaestus agreed, looking directly at Boreas. 'I have also found data pertaining to a particular type of power plant, of which they picked up several before coming to Piscina.'

'And what does that mean?' Damas asked.

'Aside from the fact that nearly all of the ship's power requirements are provided for by its plasma reactor, the pattern of energy cell they brought on board is the same as that used in our own backpacks,' the Techmarine explained. 'An inventory of the ship's armoury and other equipment includes nothing that would require similar power cells. A suit of power armour is the only reasonable explanation.'

'So the Fallen have been aboard,' concluded Boreas.

'At least one, probably several,' Hephaestus added.

'Anything else?' Boreas asked.

'Most of the data storage was erased or destroyed when we took the bridge,' the Techmarine replied with a shake of his head.

'What are your orders?' Nestor asked, shouldering aside a corpse that had drifted into him.

'Damas, contact Sen Neziel, tell him to despatch a Thunderhawk to retrieve us,' Boreas said, straightening up, full of purpose again. 'Order him to load torpedoes for full spread and prepare to target this vessel. Hephaestus, transmit the navigational directions to the *Blade of Caliban's* bridge crew and have them lay in the most direct course to Piscina II.'

'Do you think destroying the ship will stop any enquiry?' Nestor said with a shake of his head.

'No, but it will destroy any evidence of the Fallen,' Boreas countered. 'We will locate and destroy their base as well, and claim to have rooted out a cadre of renegades.'

'A lie?' Nestor asked.

'A half-truth,' Boreas replied. 'We will leave sufficient evidence that Traitor Marines had been operating in this system. No one will ask which Legion they came from.'

'Do you think that will allay suspicion?' Damas asked.

'We have hunted the Fallen for ten millennia and concealed the true purpose of our quest,' Boreas explained carefully. 'The Inquisition will see what we want them to see. They may have their doubts, but there will be insufficient cause for them to act or inquire further.'

'This makes me uncomfortable,' Thumiel admitted, turning his head to look at each of the others. 'I feel this deception dishonours us.'

'The dishonour is already ours!' rasped Zaul. 'Did you not hear the Brother-Chaplain's words? Did you not consider the oaths of secrecy we swore? Our past already damns us in the eyes of the Emperor, and we shall never be able to atone for that sin if that shame were discovered. Boreas is right, we would be hunted down as traitors, ten thousand years of service and loyalty tarnished by a moment's weakness. Do you wish the Dark Angels to be remembered in history as heroes, or alongside the likes of the World Eaters and Alpha Legion?'

'Enough of this!' barked Boreas. 'Hephaestus, lead the way to the docking bay, we shall talk of these matters later. First, we must destroy this tainted ship and dispense with Captain Stehr and the *Thor Fifteen*. Then we will track the fiends to their lair and eliminate them. That is our only concern for the present.'

'As you command,' the others choroused.

BOREAS STOOD ON the bridge of the *Blade of Caliban* and watched the slowly expanding cloud of gas, plasma and debris that used to be the *Saint Carthen*. He felt relief as he watched the glittering mass dissipating across the backdrop of stars. The feeling went deeper than the elimination of a possible threat did, right to the core of his soul. Since he had first heard the ship's name again after the riot, it had been like a thorn in his mind, a reminder of Astelan. Though he was almost physically incapable of fear, the ship had come to represent something dreadful in the Interrogator-Chaplain's mind. Seeing its destruction exorcised that anxiety, banished the lingering doubts and worries that had plagued him recently.

'Lord Boreas?' the comms officer interrupted his thoughts. 'We are being hailed by Captain Stehr.'

'Very well,' Boreas said with a nod, striding to the communications panel. He activated the speaker. 'Your presence is no longer required, captain, I wish you a speedy and uneventful journey back to orbital dock.'

'This is intolerable!' Stehr's voice ranted back over the link. 'That vessel was a prize of the Imperial Navy, you had no right to destroy it.'

'I not only had the right, but the authority and a duty to do so,' Boreas answered sternly. 'I deemed the continued existence of the traitor vessel to be a threat and have acted accordingly. I do not understand your misgivings.'

'That ship was a legitimate salvage by right of capture,' Stehr protested. 'My crew would have been paid handsomely for recovering her.'

'Service to the Emperor is its own reward,' Boreas replied bluntly. 'Your financial status is not my concern.'

'I shall inform Commodore Kayle of this unprovoked action,' Stehr continued. 'Not only have you fired upon a vessel of the Imperial Navy, you wiped out an entire ship's crew and destroyed a prize ship.'

'I trust you will give Commodore Kayle a full and detailed report of the action,' Boreas said. 'Be sure that you include mention of your disregard for my orders not to board the *Saint Carthen*. You should also take pains to tell him how your disrespectful behaviour has angered me.'

'You launched torpedoes at us!' Stehr's voice was almost a shriek.

'I launched torpedoes close to your vessel to prevent you coming to further harm,' Boreas corrected the naval officer. 'However, I demand that you leave this area immediately and do not attempt further contact with the *Blade of Caliban* otherwise my next torpedo salvo will not be aimed to miss. I will tolerate this insubordination no longer.'

'I shall see charges brought against you for this,' Stehr replied. 'Even if it means I'm brought before a court martial for disobeying orders. I will go to the highest authorities if I have to.'

'Your threats mean nothing to me, Captain Stehr,' Boreas replied. 'We are not of the Imperial Navy, neither Commodore Kayle, nor your admirals or even the Lord Admiral of the segmentum has any authority over us. Even Imperial Commander Sousan does not have authority over us, we answer only to the Supreme Grand Master of the Dark Angels and the Emperor himself. We fight alongside you because we share a common foe, but it is wholly at our discretion how we choose to fight the enemies of the Emperor. And now you are here only at my sufferance, and your continuing prattling threats begin to wear my patience. Your presence here also presents a threat to the security of my vessel and my battle-brothers, and if I do not see you leaving within the next fifteen minutes I shall take action myself.'

Boreas slammed his hand down on the comms rune to cut the link, cracking the wooden panel around it.

'Power to starboard broadsides, target the *Thor Fifteen*,' he commanded, and this time the crew acted without hesitation. Several minutes passed before one of the monitoring officers reported the *Thor Fifteen* powering up her plasma engines and picking up speed. Boreas ordered the gun deck crews to stand down and swept out of the chamber, his mood foul.

It would take the *Blade of Caliban* six days to achieve orbit over Piscina II. Boreas felt the time passing slowly. Though the destruction of the *Saint Carthen* had been a deserved victory, they had yet to root out the Fallen themselves. Boreas was hopeful that whatever diabolic plan they had been trying to enact had been undone with the destruction of their ship. There was no way to be sure though, and the only course of action available to him was to follow the little evidence they had in the hope of finding the Fallen stranded in their base on Piscina II.

But there was another matter he had to address. On the day after the boarding of the *Saint Carthen*, he called his command together again in the briefing chamber.

'You are about to face a foe unlike any you have fought before,' the Interrogator-Chaplain began. 'You have all battled renegades in the past, but to fight the Fallen is to fight against a dark reflection of yourself. Some are utterly depraved, as physically corrupted as a Berzerker or Plague Marine, but others appear no different from you or I. They wear the livery of the Dark Angels Legion, they carry the same symbol upon their shoulder as us. But remember that they are not like us. They are traitors and heretics who turned upon the Lion and the Emperor.'

'This is nothing new to us,' Thumiel said, leaning forward. 'We are ready for them, as we were ready for them before.'

'You may think you are prepared, but you must steel yourselves for the reality,' Boreas warned. 'They will try to talk to you, to appeal to you as brother Space Marines. They will twist the teachings of the Lion, to sow doubt and weaken your resolve. Do not heed their words! Harden yourself to their lies, their falsehoods and warped philosophies.'

'I will hear nothing over the roar of my bolter!' exclaimed Zaul with a snarl. 'Let their corpses try to corrupt us!'

'And therein lies the danger,' Boreas said slowly. 'For the Fallen are not a foe we can execute out of hand.'

'What do you mean?' demanded Hephaestus. 'The punishment for treachery such as theirs is death and damnation.'

'But the quest, this crusade, is not just to erase the evidence of our dishonourable past,' Boreas said, his gaze directed over their heads, as if he could see through the wall to the chapel beyond. 'It is to expunge the sins of the past. It is not enough that we simply kill the Fallen, for the stain on our souls still remains. Yes, they are deserving of death, and we shall be the ones to bring it upon them. But first it is our duty to allow them to repent their sins. Only by offering them salvation for their souls can we hope to achieve forgiveness for ourselves.'

'Salvation?' Zaul almost spat the word out and Boreas looked at him sharply. 'It is they who brought this curse down upon us, what hope is there of salvation for them? Kill them swiftly and rid the galaxy of their harmful presence and we shall have atoned enough.'

'It is not for us to judge the wisdom of ten thousand years,' Nestor cut in before Boreas could reply.

Zaul looked at Boreas, his expression full of consternation.

'Kill the mutant, the witch, the heretic, the alien,' the battle-brother said stubbornly. 'That is what we were taught.'

'And you have learnt well,' Boreas replied with a faint smile before his expression hardened. 'But now you must learn a new lesson, and learn it quickly. If we encounter the Fallen, they are to be captured alive. We will hold them until the Tower of Angels arrives, and then they will be passed into the hands of my Brother-Chaplains.'

'And then?' Zaul demanded. 'And then they die?'

'Yes, but not before we have laid bare the full extent of their crimes,' Boreas said. 'Not before they have the chance to save their souls by admitting their treachery.'

The others said nothing, guessing rightly what the Chaplain's words implied. The quiet of the briefing chamber was only broken by the background noise of humming power lines, the throb of the engines through the hull and the distant clank of machinery. Boreas looked at Zaul, staring deep into his eyes.

'If it is your will, Brother-Chaplain, that we take the Fallen alive, then it shall be so,' Zaul said eventually, dropping his gaze to the deck.

'It is my will,' Boreas replied.

THE DISPLAY SCREEN of the briefing room flickered and shimmered with an image of the moon's surface. At the centre of a superimposed white grid sprawled the Fallen's base of operations in grainy red monochrome. Unsure what defences protected the renegades' station, Boreas had ordered the *Blade of Caliban* to approach cautiously, edging into orbit a few kilometres at a time, ready to pull back from any fire from the surface. No strike came, and now the rapid strike vessel hung just two kilometres above the moon's thin atmosphere, its augurs and surveyors directed towards the cratered surface.

At the heart of the base, Boreas could make out the blocky, square-nosed shape of a landing craft, some three hundred metres in length and fifty metres wide. The rest of the buildings expanded outwards from the landing craft like a ferrocrete spider web of enclosed walkways and bunkers half buried in flows of dust and grit. Thin shafts of light spilled from windows and ports.

The others were standing next to the Interrogator-Chaplain examining the image, pointing out features that looked like power generators, comms arrays and surveyor dishes.

'They have no weaponry capable of orbital attack,' Hephaestus said, confirming what Boreas already suspected. 'However, with the scanning equipment of the central ship, boosted by the relays to the sub-stations, I think we must assume they are now aware of our presence, even if they are unable to act.'

'These look like weapons turrets,' Damas said, pointing at three separate emplacements, one on the ship itself and two others in towers a few hundred metres away to form a triangular defence. He traced his finger across the large screen to indicate their converging fields of fire. 'They're positioned well, no easy attack route. Wherever we strike from, they will have us targeted by at least two turrets.'

'They look like energy weapons, am I right?' said Boreas, glancing at Hephaestus. The Techmarine nodded.

'Yes, you can see the armoured power conduits running from relays built into the lander's central engines,' he said. 'Lascannons, I would say, by their appearance. Given their elevation and the low defraction of the atmosphere they would have an effective range of four or five kilometres, able to hit us as soon as we entered the upper atmosphere.'

'Perhaps an orbital strike to knock out their generators,' suggested Thumiel. 'The target is quite large, I am sure the gunners could hit them from orbit.'

'That would be too risky,' argued Boreas. 'A stray hit could destroy the main structure, burying our prey. Even if the target were struck, there's no way we can tell if a chain reaction wouldn't have equally catastrophic consequences.'

'And they would know for sure what we intended and be ready for us,' added Damas. 'We assume they are aware of us, but we may still hold an element of surprise which would be lost the instant we opened fire.'

'The atmosphere down there is barely breathable by humans, and here on the dark side the temperature will be considerably below freezing,' Nestor observed. 'Perhaps an initial strike to pierce the structure in several places to kill off the majority of any non-Space Marine soldiers will weight the odds in our favour.

'That will not guarantee our success,' Hephaestus said with a shake of his head. 'By its construction, the whole base looks compartmentalised, and each junction is probably sealed. We would have to crack open every part of it first. Also, it is unlikely that the Fallen themselves constructed this on their own, and so their minions would have to be equipped with environment suits to operate outside the controlled interior. We might kill some of them inside, but we could not strike quickly enough to eliminate them in significant numbers before they suited up.'

'We managed to overpower the crew of a starship,' Zaul pointed out. 'These headquarters are not large enough to accommodate even half the number of men aboard the *Saint Carthen.*'

'We had surprise and a clearly obtainable objective then,' Boreas sighed, turning away from the screen. 'If only this ship were equipped with drop pod bays, we might have been able to launch a shock assault, dropping empty pods as decoys for the turrets. As it is, we will have to go in with a Thunderhawk assault, and we cannot even risk orbital fire support to cover our approach.'

'Perhaps if we land over the horizon and attack on foot?' suggested Nestor. 'The environmental reports indicated about two-thirds Terran gravity. We could cover five kilometres in under ten minutes.'

'If we are detected, the lascannons will be able to pick us off in short order,' Hephaestus warned. 'It will take several hits to disable a Thunderhawk, giving us some measure of additional protection against those batteries. If we had known we were going to be involved in more than a boarding action, we could have brought a Rhino with us. An armoured assault would have allowed us access to the base in relative safety.'

Boreas sat down on the front bench of the auditorium, the wood of the seat creaking under the weight of his armour. He glanced at the screen again and shook his head. The others gathered around him as he pensively stroked his chin.

'There will be no easy way for us to end this quickly and conclusively,' he told them, leaning back. 'However, just like a boarding action, the narrow confines of the corridors and chambers will prevent the enemy being able to use numbers against us. We will strike as hard and fast as we can, gain entry and cleanse the base room by room, passage by passage. Zaul, you will carry a flamer, it will prove invaluable in the close confines. Everybody should take as much ammunition and as many grenades as you can carry. Ready your equipment then I shall conduct the pre-battle prayers in the chapel. Hephaestus, have the crew prepare a Thunderhawk for launch, fully armed.'

'I shall bless the missiles myself,' Hephaestus said with a nod, taking a step towards the door before turning back. 'I think we will need the Emperor, the Machine God and the Lion all to watch over us this time.'

'Their eyes are upon us, and we shall not fail,' Zaul said, touching a hand to the Dark Angels' symbol on his chest. 'Praise the Lion!'

BOREAS STOOD IN the cockpit of the Thunderhawk and looked over Hephaestus's shoulder through the armoured canopy. The *Blade of Caliban* had moved to the permanent dayside of the moon before they had launched, and the external environment indicators showed that the interior of the gunship was growing hotter and hotter, though the Space Marines' armour easily protected them from such extreme temperatures. Their plan was to enter orbit out of sight of the enemy base and approach at nearly ground level. They would perform a rapid attack run before turning and landing on the opposite side of the installation, coming to ground as close as possible to the complex.

The bright white of the moon's pockmarked surface almost filled the view from the cockpit, and the gunship began to shudder slightly as the atmosphere thickened. Hephaestus pushed forward on the control column to plunge the nose of the Thunderhawk down, heading at speed towards the surface. Only a few hundred metres from impact, he levelled their flight path and the gunship roared over craters and savage trenches, climbing over the odd low peak and diving into the wide rifts that cracked open the moon's surface.

'Time to attack run, eighteen minutes,' Damas announced from the gunner's position next to the Tech-marine.

'Primary targets are those gun towers,' Boreas told the veteran sergeant. 'Secondary targets at your discretion.'

'Understood, Brother-Chaplain,' Damas replied with a firm nod, his gaze not moving from the tactical screen casting its green light onto the face of his helmet.

Boreas walked into the main compartment where the others sat silently on the benches, their weapons check finished. Zaul had his combat knife in his hand and was etching something into the casing of the flamer. Despite the bumping and rolling of the Thunderhawk, his movements were controlled and precise.

'What are you writing?' Boreas asked, sitting next to the battle-brother. Zaul lifted up the flamer for Boreas to see. Carved in neat script were the words, 'Cleanse the Unclean.' Boreas knew the rest of the verse, it was part of a dedication to the Machine God – *Chastise the Unholy with the Sacred Bolt, Cleanse the Unclean with the Fire of Purity, Cleave the Impure with the Blade of Hatred.*

'Armour your Soul with the Shield of Righteousness,' Boreas said, starting the next verse.

'Guard your Heart with the Ward of Honour,' Thumiel continued.

'Strengthen your Arm with the Steel of Revulsion,' Nestor finished the prayer.

Smiling to himself, Boreas took his crozius from the weapons locker beneath the bench. It felt good in his hands, his badge of office as well as a deadly weapon. Fifteen Interrogator-Chaplains before him had carried this crozius; he had learnt their names when he had been presented with it. He wondered for a moment what they had been like, what it had been like to live during the Age of Apostasy and taken part in the crusades that had followed the Conclave of Gathalamor. He felt that such times were coming again. His instincts told him that the rumours, the hearsay, the omens and portents were more than just idle superstition. The very presence of the Fallen so close to a Dark Angels' world could not be mere coincidence. Forces were stirring, in this reality and in the warp, and he could only guess at what part he might play in events yet to come.

Lost in his musings, the time passed quickly and it was a slight surprise when Boreas heard Damas declare they were only a minute from firing range.

'We are detecting some form of scanning field,' Hephaestus announced as the Thunderhawk's instruments scrolled data across half a dozen different screens.

A few seconds passed and then three blinding flashes of white shot out of the darkness ahead, passing below the gunship. Another volley of high-energy lasfire zipped past from a slightly different angle, crossing the path of the Thunderhawk over a hundred metres ahead.

'Let us hope their aim does not improve dramatically,' laughed Damas as he took up the weapons controls. 'Our missiles' machine spirits are becoming aware of the targets,' he added, his voice solemn again.

Another salvo of fire flashed towards them, only a little closer than the first shots had been. Hephaestus steered the gunship even lower until it was barely thirty metres above ground level. The approach was fairly smooth, a slight incline up towards the wide brow of the hill on which the base was built.

'Firing missiles,' Damas announced as he pressed the launch stud. Twin streaks of fire soared away either side of the Thunderhawk, splitting apart as the tiny metriculator in each warhead guided itself to the designated target. A few seconds later, explosions blossomed to the left and right.

'One target confirmed destroyed,' Damas announced. 'Unsure of the other, definite damage inflicted.'

His answer came only a moment later as two bolts of white energy smashed into the nose of the Thunderhawk, causing the windshield to shatter into a thousand shards and the cockpit consoles to explode with multi-coloured sparks. The gunship lurched to starboard as Hephaestus wrestled with the suddenly unresponsive controls. Boreas and the others were slammed into the side of the hull. The wing dipped alarmingly and Boreas could feel them rapidly losing altitude.

'Brace for crash!' Hephaestus warned, letting go of the controls and seizing hold of the grab rails set into the hull over the pilot's chair.

The starboard wing clipped an outcrop of rock first, causing the gunship to yaw violently amidst the shrieking of torn metal and roar of exploding engines. Spinning fast, the Thunderhawk smashed into the lip of a crater and flipped, sending the Space Marines inside tumbling over and over as the hull buckled and flames erupted from the severed fuel line where the wings had sheared off. Four times the gunship rolled before skidding to a stop, its nose buried under tonnes of gouged rock. The Space Marines were left in a pile on the floor, Thumiel lying across Boreas's chest, Zaul and Nestor entangled with each other just outside the cockpit.

Ignoring the flickering flames, barely hot enough to start peeling the paint on his armour, Boreas pushed Thumiel away and clambered to his feet. He checked on the others and they reported no serious injuries, just minor damage to their armour and a few bruises.

Boreas forced his way through the tangle of buckled spars and crumpled bulkheads to the exit ramp. The hydraulics were a mangled mess spewing fluid over the decking, and he detonated the explosive bolts that held the ramp closed, giving silent thanks to the Machine God that the emergency mechanism had not been broken in the crash. The ramp cartwheeled away from the gunship before coming to a halt in the score marks carved into the rock by the gunship's crash.

The aft of the Thunderhawk was several metres above the ground, and Boreas had to jump down, his boots throwing up plumes of dust as he landed. He reckoned that they had crashed about a kilometre short of the base's outskirts, but pulled his bolt pistol free all the same and conducted a sweep of the crater's perimeter while the others clambered free of the wreckage. They took up defensive positions around the shattered gunship as Boreas considered what to do next.

'Can you confirm our position?' he asked, looking back at Hephaestus.

'Just under a kilometre in that direction,' the Techmarine answered, pointing towards a part of the crater's rim that was shallower than the rest. 'I have notified the *Blade of Caliban* of the situation and they stand ready for your orders, Brother-Chaplain.'

'We continue with the attacks, advance by pairs,' Boreas said. 'Hephaestus and myself, Zaul and Nestor, Thumiel and Damas. Fifty-metre intervals, Zaul and Nestor cover the right flank, Thumiel and Damas the left. We must endeavour to gain entry to the closest part of the enemy headquarters, and attack them from within.'

'Understood, Brother Boreas,' Damas acknowledged, tapping Thumiel on the arm and pointing to the left. The sergeant nodded in reply and they set off with long bounding leaps. Boreas led Hephaestus ahead while the other two covered the ground quickly to the right.

In a few moments, they were at the lip of the crater. Boreas looked cautiously over the top and could plainly see the lights of the Fallen's lair against the dark sky. He could also see the silhouettes of dozens of figures advancing across the ground towards their position.

'Attack! Attack!' Boreas bellowed, rising from his position and raising his crozius above his head. The opportunity for subtle plans and complex strategies had been taken from them the moment the Thunderhawk had crashed; now all that they could rely on was their superior weapons and superhuman abilities. 'In honour of the Lion, attack!'

Muzzle flashes sparkled in the darkness as the traitors opened fire, but half a kilometre away their opening shots were wide of the mark. Boreas threw himself forward, covering the ground in five metre strides, preferring to close the range rather than fire. To his left, Thumiel paused and fired several rounds from his bolter, and Damas added his covering fire as well. Fifty metres on, Boreas skidded to a halt and levelled his bolt pistol as Zaul and Nestor advanced to his right. Thumbing the fire selector to semi-automatic, he emptied the magazine in five short bursts, the explosive bolts tearing through a knot of enemy about three hundred metres in front of him.

The Interrogator-Chaplain could see the foe much more clearly now. They wore an assortment of heavy enclosing suits, visors and breather masks, their bulky protective clothing slowing their movements, making them clumsy. They carried a mix of autoguns and light machine guns, spewing tracer bullets out of the night. Having reached their next position to Boreas's right, Zaul and Nestor halted and opened fire, the flickering trails of their rocket-propelled bolts bright in the darkness. Boreas pulled the empty clip from his bolt pistol and tossed it aside, grabbing another from his belt and slamming it home. Glancing to his left he saw Hephaestus on one knee taking aim with his plasma pistol. A searing ball of blue energy erupted from the muzzle, casting flickering shadows as it sped into the chest of a traitor, ripping through his suit and punching out of his back before its energy dissipated.

Bolt shots from ahead and to the left indicated that Zaul and Damas had advanced to their next firing position, and Boreas sprinted forward again, this time snapping off single rounds as he ran. The display imposed over his vision swam with targets, some of them running in his direction, others hunkering down behind boulders and in shallow hollows. Every time the crosshairs glowed red, Boreas squeezed the trigger and another enemy was toppled to the ground a second or two later.

For six hundred metres they advanced in formation, four providing covering fire as the other pair ran forward. Slowly the traitors were driven back before their relentless onslaught. Boreas's audio sensors relayed the crackle of enemy gunfire, and as the range closed, the shots began to strike home, chipping off slivers of ablative ceramite, burying into the plasteel shell beneath. Discarding his fourth empty magazine, Boreas spared himself a second to assess the battle.

Forty to fifty bodies littered the ground between the Space Marines and the nearest outcropping of the traitor base. A few still moved fitfully as those who had survived their wounds suffered oxygen starvation and froze to death because of their ruptured suits. There were still over twenty enemies, more secure in places of cover, firing sporadic salvoes at the advancing Space Marines. More shapes came piling out of the nearby doors, many cut down instantly by a lethal crossfire from Zaul and Thumiel.

'Press on to the buildings,' Boreas ordered, setting off once more, his targeter tracking a traitor as he ran awkwardly around a corner. He snapped off a shot that shattered the man's thigh and spun him to the ground, his gun spilling slowly from his grasp. 'Secure entry immediately. We will eliminate any survivors once we have cleansed the interior.'

Damas headed forward, and the enemy concentrated their fire on him, bullets screaming past the sergeant and ricocheting off his armour. He made it to an entry point a hundred metres ahead to Boreas's left. Pulling a grenade from his belt, he tossed it into the opening and a moment later the explosion billowed out, flinging the ragged corpse of a man at the veteran's feet. Damas disappeared inside, and a few seconds later, his voice crackled over the comm.

'Light resistance encountered,' he reported, the dull crack of his bolter punctuating his words. 'Entry point secured.'

Boreas waved Hephaestus and Zaul ahead, and turned to give covering fire for Nestor and Thumiel as they ran across in front of him. A bullet struck his helmet, cracking through the lens of his helmet's right eye and driving into the bionics behind. A sudden surge of pain flooded Boreas's face and he stumbled backwards and lost his footing. He just managed to balance himself before he fell completely, but went down on one knee. His head throbbed and his vision swam as he tried to steady himself. The augmetic eye sparked again, burning at him from the inside and he gritted his teeth against the pain. He saw vague shapes running towards him and raised his pistol to open fire.

'Cease fire, Brother-Chaplain!' he heard Nestor tell him and he relaxed his finger on the trigger. His vision still blurred, he saw the pale outline of the Apothecary's armour as he loomed close, one arm outstretched to help Boreas to his feet. Pushing himself upright, he leant on Nestor for a moment while his dizzied senses settled. The pain in his face had gone. He could feel the soothing combat drugs injected into his blood by his armour. His thick blood was already clotting on the wound, but he could feel air leaking out of his helmet. He stumbled a few steps and then regained his balance. He could now make out the doorway where the others were holding position, and broke into a loping run, Nestor beside him.

The interior of the building was narrow, only wide enough for them to advance one at a time. Damas held the far end of the corridor, bolt pistol in his hand.

Hephaestus stood a little way behind him, astride a pile of suited bodies.

'Zaul and Thumiel are holding junctions ahead,' Damas reported. 'Still encountering only light resistance.'

'It's almost deserted,' Thumiel added. 'The rooms we have swept were bare.'

'You think they have evacuated and left behind a rear-guard?' Boreas asked, an uneasy feeling growing in his subconscious.

'Not just deserted, Brother-Chaplain,' Thumiel replied. 'Bare. Completely empty, as if there was nothing in them in the first place.'

'That makes no sense,' Nestor said. 'A facility of this size could house several hundred men.'

'Perhaps this is a new addition to the complex,' suggested Hephaestus. 'Not yet finished. It is at the outer reaches of the station after all.'

'Hold position,' Boreas told them, giving himself time to think.

His mind was still reeling from the gunshot to his head and it took him a few moments to collect his thoughts. Pulling the auspex from his belt, he set the scan to maximum range. At full power, it would not provide detailed information but it would confirm or deny his growing suspicions. It took several seconds for the power pack to warm up, and the screen hazed into life. There were a few vague patches of brightness to indicate life forms, but it was a very low signal. The silence from outside attracted his attention and he looked back through the door. Looking left and right, he could see nothing except rapidly cooling bodies. The twenty or so rebels who they had pushed through were nowhere to be seen.

'The base is all but deserted,' Boreas announced, shutting down the auspex and hanging it back on his belt. 'It matters not whether it is because it has been evacuated or because it has yet to become fully operational. We must get to the control chamber as quickly as possible. With the Lion's blessing we will find answers there.'

'What of the cleanse?' asked Damas.

'There is next to nothing to cleanse!' snapped Boreas, exasperated by this unlikely turn of events. 'Make all speed to the central craft, sweep aside any resistance and press through.'

'Affirmative, Brother-Chaplain,' Damas replied. 'Thumiel, Zaul, lead the way.'

As they advanced, Boreas saw just how accurate Thumiel's brief report had been. There was nothing at all in the corridors they ran through, or the chambers they passed, just bare grey ferrocrete. There were no stains, no litter, no furnishings or anything else to indicate that this place had been lived in. Only the dim glow-globes overhead betrayed the fact that the area they were passing through was even wired in to the main power generators. Sporadic bolter fire from ahead occasionally broke the quiet, and as he continued, Boreas passed the odd vacuum-suited body missing a limb, head or chest. Glancing down the side passages they passed, Boreas realised that many were barely finished: the whole base looked as if it had been flung together in a short space of time and then left.

It was only when the drab grey walls turned to tarnished metal that Boreas realised they had passed into the body of the landing craft at the centre of the web of corridors and rooms. Crude paintings and mottos had been daubed onto the walls. Stopping to examine them, Boreas felt his stomach tighten as he realised that they were poor imitations of the great murals of the central chapel in the Tower of Angels. Poorly rendered black figures striding through gaudy yellow flames looked like the painting of the Cleansing of Aris.

'This is a mockery!' declared Zaul, as they gathered in a circular chamber. The ceiling was layered with flaking paint, the peeled picture a clumsy reproduction of the

Salvation of the Lion, depicting the Dark Angels primarch in the dark woods of Caliban, surrounded by knights. A figure of pure white was holding out his hand to the half-feral man. Boreas snorted in disgust when he recognised the figure as Luther, made out to be an angelic saviour.

'This borders on the worst kind of desecration,' Zaul rasped, raising his bolter and firing into the mural. Splinters of metal and sprays of dust cascaded down onto him, covering his bone-coloured armour in a fine layer of speckled colours. 'Such barbarity cannot be tolerated!'

'The Fallen did not paint these,' Boreas said, gazing up at the scarred scene above. Like the first, it was not simply crude in its technique, but in composition and proportion. Only their actual content bore a vague resemblance to the paintings they imitated. 'Any one of us, though not artists, could replicate the great chapel more accurately. These were crafted by those who have never seen the originals. They were painted by the Lutherites' servants, based on descriptions and their masters' memories.'

'Why?' Zaul demanded, swinging around to face Boreas, smoke still drifting from the muzzle of his bolter.

'As worship,' snarled Boreas. 'They idolise the Fallen, they have been corrupted by them and now worship not only them, but the twisted ideals they represent.'

'We should not tarry here,' Damas interrupted. 'You said to proceed to the control centre.'

'It should be that way,' Hephaestus said, pointing ahead and to the left. 'There should be a direct route from the central passages, just turn left when we reach a main corridor.'

'Proceed with more caution,' Boreas ordered, remembering the scattered concentrations of life signals the auspex has detected. 'The Lutherites could still be here.'

With one last glance at the heretical paintings, Zaul set off, Thumiel close behind him.

About a hundred metres further in, they came across a wide junction, with passages leading off in eight directions. One was obviously the route to the landing craft's control centre, its walls daubed with all manner of graffiti deifying Luther and extolling the feats of the Fallen. The armoured doors at the far end were open, and Boreas caught glimpses of movement inside.

Thumiel had already seen it and moved forward quickly, bringing up the muzzle of the flamer. Two quick strides took him to the doorway and he opened fire, a sheet of flame engulfing the inside of the control room. High-pitched screams mingled with the crackling of the flames and a burning figure flailed into view. Damas's bolt pistol roared once and the flaming man's head exploded, hurling his carcass back into the room.

'We need a prisoner for information!' Boreas yelled as the rest of the squad launched themselves forward, weapons ready. 'Take one alive.'

As he burst into the chamber, Boreas saw that it was high and narrow, filled with banks of scorched, dead consoles, pools of burning flamer fuel scattered across the floors and walls. Charred and smoking bodies were scattered across the floor, crouched behind panels and chairs where the traitors had tried to take cover. Several still writhed around on the ground, howling in agony or their faces wracked with noiseless screams.

A few had survived and opened fire, shotgun shells and bullets smashing into Thumiel, the first who had entered. Zaul returned fire from behind his battle-brother, his fusillade smashing apart display panels, gouging through banks of dials and readouts and ripping through the bodies of three of the Fallen's servants.

There were two others alive, and Boreas quickly took them down with shots to their legs. Like the others, they were dressed in drab environment suits, their eyes wild behind the tinted visors of their face masks. One tried to raise his autogun to fire again, but before his finger closed on the trigger, Nestor had pulled out his combat knife and hurled it into the man's shoulder, causing the weapon to tumble from his grasp.

Boreas holstered his pistol and strode towards them. They tried to crawl away, and backed up against a workstation topped with a cracked and sparking comms unit. Boreas grabbed the nearest by the pipe of his breather and dragged him up so that he was dangling off the ground. The other started inching away until Boreas stood on his injured leg, pulverising the bone and ripping a muffled scream from the man.

'*External address.* Where are they?' demanded Boreas, the skull visage of his helm a hand's breadth from the man's face.

He shook his head dumbly, his eyes casting to the left and right, but there was no avenue of escape, only five more vengeful Space Marines.

'Answer me!' Boreas yelled, the speakers in his helmet amplifying his words to a deafening bellow that caused the man to shake in the Chaplain's grip. 'What is your name?'

The prisoner glanced down at the other survivor, who shook his head vehemently.

'Don't say anything!' the man on the ground gasped through his breather. 'Remember our oaths!'

Boreas put the man down and pushed him back so that he was sprawled over the comms unit. Holding him there with one hand, he turned to the other rebel. He reached down and grabbed the man's shattered ankle and lifted him up like a child.

'Your friend will die quickly,' Boreas said, swinging his arm back and then forward, dashing the man's head against the bottom of the workstation, his neck snapping violently. Tossing the corpse aside, the Interrogator-Chaplain placed his hand around the throat of the lone survivor, crushing the air pipe of the breathing mask. 'You will die slowly.'

'Es... Escobar Venez!' the traitor shrieked. He fought lamely against the implacable strength of the Space Marine's grip for several seconds before giving up and flopping backwards again.

'I am Interrogator-Chaplain Boreas of the Dark Angels Chapter,' Boreas told him. 'I have the skill to cause a Space Marine to writhe in agony and tell me his deepest secrets, his darkest fears. It will take me mere moments to make you talk. There is no point resisting.'

'I don't want to die,' Venez said.

'It is too late for that,' Boreas told him. 'All that remains to be determined now is whether you die slowly and painfully, or you tell me everything I want to know and your torment will be ended quickly.'

'If I talk, it will be quick?' the traitor asked. Boreas nodded once.

Tears began to gather in Venez's face mask, welling up in the eye plates. He looked at Boreas, and then at the others, and then back at Boreas. With a sob, he gave a shallow nod. Boreas released him and stepped back. Glancing back, he saw Damas and Thumiel at the door, ready for attack. Zaul stood close by, intent on the prisoner, his bolter aimed at the man's midriff. Hephaestus and Nestor stood a little further away.

'Where are your masters?' Boreas asked again.

'They left, a long time ago,' Venez told him. 'Twenty, maybe twenty-five days ago.'

'Where are they now?' Boreas said, leaning forward again, resting against the broken panel, towering over the rebel.

'I don't know for sure,' Venez replied. Boreas leaned closer, and Venez shrunk back. 'Piscina IV! They were heading to Piscina IV on the ship.'

'Which ship?' Zaul snapped from behind Boreas.

'The *Saint Carthen*,' said Venez, his stare not moving from the death-faced Chaplain.

'What are they doing on Piscina IV?' Boreas asked, trying to keep calm. Inside, he was furious and full of trepidation. As he had feared all along, his actions had taken him further and further from his prey, not closer.

'I don't know the details,' confessed Venez. 'But I over-head the masters talking about some sort of code – a failsafe code.'

'A failsafe code for what?' Boreas demanded. 'What did they need the code for?'

'I don't know!' screamed Venez, looking away and scrunching his eyes closed. 'Something to do with your keep, that's all I know.'

'Tell me everything!' Boreas hissed.

'I don't know what they planned, I swear!' the prisoner begged. 'The *Saint Carthen* took them to Piscina, and they knew you would chase it and not stop them.'

'What else?' Boreas asked, his skull-masked face a few centimetres from Venez's.

'They were going to wait for you to leave and go to your keep, that's all I know,' Venez sobbed. 'We were to delay you as long as possible. This whole outpost is just a ruse, to fool you and lure you further from them.'

'Who are they, what are their names?' Boreas demanded, Venez flinching at every word.

'Two groups... They came in two groups,' Venez babbled. 'We followed Lord Cypher, but we met others who came with the *Saint Carthen*. Sometimes they argued with each other, I think they had different plans. We didn't see them very often, they never spoke much when we were around. I don't think Lord Cypher knows about the failsafe plan, I think he is after something else in your keep. That's all I know, that's everything!'

Boreas's hand moved fast, his fingers driving through Venez's ribcage and rupturing his heart. Blood bubbled up his face as he slid to the ground. He thrashed around for a few seconds before his movements became more feeble, his accusing eyes locked on the Chaplain.

'Promises to traitors have no validity,' Boreas snarled before turning away. 'Die in pain.' Venez's fingers flapped ineffectually at the Interrogator-Chaplain's boot before he slid sideways and sprawled across the metal floor.

'We must leave now,' Hephaestus said heavily, stepping close to Boreas.

'Did you understand what he was talking about?' Boreas asked. Hephaestus looked away, saying nothing. 'Tell me!'

The Techmarine took a few paces away and then turned back to face them. They were all looking at him, even the two Space Marines at the door,

'The failsafe is a device built into the vaults of the keep,' the Techmarine explained, looking at his battle-brothers. 'It's called the annihilus. After the fighting over the basilica with the orks, it was decided when the new keep was constructed that it should never be allowed to fall into enemy hands. Since the only way the keep would fall were if the rest of the Piscina IV was also subjugated, it was also intended to deny the planet to any invader.'

'What do you mean?' Boreas asked, full of foreboding. 'How does this failsafe device deny a whole planet to the enemy?'

'It's a virus weapon,' Hephaestus answered flatly, staring directly at Boreas. His expressionless helmet told Boreas nothing, but the tone of the Techmarine's voice spoke volumes of the fear he was feeling now.

Boreas was stunned. He was about to say something and then stopped, the words meaningless. He tried to encapsulate his feelings, communicate the dread and the anger that was welling up inside him, but there was no way to express them.

'The keep under my command, our outpost on that world, contains a device designed to wipe out every living thing on the planet,' Boreas said flatly. He felt fatigued and numb. 'And I was not told of this?'

'You were not supposed to know of its existence unless it was absolutely necessary,' Hephaestus replied. 'The Grand Masters were quite specific with their orders.'

'And yet the Fallen, the worst of our enemies, came by this knowledge!' Boreas roared, striding towards the Techmarine. He yanked his crozius from his belt and thumbed the stud, its head blazing with cold blue light. Nestor's hand closed around his wrist as he swung his arm back for the strike.

'This will solve nothing,' the Apothecary said quietly. 'Inquiry, and if necessary justice, can wait until we have averted this disaster.'

Boreas stood there for a moment, Nestor's words seeping through the rage that boiled within his mind. Relaxing, the Chaplain nodded and the Apothecary released his grip. Boreas looked at the crozius, at the winged sword of its head. With a wordless snarl, he let it drop to the floor.

'Signal the *Blade of Caliban* to send a Thunderhawk, Brother-Techmarine,' he snarled and stalked towards the door, leaving the crozius on the floor next to the dying Venez.

THE TALE OF ASTELAN
PART FIVE

THE FORMER CHAPTER commander gathered his thoughts before he started, pushing himself back up onto the table. He spoke slowly, purposefully, his voice betraying none of his physical and mental frailty.

'You can disregard everything I have told you, if you wish. It is a remarkable tale, I cannot deny that, and one you might find hard to accept. If you cannot recognise my arguments on the strength of what you have already heard, then your masters have trained you well, and your loyalty does you credit. But your loyalty is misplaced. It is devoted to those who are undeserving of it. Your only loyalty is to the Emperor and to mankind, never forget that. Consider that fact when you listen to what I tell you now. Of the many truths I have to reveal to you, this is the most important. The Dark Angels considered themselves damned by the shame of the events of the Horus Heresy. They are wrong. Their damnation began when

231

Caliban was rediscovered, and Lion El'Jonson took command of the Legion.'

Astelan paused and watched Boreas's face. It was as expressionless as ever, his stare dark and intense.

'Continue,' the Chaplain said.

'For ten thousand years, the Dark Angels have sought to atone for what happened on Caliban. This I learned from Methelas and Anovel, and you have confirmed it through your own actions and words. You have shrouded yourselves in secrecy, suppressed all knowledge of those events, and eliminated all evidence that the Fallen exist. Even within your own ranks, you have created tiers of secrecy so that even the battle-brothers of the Chapter are unaware of their true origins. Like a coven of malcontents, you whisper to each other in the shadows. You conspire to carry out your quest away from the eyes of others. A veil of shadow covers everything you do.

'It is not because of the Horus Heresy, it is not because Luther and I, and others like us, fought with our own brethren. It is not because the shame of our sins must never been known to others. All of these are excuses, fabrications, justifications to hide the truth. And the truth is so simple, it is shocking. There was a darkness within Lion El'Jonson. A darkness you all carry within you. It surrounds you, yet you are blind to its presence. Intrigue, secrets, lies and mystery: this is the legacy of your primarch.'

'And what makes you think this?' Boreas asked.

'It is a long explanation, but listen to it in its entirety,' Astelan told him. 'It begins before the dawn of the Age of Imperium. Ancient Earth suffers from discord and anarchy as the Age of Strife engulfs mankind. A visionary sees the way to lead humanity out of the darkness, devises a way to guide man back to the stars. We know him only as the Emperor, and He is far from an ordinary man. Creating an army of superior warriors He subjugates the barbarian tribes that dominate Ancient Earth and creates a new society, that of Terra, the foundation of the Imperium He plans to build. Though His warriors are strong, fast, intelligent and loyal, He strives even further to perfect His vision, and creates the beings known as the primarchs. This I learned as a Chapter commander of the Dark Angels.

'The primarchs were the perfect creations, far superior to any mortal man, wholly unnatural in their birth but imbued with altered genes that would make them matchless in the galaxy. Quite what the Emperor intended will never be known, for the primarchs were taken from Him, in much the same way as you say those of us who sided with Luther were taken from Caliban. The Emperor, perhaps, thought them lost, or maybe he knew that they were out there in the galaxy, awaiting rediscovery. The primarchs could not be recreated, or the Emperor was unwilling to try, and He founded the Space Marine Legions instead. Using what gene-seed He had remaining of the primarchs, He created us, the Dark Angels, and the other Legions, and so the First Founding was complete.

'The Great Crusade began and we swept out into the stars on a great war of conquest. As planets fell to us, or were brought back into the fold of the growing Imperium, we raised new warriors and created new Space Marines from that same gene-seed, and thus the Legions were kept at full strength.

'Over time, the primarchs were rediscovered. They had not been slain, but instead had been flung to the corners of the galaxy, awakening as infants on human-settled worlds. Here they eventually grew up in human society, and were rediscovered by the Emperor and the Legions which had been created from them. Each was given command of the Legion that bore their gene-seed, and the Great Crusade continued.

'Much of this is known to you, I am sure. However, there amongst the legends, you can still see the evidence of what I am about to tell you. Some of the primarchs were flawed. It might have been that their gene-seed was not as perfect as the Emperor thought, or perhaps the dark powers had gained influence over them while they were separated from the Emperor. But there is another, much simpler explanation.

'The primarchs and their Legions became as one. Their gene-seed was used directly to raise new Chapters for the Legions, and they became the commanders. Their personality and that of their homeworld was indelibly etched on to the Legions, so that their battle-brothers became but lesser reflections of their primarchs. They, of course, shared a common homeworld, their people had raised the primarchs as their own. Still, this does not explain fully the effect the primarchs would have on the Legions they commanded.

'The reason, I believe, that the primarchs and their Legions became as one with each other is because the primarchs learned how to be human from their homeworlds. When Leman Russ awoke on Fenris, he found himself on a savage ice world ruled by barbarian warriors. He grew up to be fiercely loyal, impetuous and unorthodox, just like those who had raised him. When Roboute Guilliman became an adult on Macragge, he had been tutored in life by statesmen, strategists and leaders of society, and was famed for his organization, from the greatest sweeping plan to the smallest detail. Think about it. The primarchs had to *learn* how to be human.

'Perhaps it was unavoidable, or perhaps it had always been the Emperor's intent to raise and educate them as his own sons. Whatever the cause, the primarchs, for all their skill, strength, speed and intelligence, were a blank slate. They learned well and they learned quickly, but at the heart of the matter is the fact that they had to learn how to be humans.

'You and I are Space Marines, and we are something far above and beyond a normal human. Our bodies bear only a physical resemblance to those of normal humans, for inside us the gene-seed and implanted organs have turned us into something far from normal men. We were not chosen on our physical suitability alone. We, like the primarchs, are intelligent, dextrous and quick of mind, and a decade of training and a lifetime of battle have honed those skills. It is said that we know no fear, and it is true, for the kind of fear a man suffers from is alien to us. We are incapable of the passion that humans speak so highly of in poems and sagas. We are no longer humans, the way we are created ensures that. It is a sacrifice, for mankind's own humanity makes it vulnerable, makes it susceptible to betrayal, to doubt, to despair and destructive ambition. We are beyond such weaknesses, and yet we will never again truly be part of humanity, we will never again be one of the creatures we have been created to protect.

'But even with that great catalogue of changes that marks us as far superior, and sometimes far weaker, than normal humans, we are still closer to mankind than the primarchs ever were. They were wholly artificial, never having had a true mother and father. We Space Marines, you and I, were once human. No matter what the training, no matter what they do to our bodies, no matter how much a lifetime of battle hardens us to it, at the core of us lies that humanity. It will never surface wholly – it is suppressed, buried far beneath our conscious recognition of it – but in our hearts and in our souls we were once and still are human, something the primarchs never had.'

'So what does that mean for Lion El'Jonson?' Boreas asked. 'He was raised by Luther, amongst the loyal, courageous knights of Caliban.'

'The very aptitude the primarchs had for learning, for adapting to those around them and their environment was their downfall. Lacking basic, unalterable humanity, they were just replicas. Physically perfect, intellectually without peer, but spiritually vacant. From the moment they awoke, they started learning, started shaping themselves into what they would become. Those around them helped this process, taught them the values they would hold dear to them for their rest of their lives. The primarchs learned their moral values from the cultures they were raised in; they learnt how to fight, how to lead and how to feel from others.'

'I still fail to see the relevance,' Boreas said with a shake of his head.

'In some, that learning was perhaps a semblance of what the Emperor intended. Roboute Guilliman was the greatest of the primarchs, and never once wavered in his dedication and service. But he was inferior to Horus in every way. He was not as able-minded, nor as charismatic, and not as physically adept. Why was it that Horus turned to the powers of Chaos, perfect as he supposedly was, when Guilliman, his inferior, is still renowned ten thousand years later as the shining example of a primarch?

'It is because Guilliman had learned incorruptibility. For whatever reason, from whatever source, Guilliman had shaped his mind to make it impregnable to the lure of power and personal ambition. He said Space Marines were unsullied by self-aggrandisement, and he spoke truly for he took all Space Marines to be as worthy as himself. Horus, somewhere in his upbringing, had learned a fatal weakness, a chink in the armour of his soul that allowed him to consider himself greater than the Emperor. He turned against his master, as did those who also had such flaws, and eventually Horus was killed and the others driven into the Eye of Terror where they stay to this day, nursing their flaws, reinforcing their prejudices.'

Boreas considered Astelan's words. 'I still have yet to hear anything to indicate why Lion El'Jonson could be to blame for the fall of the Dark Angels. If what you say is true, and the Lion was flawed, then it is the fault of Luther, the man you claim to be the Dark Angels' vanquished saviour. If Luther had raised Lion El'Jonson in the correct way, then it was Luther who turned from the Emperor, and thus it is still his sin.'

'That would be true, but for one thing,' Astelan continued. 'Our primarch, the great Lion, commander of the Dark Angels, was imperfect when Luther saved him from the guns of the Caliban hunting party. He had awoken in the deeps of the Caliban forests. They were wild, dangerous places, swathed in near-darkness, where the sun penetrated the canopy only rarely. In the shadows lurked terrifying, mutated creatures that could kill a man with a single bite of their monstrous jaws or a swipe of their lethal claws. There they stalked and hunted each other, a vicious play of predator and prey.

'This is the world that Lion El'Jonson grew up in and learned from. He learned that the dark shadows could hold hidden dangers, but also that they gave sanctuary. He became a creature of darkness, a thing that avoided the light, for it made him vulnerable and exposed him to danger. When Luther found him, El'Jonson was completely feral, incapable of speech, little more than an animal. He found a hunter, and also the hunted.

'It mattered not what Luther taught him, how well he raised him, what values he passed on to his adopted son. Although on the outside the Lion became a cultured, eloquent, intellectual man, on the inside he was still that hunted, fearful creature. The flaw was already there, it simply became covered with layers of civilization and learning.

'And so there was conflict in the heart of the great primarch. Though I once cursed his name and wished him dead, I have grown beyond such feelings now. One cannot hate the primarchs for what they are, any more than one can truly hate the orks for being alien warmongers, or a gun for shooting you. They are simply what they have been created to be. We come to loathe their actions, to abhor what they represent, as I have come to loathe and abhor the primarchs for what they became and what they did. But it is the symptom we hate, not the disease; it is the effect we despise, not the cause.'

'A fanciful theory, but that is all,' Boreas said. 'Theories are not the truth, and that is what you promised I would hear.'

'Is it proof that you require? Will your doubts be swept away with evidence? If that is the case, then we shall leave the theories for now, and you shall hear the end, or really the beginning, of my tale.'

Astelan took a deep breath and stretched his aching, scarred limbs. He pushed himself off the slab and bent down to refill the goblet with water and took a long draught. Boreas watched him with his unbreaking stare, his eyes never wavering from Astelan's face, perhaps trying to divine the truth from his expression alone.

'When we first learned that our own primarch had been found, we were overjoyed,' Astelan continued, leaning with his back to the stone table. 'It was like a long lost forefather returning to us from the grave, and in many ways that is a literal truth rather than a useful analogy. Part of him was used to make us, and we owed much of what we were to him. It was another two years of fighting before I could take my Chapter to Caliban itself and meet our great commander, but the encounter was pleasant. More than pleasant, it was reassuring. We had once fought for the Emperor himself, and now we had a new commander. It had been a time of uncertainty, for though we trusted the Emperor implicitly, and if he gave command of the Dark Angels to Lion El'Jonson it must have been the right thing to do, we were unsure of the implications.

'But when I met our primarch for the first time, when he gripped my shoulder and looked into my eyes, my fears were banished. Only the eyes of the Emperor himself held more wisdom than that immortal gaze. Dark, penetrating, all-seeing, the Lion's eyes stared into your soul. If only then I had seen the madness that lay behind that intensity, history may well have been very different. But perhaps not. Perhaps even if I had somehow cut him down on the spot, it would have been too late. His legacy had already been bequeathed to the Dark Angels for ten thousand years.

'It is hard to explain what one feels when in the presence of a primarch. Even I, a hardened Chapter commander of the finest Legion, felt awed and humbled. It is not unsurprising that the legends tell of how normal men were known to faint in their presence. The Lion exuded power and intelligence, every action was perfectly executed, every word perfectly considered. Far from being afraid, I was inspired. It had been many long years since the Emperor had truly led us, for the Imperium had grown vast in that time and his labours and cares had grown in proportion. So, standing in front of our primarch, feeling his raw strength like a heat that prickled my skin, I swore a new oath of allegiance, to the Emperor, to humanity, to the Dark Angels and to Lion El'Jonson.

'The Great Crusade was at its height then, and I spent only a few days on Caliban, marvelling at its beauty. Our primarch was a reflection of his homeworld, I realise now. The surface was breathtaking, but underneath lived darkness.

'My Chapter returned to the fore of the expanding frontier of the Imperium, and we continued to battle against the foes of mankind, pressing further and further into the darkness. It was then that things started to change. Slowly, subtly, the influence of the Lion was being felt and the Legion altered in accord. When we had fought for the Emperor, we had virtually free rein. We had a mandate, a destiny to fulfil, and we understood implicitly what was expected of us. It is the same vision that I spoke of earlier, and I can see now why you find it so difficult to understand. You who were not there, who did not hear the Emperor's speeches, who did not swear allegiance in front of the Emperor himself, will never understand. That destiny is a part of me as much as my secondary heart.

'Where once the Emperor had sent us forth in the knowledge that his will was our will, now our primarch introduced greater controls. At first it seemed eminently appropriate, after all he was indeed a strategic genius and with him to co-ordinate our efforts surely there was nothing that could stop us. But slowly, year after year, more power was taken from the Chapter commanders to act independently, to devise their own course of action. More and more, the Lion held the reins of the Legion tight.

'It was then that an incident occurred which began to stir my suspicions. It was nothing much, on the face of it. My Chapter had dropped from the warp into a particular star system and we were making our way towards its core to see if there were any inhabitable worlds. As we approached the inner planets our scouts sent back word of another fleet on a closing course. We moved to battle stations to prepare for immediate attack, and we began to manoeuvre to gain the best advantage. When I was happy that our fleet held the upper hand, I gave the order to attack. Very dearly that order could have cost us, if it had not been for the alertness of the captain of one of our ships in the vanguard. He refused the order to open fire and urgently reported back. The enemy fleet was no enemy at all! We were about to engage the ships of the Twenty-third Chapter, under Commander Mentheus.

'The near-catastrophic attack was aborted, and no more was said about it, but I began to think. Why had Mentheus been there? Why would El'Jonson have sent two fleets to the same system? I thought perhaps that at first our primarch had made a mistake. But that was impossible, the exactitude of his planning and co-ordination was one of the Lion's greatest strengths. He never made mistakes of that nature. That left the possibility that Mentheus or myself were in error, but after conferring with each other, we were both in agreement that we were following our specific orders.

'That left only the possibility that Lion El'Jonson had intended for us both to be there. I could think of no reason why two Chapters had been required, the system was uninhabitable. There had been nothing to indicate a threat worthy of two Chapters, both recently refreshed and at full strength.

'There was no reason I could think of, and for a while I ignored the thoughts that had begun to nag at my subconscious, until they took me onto a new track. The fact that we were both heading to the same system had not been communicated to me. What was more worrying, perhaps, was that our primarch had not seen fit to even tell me that we were fighting in the same sector, though Mentheus had been well-informed. This made me realise that, with the primarch's greater control over every Chapter, the communication between Chapter commanders was virtually non-existent. At the dawn of the crusade, we would regularly confer to devise strategy, to co-ordinate our efforts for the maximum chance of victory and success. Now, we received our orders and simply followed them.

'It was as if El'Jonson was attempting to isolate us. The fear and distrust that had been ingrained into his soul during his infancy was turning to paranoia, perhaps. The instinct for survival on the most basic level was now twisted with the teachings of Luther and the upbringing Lion El'Jonson had received. Where once he saw enemies and prey in the shadows, now he saw them again but in the galaxy around him. I think that our primarch began to fear us, and that through no fault of his own he began to see everything around him as a threat.

'I resolved to counter some of this growing isolation and made more vigorous inquiries. My suspicions were still not aroused at this point, I merely saw a problem developing and sought to avoid it. As I gathered more information, the picture became more clear. Each of the old Chapters, those founded before the rediscovery of Caliban, had a shadow, a new Chapter, founded on Caliban with Lion El'Jonson's own gene-seed, within five sectors or less of it. You could argue that this was coincidence, or more likely for mutual support, and I would agree were it not for the fact that many of the new Chapter commanders seemed to be aware of the presence of the old Legion, but the commanders who had served alongside me throughout the Great Crusade rarely knew of the proximity of their companions. We were being watched.

'Perhaps you now think that it was I who was afflicted with paranoia, and not the primarch at all. Perhaps you are right, perhaps his taint had somehow touched me, and I must stress to you that at this time I had no real concerns, no genuine grievances, just a disquieting feeling, an instinct that something was wrong. That instinct began to focus when I made another discovery. Our primarch was always lauded for his activity, for fighting on the front line of conquest even while directing the resources of his entire Legion. But it appeared that his attention was not evenly spread across the Legion.

'For a primarch who was said to love his homeworld more than any mortal inhabitant of Caliban, the facts painted a curious picture. Rather than an understandable, though still worrying, favouritism for the Chapters who shared the world of his birth, the Lion actually spent more time leading the old Legion Chapters. Though two-thirds of the Dark Angels were now from Caliban, our primarch accompanied those Chapters less than a quarter of the time.

'I came to a shocking and inevitable conclusion: the primarch of the Dark Angels, our commander, did not trust us!'

Astelan stopped there to allow the import of what he was saying to sink into Boreas's thoughts, but the Interrogator-Chaplain's expression did not change. It was as if nothing Astelan was saying had even the slightest meaning for the Chaplain at all.

'Do you not understand?' the former Chapter commander asked.

'Explain it to me more clearly,' Boreas replied.

'We were the Dark Angels! We were the first, the best of the Emperor's Legions! The Emperor himself oversaw our founding, our training and our wars. We were the finest warriors in the Imperium, none had conquered more, and none had showed more zeal in battle and more dedication to their duties. And now our primarch did not trust us!

'It hit me like a shot and the realisation stunned me. I see now why perhaps you cannot understand. You have been raised by the children of Lion El'Jonson, and his legacy is within you, so that distrust and secrets are second nature to you. Not me! I sought desperately for some other rationalisation, to offer myself some alternative conclusion, but there was nothing else that could explain the actions of our primarch.

'And still, I never once doubted the Lion. I did not think the blame was his, I did not realise that it was his madness, his mistrust that had led to this. My first thought was that perhaps he had just cause, that perhaps the old Legion was failing in some way. Maybe we were not aware of it, but perhaps we fought less valiantly under El'Jonson than when we fought for the Emperor himself. Perhaps our achievements matched poorly to those of the new Chapters. Perhaps our attention to our duties had diminished in some fashion.

'This became a singular worry to me, especially when I received word from the primarch himself that he would be taking command of my Chapter for his next campaign. It was almost an accusation, and when I told my company captains I emphasised the need for us to excel, to fight harder and with more dedication than ever before. I impressed on them the need for us to shine in battle when the eyes of the primarch himself were upon us. This message they took to the battle-brothers and as we travelled to the Altyes system we trained harder than ever, so that we might not fail in our primarch's eyes.'

'And so it was at this point that you started to subvert your own Chapter against the primarch?' Boreas said heavily. 'It was then that your heresy began?'

'I voiced my concerns to no one, and my research had been circumspect and secret for I hoped that my growing suspicions were unfounded,' replied Astelan. 'Let it not be said that I jumped straight to accusation of Lion El'Jonson, that I saw myself somehow as his judge and found him at fault from the outset. No, it was only later, during those long days on Caliban, and even later still while I wandered the wastes of Scappe Delve, that the pieces all coalesced into a single picture, that the instincts, the subconscious observations became focussed into a whole. For I had plenty of time to ponder on my life at that point, and then when I came to leave Scappe Delve, the vision of the Greater Imperium began to take shape and occupied my thoughts. Only now, to you, have I shared these truths.'

'A dubious honour, you can be sure,' Boreas said. 'As you have pointed out yourself, there are explanations for these events, even if I were to discount your obvious paranoia and megalomania. None of what you have told me can justify your actions on Caliban, particularly your attempt to kill the primarch himself. When did your heresies begin, Astelan? When did they really begin? Only when you confront them fully will you see them for the acts of treachery they are, and then be able to repent what you have done.'

'It began, it truly began, in the Altyes system. Signals had been detected, human in origin, and our primarch wished to investigate them. We proceeded vigilantly as ever, for the Great Crusade was a war to bring light into the darkness. We never knew what waited for us out in the stars and in the shadows between the starlight. Ancient races with arcane weapons, barbaric human civilisations, worlds in the grip of unfettered technology, human settlements enslaved by aliens, all these things and more were out there.

'So you can understand that whenever we entered a new system we treated it as hostile, not knowing what to expect. Aggression, speed and determination were our greatest weapons, tempered with purity of purpose. All were needed when we arrived at Altyes.'

'What did you find there?'

'The faint signals and their origin proved to be true. There were indeed humans living in Altyes. They had retained much of their civilisation, and would be a great addition to the growing Imperium but for one obstacle. Altyes was over-run with orks. The greenskins had come a century earlier, and overwhelmed the Altyans and now the whole planet was enslaved. The human population had been put to work in great factories to build ships and weapons for the orks, who covered the world in a teeming mass.

'We struck at once. To the Altyans it must have been like a bolt of lightning from the skies, to the orks it was as if the galaxy itself had turned on them. As we descended in drop pods and transports, the fleet opened fire on the planet below. We hardened our hearts to the fact that thousands of Altyans lost their lives alongside the orks, for it was the world that we were trying to save, not individuals.

'How often have the Dark Angels gone to war as a whole Chapter in your lifetime, Chaplain Boreas?'

'Never in my memory, the largest engagement I have been involved in had five companies involved. Why?'

'It is a truly inspiring sight, a whole Chapter at war! Over one thousand Space Marines embodying the Emperor's wrath. The skies fill with the shrieking of jets and blacken with drop pods and gunships. The ground itself explodes with laser blasts, missiles and plasma, tearing at the heart of the enemy, ripping their will to fight from their chests with a single stroke. Even then, with a whole Chapter to command, a thousand Space Marines is few warriors to subjugate a world, but they are enough to destroy any enemy.

'With decisive strikes, we destroyed and captured the largest factories and laid waste to them. Using speed and precision, we struck at the roads and bridges, the fortifications and landing pads. In orbit, our fleet engaged the ork ships and drove them into the atmosphere or reduced them to blazing hulks. Within two days we had forged ourselves a foothold on Altyes.

'From that breaching point we expanded outwards, driving the orks back, catching them in ambushes, pushing them into ravines and to the coasts. Slowly, surely, their resistance wavered, and we continued to push them hard. We had them surrounded though they outnumbered us by hundreds-to-one, through mobility and co-ordination we divided them and sub-divided them and continued to break them up and exterminate them one part at a time.

'Once orks have landed on a world it is polluted, and we rigorously cleansed Altyes of their presence, eradicating every shred of their contamination. They struck back where they could, but against the battle-brothers of the Dark Angels, their disorganised, lacklustre attacks were all but useless. Their ferocity was as keen as ever, but against the Lion they were doomed. They were out-matched in every single way. In firepower, in manoeuvre, in orbital supremacy, and in sheer fervour, we were always in a position of power. Where they gathered in strength, we pounded them with our ships. Where they were scattered, we sent our rapid strike forces to wipe them out before they could muster a resistance.

'Skilled and as experienced as I was, I learned much on the Altyes campaign. I studied the Lion, the way he planned, the way he directed our strengths and employed stratagems I had never conceived of, never mind put into practice. Yes, I studied hard and learned well, but it was not until Tharsis and the quashing of the rebellion that those lessons were to be employed again by me.

'Despite our unparalleled success, despite the valour of the battle-brothers, destroying a world full of orks is no quick matter. The days turned to weeks, then months, and then a year. But at the end, only one pocket of serious resistance remained. Several thousand orks had taken shelter in one of the passes that split the mountains at the heart of the southern continent. While half my Chapter eliminated all trace of the orks across the rest of Altyes, El'Jonson and myself mustered five companies to wipe out the final ork encampment.

'It was then that Lion El'Jonson revealed his true nature. The orks attacked unexpectedly, perhaps driven by desperation or perhaps by seeing some weakness in our battleline. They charged out of the pass even as we prepared to attack, and smashed through the Eighth Company. But rather than stop to turn east or west, they drove north towards the city of Keltis. Our primarch instructed me to allow them to take the city. This was folly of the highest order, in my opinion, as to do so would endanger half a million Altyans needlessly.'

'But you yourself have already told me of the casualties inflicted on the Altyans during the initial attack,' countered Boreas. 'What was different about the fate of Keltis?'

'There are unavoidable civilian casualties in war,' Astelan answered carefully. 'Not only would great caution have risked the entire start of our campaign, it would have slowed us and, through our lack of speed, put even more Altyans at risk. At Keltis, there were no such considerations, I believe it was merely El'Jonson's disregard for the worth of human life, his selfish preservation of those under his command, that led to his plan.'

'So, having arrogantly decided that the primarch was wrong, what did you do then?' Boreas asked.

'My Second and Fourth Companies were in a position to cut off the ork attack and hold them up while the rest of the Chapter responded,' explained Astelan. 'It was then, as I looked at the tactical displays that both the genius and the darkness of the Lion were revealed. The Second and Fourth Companies were positioned perfectly for an attack on Keltis, and the primarch's plan was to encircle the orks in the city and eradicate them. It also became clear to me that the chink in our armour, the scattered disposition of the Eighth Company, had been meticulously ordered by the Lion to tempt the orks from the maze of valleys and canyons. Not wishing a potentially bloody assault on the orks' position, he had pulled them out into the open, using the people of Keltis as bait!

'The plan had so far been a complete success, but to my eyes the sacrifice of Keltis was unnecessary. Now that the orks were on the plains, we could attack in force before they even reached the city. I requested that the Second and Fourth Companies be moved to block the ork advance.

'Our primarch refused. He told me to allow the orks to sack Keltis and we would then converge on them in force and destroy them utterly. He was worried that if we attacked on the plains the enemy would have a chance to scatter or even retreat, costing us many more months of fighting, as well as many more Space Marine lives. I asked him how he could justify half a million deaths to save us a few battles and he said that these half a million deaths would save the lives of a hundred Space Marines.

'I was shocked. It is not for us to reckon our worth against the lives of those we protect. Our duty was to defend mankind from aliens, not use them to save ourselves. While death in the populace of a contested world is undesirable, it is often unavoidable. Keltis however, could easily be saved, and thus I argued with El'Jonson, but he would listen to no counsel of mine. So it was with a heavy heart that I ordered the Second and Fourth Companies to intercept the orks and make a stand before they reached Keltis.'

'You disobeyed the Lion?' Boreas's voice betrayed his genuine shock.

'I did, and I would do so again. The Second and Fourth Companies took heavy casualties as El'Jonson had predicted, but they held against orks until we could counter-attack in force. Also as El'Jonson had predicted, the orks retreated back across the plains, harried by us, but the conclusive victory he had anticipated never happened. Keltis was saved though and I consider myself right to have done what I did.'

'So what happened next?' Boreas asked.

'El'Jonson was enraged,' Astelan answered, eyes closed, shaking his head. 'He banished me and my Chapter back to Caliban, and we were replaced on Altyes by Mentheus's Twenty-third Chapter. Oh yes, is it not convenient that they were only three sub-sectors away? Our shadows had been there all the time. I protested but El'Jonson would not even give me an audience. Thus it was that our exile on our homeworld began.'

'And so you started the first steps along the road to ultimate betrayal of your primarch and your Legion,' sighed Boreas. 'With that simple act of disobedience you condemned the Dark Angels to a legacy of fear and secrecy. It was not the Lion who created that grim future, it was your lack of faith in him, your own rebellious nature and jealousy.'

'That road had been laid down for me ever since Lion El'Jonson had been discovered in the woods of Caliban by Luther,' argued Astelan. 'It was the coming of the primarchs that nearly destroyed the Imperium, and I do not mean just those who turned during the Horus Heresy. At the start of the Great Crusade it had been just us, the Space Marines, and the Emperor as one. But when the primarchs took command of the Legions, another force became involved. Their individual pride, their honour, their ambitions and their traditions cluttered the clarity of the Emperor's vision. It was from that moment that the Imperium was doomed to fall once more.'

'And yet the Imperium still prevails, ten thousand years later. Despite what you say, we are still here.' Boreas pointed out, looking pointedly around the cell.

'But the Great Crusade is a legend, a distant memory. It was never meant to be that, it was never an event, it was a state of mind. It was the primarchs who gave the power to weak, fallible humans after the Horus Heresy. Not from ill intent, but from ignorance. Humans were never supposed to control their own destiny, they are incapable of doing so. What has become of the Imperium? It has become a labyrinth of organisations and politics, bickering Imperial commanders, and is run by intermediaries, not leaders. The Space Marine Legions were broken down into Chapters, and the Imperial Guard that had risen up in our wake had its ships taken from it and the Imperial Navy was created.

'Even now, I sit in this cell condemned because of the same fear. It is the fear of great men, the love of mediocrity, that the Imperium thrives upon. Humans, and the primarchs who became their puppets, have condemned themselves and us to a slow, lingering death. The Dark Angels fear the humans they protected. Is it not a strange irony that the sacrifice that I made has led to ten thousand years of skulking in the dark? That the bright stars in the firmament of battle have become shadows, afraid to show themselves for what they are, afraid of themselves for what they know lies within them. Ignore my words if you will, but when the time comes, look inside yourself, feel the spirit of the Lion within you. The taint is there. I will say it once more so that you might remember it. There was a darkness within Lion El'Jonson. A darkness you all carry within you. It surrounds you, yet you are blind to its presence. Intrigue, secrets, lies and mystery. These are the legacy of your primarch.'

Boreas did not reply but stood there for a long while in contemplation. Finally, he looked back at Astelan, but said nothing. With a barely perceptible nod, he turned and walked towards the door. Swinging it open, he stopped, his head turned to one side.

'Am I done, Grand Master?' he asked, and Astelan was confused.

'You have done well, Brother-Chaplain,' a deep voice said from behind Astelan. 'You have earned yourself a black pearl for your rosarius. I will deal with this traitor myself.'

Astelan looked around, but at first could see nothing. He heard the door clang shut and the cell was dark again. A movement caught his eye, and he looked more closely in that direction. From the shadows a skull emerged, and he saw that it was the mask of a man swathed in a robe of blackness. The man stepped forward into the dull light of the brazier. Astelan recognised him as the other Space Marine who had been in the chamber when he had first been brought here.

'You have heard everything, you have been here all this time?' he gasped in disbelief. 'Who are you?'

'I am Sapphon, Grand Master of Chaplains, the Finder of Secrets,' the man told him, his voice slow and deliberate. 'I have indeed been here all along. A simple trick, to misdirect your eyes, to focus your attention on other things and not my presence.'

'What will you do with me?' Astelan asked.

Sapphon pointed over Astelan's shoulder, saying nothing. The door opened and two more figures wearing skull

masks and black robes entered. They grabbed Astelan
with gauntleted hands. He struggled vainly but he was
powerless to resist, his strength sapped by days of torture.
They dragged him to the door until Sapphon raised his
hand and they stopped.

'You will be taken to the deepest recesses of the Rock,
and there you shall stay, tended to by the best of our
Apothecaries,' said the Grand Master in his deep voice.
'There will be no repentance, there will be no end, swift
or otherwise. There you will hear the cries of the Betrayer,
and you will come to understand what it is that you have
done.'

'Luther, Luther is here?' Astelan said, his thoughts
whirling. 'How? Why? Did he not die at the hands of the
Lion on Caliban?'

'He did not,' Sapphon told him. 'He is ours, held in the
deepest cell of this rock. As his cries for forgiveness echo
in your ears, you will learn to beg for mercy as well.'

'I do not understand,' Astelan pleaded.

'You are fond of the sayings of the Imperium,' Sapphon
replied with a gesture to the Space Marines holding his
prisoner. 'You said they have deeper meaning than many
give them credit for. I too understand the wisdom that
lies behind the proverbs and curses of the common folk.'

Astelan nodded. He heard Sapphon's voice as the
guards pulled him out of the cell and closed the door.

'Knowledge is power, guard it well,' the Grand Master's
voice called after him.

THE TALE OF BOREAS
PART FIVE

WITH THE *Blade of Caliban's* reactor at dangerously high levels, it was still a twelve-day journey back to Piscina IV. As soon as the Space Marines were back on board, the ship got under way. Boreas headed directly for the chapel and sealed the door behind him. For ten days he remained there.

Sustained only by the support systems of his armour, the Interrogator-Chaplain knelt unmoving in silent vigil before the altar. If anyone had been there to see him, they might have taken for a statue. But for all his physical immobility, the Interrogator-Chaplain's brain was in a feverish storm. He tried to quiet his tumultuous thoughts with prayers and chants, reciting every hymnal and catechism he knew for hours on end, but to no avail. Despair turned to anger, anger turned to fear, and fear turned back to despair in the whirlwind of his mind.

He searched desperately for reason and calm, but madness crept into his thoughts, battering his conscience, ripping at his pride, fuelling his guilt. Shame burned within him as he thought how rash and foolish he had been. Remorse tortured him until he mentally lashed out, cursing the Grand Masters for their secrecy, damning Hephaestus for his mistrust. Most of all, he was wracked by the futility of his situation. He was helpless, and his emotions, for so long kept in check by iron discipline and training, drifted and raged.

He prayed fervently for guidance, for some sign of what to do, but there were no answers, no revelations. And always the feeling of betrayal rose up in his thoughts. Betrayal by those he served, and betrayal by those he served alongside. Mocking laughter taunted him, and he began to hallucinate, seeing apparitions of a barren Piscina, the ground littered with millions of bones. Contorted, grinning faces swathed in shadow filled his vision, cackling at his ignorance.

Most painful of all was the thought that he had lost. The Fallen had led him by the nose all the way, teasing him onwards, luring him from Piscina. Worse, he felt they had corrupted him spiritually as well as fooling him. He had abandoned his sworn duty to protect Piscina and its inhabitants. They had set him against forces loyal to the Emperor. The sheer scale of what they had done confounded understanding. It had all been an illusion, an elaborate shadow play to pull him further and further from their true purpose.

It seemed so obvious to him now that the riots had been engineered by the Fallen to attract his attention. There had been no mutilated Navigator, it was all a pretext. How long had the agents of the Fallen been manipulating the citizens of Kadillus Harbour, planting the seeds of their lies, scheming in the heart of the realm Boreas had sworn to defend? They would have known he would eventually hear about the *Saint Carthen's* presence. From then on, their complex plot was set in motion. The Fallen Angels had pitilessly sacrificed their followers to further their plan, knowing that the Dark Angels would be merciless in their hunt. They had left just enough information for him to follow the trail to a false base, to draw him far from where he needed to be.

The most damning part of the plot was its sheer audacity. In his moments of lucidity, Boreas pieced it together, and it was these deductions that caused him to despair of saving Piscina IV from the horrific fate the Fallen had planned. And if Piscina IV fell, then Piscina V would doubtless be the next target. When the *Saint Carthen* had arrived and set in motion the chain of events that had drawn Boreas away, the Fallen had been there, dropped on Piscina. The more he chased the ship, the greater the distance between him and his real quarry. It was a calculated and cruel irony, inspired to cause him the greatest torment. Like puppeteers, his enemies had manipulated him at every turn and had plotted for this moment. Not content with destroying the world under his protection, they had done it in such a way as to damn his soul in the process.

Boreas knelt on the floor of the chapel, head bowed before the altar, and begged the Emperor and his primarch for forgiveness. But he knew there would be none, because he could not forgive himself. It was that shame, the dark coil of sin that writhed inside him, that kept him locked in the shrine. How could he ever leave and face Hephaestus, who unwittingly had damned him? What could he say to Zaul, who had been the most fervent amongst them, and who thought Boreas a hero of the Chapter. And the others – Nestor, Damas and Thumiel – their accusations would be silent but no less crippling. Boreas could not face it. He had none of the answers they would need. They would look to him for strength and courage, but he had none to give.

On the tenth day, half-delirious, derided by daemons of his own creation, Boreas drew his pistol and held the muzzle against the weaker joint of his neck armour. The bolt would tear into his throat and blow out his spine, ending the pain forever. For half a day he sat, thumb through the trigger guard, imagining the blissful oblivion just a simple motion away.

His mind became still and calm. Everything dropped away from his thoughts, his emotions shrinking to a single, focussed point inside his head. The galaxy disappeared, the ship, his battle-brothers, all of them slid from conscious thought. All that remained was him and the pistol. Life and death.

At that moment, he looked up with his one good eye and saw the Chapter symbol of the Dark Angels on the wall in front of him. It was beautifully crafted, the sword at its centre shaped from pure gold and silver, the dark wings to either side delicately chiselled from black marble. Boreas stood, the bolt pistol dropping from his fingers. He stretched out his hand towards the embodiment of everything he had lived for, everything he had been created to uphold. He took a couple of faltering steps forward and then strode more purposefully around the altar and laid his hand against the sword. Removing his scarred and battered helmet and tossing it to one side, he leaned forward and rested his forehead against the hilt of the sword, feeling the pulse and hub of the ship vibrate through his torn face. Closing his eyes, he bent lower and delicately kissed the blade in thanks.

'Praise the Lion,' he whispered. 'Praise the Lion for his strength, wisdom and fortitude. His blood runs in my veins. His spirit lives on in my soul. Praise the Emperor for his courage, his guidance and his purpose. By his hand, I was made. By his will, I live. There is no peace, no respite. There is only war.'

BOREAS FOUND THE others gathered in the reclusium, seated in silent meditation, dressed in their robes. It was Zaul who looked up first, his expression of surprise quickly turning to joy.

'Brother Boreas!' he exclaimed, jumping to his feet. The others broke out of their trances and stood, their reactions a mixture of curiosity and relief. Only Hephaestus remained seated, staring at the ground.

'Brother Hephaestus?' Boreas said, walking over to stand in front of the Techmarine. He saw that his hands were cut and bruised, and there were stark weals across his chest and shoulders. There was a haunted look in his eye as he raised his gaze to the Interrogator-Chaplain. Boreas offered his hand, and after a moment's hesitation, the Techmarine grasped it firmly and pulled himself to his feet, a faint smile playing on his lips.

'Nestor was correct,' Boreas said, turning to address them all. 'Now is not the time to judge, or for recriminations. Now, more than ever, we must be united. They want to divide us, to pit us against each other and ourselves. We shall not let them conquer us, we are stronger than they.'

Zaul hurried forward and clapped a hand onto Boreas's left shoulder, still grinning.

'We were vexed by your absence, Brother-Chaplain,' Zaul said, his grin replaced by a look of consternation. 'We were lost without your guidance, your words of wisdom.'

'We debated much over what to do,' explained Damas. 'We were unsure of the best course of action.'

'As was I,' admitted Boreas, clasping Zaul's shoulder in return. 'I wandered a lonely path, but the Lion guided me back.'

'What are your orders?' asked Nestor. 'I think it is paramount that we return to the citadel as soon as we arrive at Piscina IV.'

'I agree,' Boreas replied, stepping back, his fists balling at his side. 'We must confirm what we have learnt. The Fallen have played a deadly game with us until now, and this may yet be another falsehood set to confound us.'

'And if it is not?' asked Thumiel. 'What then?'

'If we can, we prevent them from succeeding,' Boreas answered quickly. 'If we are too late, then we mourn the loss.'

'And what of the Fallen?' Damas inquired.

'We shall seek justice and exact punishment, as we have done for ten thousand years,' Boreas replied.

They stood there for a moment, this one thought joining them together. Boreas stepped up to Damas and plucked at his robe with his finger.

'You are out of your armour, brother-sergeant,' Boreas said with a slight smile. 'As are you all. I do not remember announcing the crusade accomplished.'

'As you will it, Brother Boreas,' Zaul replied. 'We shall arm ourselves for the continuing fight. But I suggest that while we do so, you eat heartily and refresh yourself. I smelt you before I saw you, and your face is as thin as an eldar's. Your search for guidance must have taken you far.'

'It was a long path,' Boreas agreed with a nod. 'A long and dangerous path, but one I shall not need to tread again.'

As THE THUNDERHAWK streaked down through the upper atmosphere of Piscina IV, the comm was filled with a cacophony of transmissions. For the last two days the *Blade of Caliban* had attempted to make contact with the planet's surface or the orbiting station, but there had been no reply. Boreas's fears had increased with the continuing silence, fearing that it betrayed the extinction of life on the world, that the Fallen had activated the annihilus and wiped out everything he had sworn to protect. Now, as the Space Marines headed towards their fortress, every frequency, every transmission medium, was bursting with almost meaningless chatter, and disturbing as it was, Boreas felt relief that there was still life on the planet below.

All attempts to make contact with the surface still failed, and the Interrogator-Chaplain could not yet decide what course of action to take. As much as he tried, Hephaestus could do nothing to filter out the messages that overlaid each other, and only scattered fragments barked from the audio unit in garbled bursts.

'...casualties at thirty-five per cent...'

'...sporadic fire continuing, falling back...'

'...desert us not in the hour of need, turn to the great benevolent...'

'...west wing in ruins, fires spreading, tenders dry...'

'...ay of the Emperor's judgment is upon us, for the sinf...'

'...evacuation stalled...'

'...abandoned us. I can't believe they abandoned us. I can't believe...'

'...o response to hails. It's as if they...'

'...Emperor protect us, there's bodies everywhere. It's like a slaughter house in...'

'...why did they do this? It doesn't make any...'

'...casualties now at forty per cent, further advance possible...'

Boreas flicked off the comm in frustration and stared out over the blunt nose of the gunship. Thick white cloud spread out beneath them, but ahead a darker patch was spreading, polluting the sky. For a few seconds, as the Thunderhawk passed through the cloud layer, the Interrogator-Chaplain could see nothing but whiteness. Then, as the gunship broke out of the underside, he caught his first sight of Kadillus Harbour.

More than a dozen columns of smoke rose into the air from across the city, and even at this altitude, he could see massive fires raging around the docks and the starport. Turning his gaze to his left he saw more evidence of trouble, explosions blooming on the volcano's slopes close to Barrak Mine at the north end of Koth Ridge.

'Head straight for the outpost, we can land in the Kandal Park,' he told Boreas, unable to tear his gaze from the scene of devastation below them.

As the Thunderhawk swooped lower over the city, Boreas could make out more evidence of heavy fighting. The ruined shells of buildings and smouldering ruins of hab-blocks sat alongside tracts of rubble, demolished factories and a mess of twisted girders and cranes.

'What could have happened?' Hephaestus asked. 'It is as if the city is tearing itself apart.'

'I think it is,' Boreas replied, pointing at the streets below. They were filled with people, tens, perhaps hundreds of thousands of them thronging the roads, setting fires, looting and fighting. They saw clusters of Imperial Guard, firing indiscriminately into the crowds. Even more disturbing, tanks rolled down the roadways, blasting at buildings and citizens with equal fury, their heavy bolters blazing, a swathe of crushed bodies left in their wake. He saw Guardsmen fighting Guardsmen, battling across rooftops, fighting street-to-street.

People on the ground began to notice the gunship overhead as it slowed and circled to land. Some threw their arms in the air, obviously pleading to the Space Marines. Bullets whined nearby as others started shooting, and lasbolts deflected ineffectually off the Thunderhawk's heavy armour.

'I can't land!' Hephaestus said. 'There is no clear zone.'

Boreas looked ahead and saw that the open park was full of people. The carefully cultured trees and hedges, the only life inside the city that was not in the Imperial commander's gardens, were trampled and burnt. The lawns and rock gardens were covered with people, and many bodies.

'Just land!' ordered Boreas, unhitching his harness and stepping into the crew compartment. Hephaestus glanced at the Chaplain's retreating back, shook his head and then directed his attention back to the controls.

THE THUNDERHAWK DESCENDED on pillars of blue fire. The crowds tried to scatter, but the press of the bodies meant that many were caught in the downwash of the jets, reduced to ashes instantly. The gunship settled heavily into the soft earth, crushing the charred corpses of those caught below, its metallic feet sinking a metre into the soil. The assault ramp swung down and Boreas stood at its head, bolt pistol in hand. People began to surge towards him and he fired into the air. Some stopped, others threw themselves to the ground, many turned and tried to flee, their screams filling the air.

A woman with a tangled mass of hair, her red woollen dress stained with soot, sprinted up the ramp, a carving knife in her hands. She threw herself at Boreas, the blade buckling on the armour of his breastplate. He shoved her aside, toppling her off the ramp onto the scorched earth.

'Cease this madness!' he bellowed, but the terrified and frenzied mob paid him no heed, stampeding forwards and backwards, trampling over those who fell, their cries of fear and pain drowned out by the shouting and shrieking.

'We must break through, use minimal force,' he said, stepping down the ramp. 'We can devise a strategy once we have ascertained whether the keep is still intact.' The others followed, looking left and right in disbelief as they descended. As the last of them stepped out, the ramp closed behind him with a loud grinding.

Boreas battered his way through the press of bodies, shoving men and women aside to get through. He grabbed an old man by the throat and hurled him away as he tried to prise Boreas's bolt pistol from its scabbard. Others scrabbled at his knife, or battered at his chest and legs, and he drove them away with bone-crunching sweeps of his hand. Looking over his shoulder, he saw that the others were making equally slow progress, the crowd surging in behind him as he ploughed forwards.

As he waded through the human morass, Boreas began to listen to their shouts. They were cursing the Dark Angels, calling them traitors and murderers. They begged the Emperor to bring his vengeance down on the Space Marines, accusing them of oath-breaking. A sick feeling grew inside Boreas as he guessed what had occurred.

The Fallen were here, or had been. The citizens of Piscina, the Imperial Guard, the security officers would have thought them loyal Space Marines. They knew little of the Horus Heresy, even less of the continuing fight against the Traitor Legions, and nothing of the treachery of the Lutherites. Boreas dared not think what atrocities they had committed, but whatever they were, it had turned the world against the Dark Angels.

'We must get through to the outpost, whatever the cost,' he told the squad, smashing his gauntleted fist into the chest of a thin, bearded man who swung at him with a metal bar.

Boreas drove forward with greater ferocity, crashing through the mob and scattering them left and right. He reached the high metal fence that surrounded the park, subconsciously noting the mangled bodies that lay along its length, those who had been crushed to death by the press of people. Without pausing, he tore two of the railings clear, and then two more, and again, until he had opened a hole wide enough to clamber through. The street beyond was quiet, the high buildings stretching up either side deserted.

Turning left, he broke into a run, pounding along the street in the direction of the keep. As his anger rose, his speed increased, until he was hurtling at full sprint along the road. Turning a corner, he ran into the wide, rock-crete killing ground surrounding the outpost. Scores of Guardsmen were there, fighting with citizens and each other. The blazing wrecks of two personnel carriers cast a bloody hue over the scene. Boreas slowed to a halt. Looking out over the mass of brawling people, he spied another troop transport, flying the banner of Colonel Brade. The flare of lasfire illuminated the grim scene as the carrier's multi-laser opened fire, the energy bolts scything through Guardsmen and maddened citizens alike.

'Clear a path. Fire to wound if possible, kill if necessary,' the Chaplain ordered, pulling free his bolt pistol.

He fired ahead as he advanced, shooting low, the bolts fracturing thighbones, ripping through hips and shattering kneecaps, until a corridor had opened up in front of him leading towards Brade. The small turret on the APC turned in his direction, and for a moment it looked as if it was going to fire at him. Then the barrels tilted downwards before another blaze of shots tore through the hellish battle, clearing an open route for him. Boreas ran forward, the other Dark Angels close behind, and stopped next to the transport. He banged on the hull and a moment later the hatch opened and Colonel Brade stuck his head out.

'Thank the Emperor you have returned, Lord Boreas,' the colonel gasped, clambering out awkwardly. He stared for a moment at the Space Marines as if it was the first time he had seen them properly. It was then that Boreas realised it probably was, at least with their present appearance. Their armour was bone white, decorated with red, green and black heraldry, and festooned with purity seals that fluttered in the wind. Dents, bullet holes, las-scorches and pieces of embedded shrapnel still scarred their armour, despite Hephaestus's best repairs in the time he had been allowed. Damas's armour was covered head-to-toe in the neat script of the Opus Victorium, and the side of Boreas's own skull helm was covered in a bare metal plate where it had been punctured.

'Tell me everything,' Boreas demanded, turning so that he could keep a careful watch on the fighting. The battle started to move away as the Guardsmen protecting the colonel forced their way to the north with fusillades of lasfire, driving the armed mob away from the keep. Bullets and las-shots still occasionally whined overhead and the air was filled with the clamour of shouting, firing and intermittent explosions.

'I hardly know where to start–' Brade said with a shake of his head, glancing cautiously around.

'Tell me about the Space Marines,' Boreas prompted, directing Thumiel and Damas to cover the other side of the vehicle with a flick of his hand. He heard the bark of their bolters now and then as they fired at rebels who had broken through the cordon of Imperial Guard.

'How did you know–?' Brade asked.

'That is not important,' Boreas waved away the colonel's question. 'You must tell me about the other Space Marines.'

'No one is sure when they arrived, they certainly weren't seen getting off any ship or shuttle that landed,' the colonel began. 'I simply heard from the commander's enforcers that Space Marines had returned to the keep and I thought nothing more of it, assuming it was you and the others. Then the orks attacked again, in such numbers I haven't seen since the invasion. They overran Vartoth in an afternoon, and we threw up a line to hold them from coming further south. They broke through early evening yesterday and now we're desperately trying to hold on to Barrak.'

'I saw the fighting,' Boreas said. 'Where are the Space Marines now?'

'I don't know,' Brade replied with a shrug. He flinched as a shell detonated against the wall of a nearby building. 'I tried to contact you at the keep, but there was no reply, so I sent a delegation to ask for an audience. That's when they came out. I only have scattered reports, I'm not sure what happened next.'

'Tell me what you know,' Boreas urged him. 'Every detail could be important.'

'Well, the first group to emerge just ignored the messengers,' Brade said, his brow creased in a frown of concentration. He looked about ready to collapse, his face haggard, his eyes heavy and dark. 'There were three, maybe four of them. They were definitely Space Marines. Their armour was the same as yours, the Chapter symbol, the badges. My officers tried to speak to their leader, but they were shoved aside, and they dared not persevere for risk of offence.'

'How did they know who their leader was?' Boreas asked.

'He was dressed differently,' the colonel explained. 'He wore long robes like a coat over his armour, and carried two bolt pistols in low slung holsters.'

'A sword in a scabbard. Did he carry a long sword in an ornate scabbard?' demanded Boreas, feeling an unfamiliar chill of foreboding.

'Yes, yes, I think the survivor mentioned that,' Brade answered, nodding slightly. 'Do you know him?'

'Only *of* him,' Boreas replied. 'It is not your concern, continue. You said survivor?'

'Er, yes,' Brade said, visibly shaken. 'The first group headed south, towards the docks, and disappeared. I don't know where they went. My men didn't know what to do. They contacted me by comm to ask for orders, and that's when the others came out. They opened fire immediately, I heard Lieutenant Thene screaming over the comm, and bolter fire. One of the officers, Lieutenant Straven, ran immediately. He was the only one who got away, the others were cut down where they stood.'

'And then?' Boreas prompted Brade, who had lapsed into deep thought.

'Then they started the massacre,' the colonel said with a grimace. 'They advanced into the city, killing anyone in their path, destroying ground cars, tossing grenades into buildings. It was carnage. We didn't know what to do, and by the time a platoon arrived, they were nowhere to be found. But it was too late by then. Panic began to spread, the word got out that the Dark Angels had turned on us. I didn't believe it, but then everything descended into anarchy. There were riots everywhere, half my own men joined in, under the pretence of hunting the Space Marines down. After that, it just got worse and worse.'

'And the situation now?' Boreas asked.

'You saw for yourself, I'm sure,' Brade said bitterly. 'The entire city is in revolt, but the Imperial commander is safe, we have tanks stationed at all the roads leading to the palaces. Northport is in ruins, no ship can leave or land, and the docks are little more than rubble.'

'I must attend to urgent matters at the keep,' Boreas said. Motioning the squad to follow, Boreas began to march towards the gatehouse of the keep. He had only taken a few paces when he turned back to look at Brade.

'Thank you for trusting in us,' Boreas said.

'I had to keep my trust in you,' the colonel replied, leaning back against the armoured carrier. 'I had to believe that you had not betrayed us. The alternative is too terrible to contemplate.'

'Yes it is, colonel,' Boreas agreed quietly. 'Hold the perimeter here for as long as you can, I shall contact you again shortly.'

THE MAIN GATE into the citadel was sealed shut. Pressing the entry combination, the door slid aside and the Space Marines entered, weapons ready. As they stepped inside, the door hissed back into position behind them.

Three bodies lay in pools of blood in the entrance hall, the red-robed gatekeepers whose duty it had been to receive delegations from the Imperial commander. Examining them, Nestor pointed at the deep knife wounds across their chests and throats. The unarmed men had been butchered, probably as they had welcomed their unexpected visitors.

As they progressed, they found more evidence of cold-blooded murder. Attendants, scribes and logisticians lay at or near their work stations, also brutally slashed and stabbed. Working their way up the tower, they found bodies on the stairs and in the hallways. With trepidation, Boreas followed Damas into the aspirants' chambers.

The veteran sergeant gave a howl of anguish and ran forward. The bodies of the youths were draped across their cots, sprawled on the floor and slumped against the walls. Damas checked each in turn, and when he got to the last he shook his head slowly.

'Their necks have been snapped,' he stated flatly, the corpses reflected in the red lenses of his helmet. He lifted up the hands of the boy at his feet, the youth called Varsin. His knuckles were bloodied and broken. 'They tried to fight, as I taught them. It would have been futile.'

'They died bravely,' said Zaul. 'They died fighting for the Emperor.'

'No!' Damas snarled. 'There was no bravery here, just desperation! Pointless, senseless slaughter. This served no purpose. None of this killing did. They were defenceless, all of them.'

There was a point, but Boreas chose not to share it with his distraught brethren. It was the final insult, the final challenge to the might of the Dark Angels. It was a statement of intent, as clear to Boreas as if it were written in blood on the walls – the Dark Angels had no future.

'We must check the vault,' Nestor said suddenly.

'The annihilus is obviously not active,' Hephaestus pointed out. 'If it were, there would be nothing left alive on the island.'

'They may have tampered with it,' the Apothecary insisted.

'Very well,' Boreas agreed. 'Nestor and Hephaestus with me. Zaul, Thumiel, check the upper storeys and the roof. Damas, go to the vehicle bay and ready the Rhino for combat.'

As he walked down the stairs, Boreas felt drained and empty. The Fallen had done more than simply kill the servants of the Chapter. By attacking here, in the Dark

Angels' own outpost, they had driven a blade into the heart of the Chapter.

They passed signs of sporadic fighting as they travelled through the keep: bullet holes in the wall, a ragged corpse draped down the stairwell, trails of dried blood on the floor.

When they entered the vaults, stepping over the bodies of three serfs who had tried to defend the entrance, Nestor carried on past the operations chamber, deeper into the tunnels. Ahead, an armoured door hung open, twisted off its heavy hinges, the locking bolts ripped aside. Nestor dashed forward into the small chamber beyond. A few moments later he reappeared, and leant heavily against the wall.

'They have taken it,' moaned the Apothecary.

'Taken what?' demanded Boreas. He knew of the Apothecary's storage crypt and assumed it contained rare or possibly volatile medical supplies.

'The gene-seed, they have taken the sacred gene-seed,' Nestor replied, his voice a hoarse whisper.

'Gene-seed?' Boreas was confused. Then the realisation struck him and his anger welled up. 'More secrets! More lies and half-truths!'

'It was for the security of the Chapter, Boreas,' Nestor said, hanging his head. 'It would be folly for all of our gene-seed to be carried in the Tower of Angels. What if the unthinkable happened? What if the Rock were lost? Destroyed in the warp, perhaps? After we survived the loss of Caliban the Lion wanted to ensure the Chapter would always endure. It was decided that some of the gene-seed would be sent to distant outposts, hidden away, its location known to only a select few.'

'What do you know about Caliban?' demanded Boreas. 'What else have you kept from me?'

'Boreas, Brother-Chaplain…' Nestor's voice was tainted with a harsh laugh, edged with insanity. 'I am six hundred and seventeen years old, did you really think that after all this time I would not be a member of the Inner Circle? That's why a veteran like myself is here, on this forsaken outpost. To protect the future, to guard the gene-seed.'

The words of Astelan sprang into Boreas's mind: *There was a darkness within Lion El'Jonson. A darkness you all carry within you. It surrounds you, yet you are blind to its presence. Intrigue, secrets, lies and mystery.* They shrouded the Dark Angels Chapter, a veil of darkness they had woven around outsiders and themselves.

'We must recover the gene-seed at all costs,' Nestor insisted, having recovered from the shock, walking between Boreas and Hephaestus. The Techmarine was standing rigidly still, stunned by the turn of events. As Nestor pushed past, he seemed to snap out of it.

'First we must check the annihilus is intact,' the Techmarine said, looking at Boreas.

'Where?' the Interrogator-Chaplain asked.

'The main control chamber, I can access it from there,' Hephaestus replied, following Nestor down the dimly lit tunnel.

Entering the control chamber, Hephaestus crossed to the central platform and activated one of the central interfaces. Around him, screens flickered into life, bathing the room in an erratic green glow, and the needles of gauges monitoring the keep's power systems wavered in their glasses. On one screen to Boreas's left, the Chaplain saw a view of the courtyard outside, and watched as rebels surged forwards against the line of Imperial Guard, some mercilessly cut down by volleys of fire, others battering their way through with fists and rocks. Tearing his attention away, Boreas watched as Hephaestus's fingers danced over a runepad.

'Hurry! Every moment wasted takes the Fallen and the gene-seed further out of out reach,' Nestor snapped from just outside the doorway.

Meaningless numerals, letters and symbols scrolled up the screen as Hephaestus worked. The screen then went blank for a few seconds before an empty white box appeared at its centre.

'Authority cipher,' explained the Techmarine as he entered a sequence of runes. The screen went blank again for a few more seconds before a message appeared.

+CIPHER ACCEPTED – ANNIHILUS VIRAL FAILSAFE ACTIVATED+

'Something is wrong,' the Techmarine warned, stabbing at keys without response.

'What's happening? Tell me what this means!' demanded Boreas, staring at the words on the display.

Hephaestus ignored the Chaplain as he continued to desperately punch in security protocols and override commands. Stepping back, he smashed his fist into the screen, sending shards of glass spinning through the air.

'Hephaestus, tell me what's happening!' Boreas yelled, dragging the Techmarine around to face him.

'One last trick,' muttered Hephaestus. He looked back at the shattered screen and then at Boreas. 'They broke into the core machine spirit and gave it new commands. As soon as I accessed the annihilus, it was primed to activate.'

'Can't you stop it?' asked Nestor, taking a pace into the room.

'No, it's impossible, there's no delay,' Hephaestus told them. 'Activation is immediate. The annihilus was always intended to be a last resort. Why take the risk of it being deactivated during a countdown?'

'You mean the virus is spreading even now?' asked Boreas, looking around him as if he might see the deadly toxin flooding the air.

'Yes,' the Techmarine answered, slumping against the console. 'We failed.'

'What happens next?' Nestor asked. 'What type of virus is it?'

'Omniphagic,' replied Hephaestus heavily. 'It will devour all living matter. It can be airborne or waterborne, and will pass by contact. Kadillus Harbour will be infected within two hours of release, the island within half a day. After that it depends on wind strength and the currents, but the virus will wipe out every living creature, destroy every organic cell on the planet, within five days. As it spreads it grows more virulent, in a cyclical effect that will strip the planet bare. Even bones will be destroyed. Were it not for our armour and helmets, we would already be dead. We have failed.'

'Not wholly,' Nestor said, causing Boreas and Hephaestus to look up sharply. Hope flared within the Interrogator-Chaplain. 'We can still retrieve the gene-seed.'

'Zaul, Damas, Thumiel, assemble in the entrance chamber!' commanded Boreas, striding off the control dais. The other two fell in behind him. As he walked, he explained the situation to those who had not been present.

'Why would they do such a thing?' Zaul asked over the comm-net. 'What is the point?'

'I cannot say for sure, but I think it is a message,' Boreas told them. 'They want our brethren to know what happened here, but for what twisted reason I cannot fathom.'

'Why risk us not activating it?' Hephaestus wondered. 'To tie the activation in with the override seems a foolish thing to do.'

'The prisoner Boreas questioned in their base spoke of dissent,' Nestor recalled. 'Perhaps some of them did not agree, perhaps they were only after the gene-seed. The others might not have had the opportunity to properly set the annihilus and so had to resort to deception.'

'Or they just wanted to ensure they were clear of the planet before the virus was released,' suggested Damas. 'It would seem likely for such a cowardly act.'

'It matters not,' growled Boreas. 'When we take them, they shall tell us everything! I will personally see to that.'

* * *

DAMAS WAS THE last to arrive in the entrance chamber, and fell in beside Boreas, who stood facing the sealed door.

'We must get back to the Thunderhawk. Kill if necessary,' the Chaplain told his squad. 'The Fallen will not escape us; I will hunt them under every rock and across every kilometre of space. For what they have done today, I will inflict pain upon them never before envisaged. I will make them live for a year and a day in agony as justice for their crimes.'

He took a step towards the door, and then stopped suddenly.

'Brother-chaplain?' Nestor inquired. 'Is there something wrong.'

'Hephaestus, tell me, where is the virus stored?' Boreas asked, turning to the Techmarine.

'In the lowest vault,' he answered. 'Of what relevance is that?'

'The first aim of the virus is to cleanse the keep of intruders, correct?' Boreas continued his chain of thought.

'Yes, the virus is released internally first, before spreading to the rest of the city,' Hephaestus confirmed.

'And how does it spread?' Boreas asked.

'Simple, if the keep has been breached or has been taken, there will be any number of ways for it to pass into the...' Hephaestus's voice trailed off as he followed Boreas's gaze towards the armoured entry portal. 'There has been no attack, no breach...'

'The tower is completely sealed,' Boreas said, looking at each of the others. 'As protection from gas or viral attack from outside, the keep is airtight. Until we break that seal, the virus is confined to the interior.'

'But as soon as we leave, the seal is broken,' said Nestor. 'I do not understand.'

'We will not be leaving,' Damas explained slowly.

'But the Fallen, the gene-seed–' Nestor protested bitterly. 'Piscina is already doomed. Although the

circumstances of its activation may have been unorthodox, the virus bomb's purpose remains the same.
Kadillus is in the grip of revolt, and the orks are attacking
in overwhelming numbers. The planet is already lost. We
shall simply be hastening its demise. The virus will
cleanse the world as it was supposed to, denying it to the
enemies of the Emperor.'

'No,' Boreas answered flatly.

'No?' roared Nestor. 'You would abandon the hope of
our Chapter's future for a world already in flames, on the
brink of destruction? You would sacrifice that for a dying
world?'

'A world we swore to protect,' Boreas reminded him. 'A
sacred oath to lay down our lives and guard it by whatever means necessary.'

'Piscina is lost!' declared the Apothecary. 'If the rebellion does not destroy this world, the orks will overrun it!
There is nothing left to save, Boreas!'

'We are not leaving,' Boreas said stubbornly, recalling
his arguments with Astelan. 'We live to serve the Emperor
and mankind, not the Dark Angels.'

'This is heresy,' Nestor barked. 'Are you renouncing
your oaths of allegiance?'

'No, I am remembering them,' Boreas snapped. 'We
swore to protect Piscina, and that is what we will do. It
matters not if the price is our lives, or even the sacred
gene-seed; this duty overrides all others.'

'I cannot let you do this,' Nestor said, taking a step
towards the door. 'My duty, my oath, was to protect that
gene-seed.'

Boreas grabbed the plasma pistol from Hephaestus's
belt and thumbed the activation switch. It began to hum
and vibrate in his grip as it charged up.

'You will not open that door, Brother-Apothecary,'
warned Boreas, pointing the pistol at Nestor's head.

'What treachery is this?' Nestor's voice, even distorted
through his suit, dripped with scorn. 'You would kill

your own brethren rather than continue the great quest of our Chapter? You, a Chaplain, guardian of our traditions and guide to our souls, would rather kill me than atone for a sin ten thousand years old? I think not.'

Nestor took three more steps and reached towards the portal runepad. Boreas pulled the trigger and a ball of superheated plasma smashed into the Apothecary, exploding on impact. His headless torso, the stump of his neck cauterised and smoking, pitched forward and slumped against the gate.

'None of us are leaving,' Boreas said, handing the pistol back to Hephaestus.

'You do realise that if we do not leave, we will die here,' the Techmarine told them. 'The virus can stay active for up to seventy days once released. That is over twenty days longer than the environmental systems in our armour can sustain us.'

'I will obey your command, Brother-Chaplain,' Zaul said. 'If it is to die here, then so be it.'

'You ARE TO achieve orbit of Piscina V, and guard against any intrusion.' Boreas stood in the control room, at the comms station, instructing Sen Naziel. 'Nothing is to land, nothing. Do you understand?'

'Yes, Lord Boreas,' the ship's officer replied.

'I will shortly transmit a coded message,' Boreas continued. 'When the Tower of Angels arrives, it is to be passed on to Grand Master-Chaplain Sapphon. No blame will be attached to you or the crew for the events and our actions of these last weeks. I commend you for your dedication to the Chapter, and your perseverance in the pursuit of your duties.'

'And when will you be joining us again?' Naziel asked. Boreas paused, unsure what to say.

'We will not be joining you,' he said eventually. 'These are my final commands. The Grand Masters will inform you of your future.'

'I don't understand, my lord.' The confusion was evident in Neziel's voice.

'You do not have to understand, merely obey your orders, Sen,' Boreas told him. 'Honour the Chapter. Venerate the Emperor. Praise the Lion.'

'Praise the Lion,' Naziel echoed and Boreas switched off the link. Turning his attention to the data log, he activated the recorder.

'This is Interrogator-Chaplain Boreas of the Emperor's Dark Angels Chapter,' he began. 'This is my final communication from Piscina, as commander of the Dark Angels in the system. Our ancient foes have struck a blow against our Chapter. The reviled enemy has wounded us severely. We are entangled in a plot that goes beyond our comprehension. The events I am about to relate stretch beyond this world, beyond the furthest reaches of this star system. Great and dark powers are at work, I see their hand manipulating us, bending us to their twisted goals.'

He stopped, choosing his next words carefully.

'For ten thousand years we have sought redemption. We have pursued that which shamed our brethren when our time of triumph was at hand. It was a grave, unforgivable sin, which must be atoned for. That is beyond doubt. But these last days, an even greater sin has come to light. It is the sin of ignorance. It is the sin of past errors repeated.

'I ask myself what it means to be one of the Dark Angels. Is it to hunt the Fallen, chasing shadows through the dark places of the galaxy? Is it to pursue our quest at any expense, foregoing all other oaths and duties? Is it to lie, to hide and to plot so that others will never know of our shame? Is it to keep our own brethren unacquainted with the truth of our past, the legacy we all share in? Or is it to be a Space Marine? Is it to follow the path laid down by the Emperor and Lion El'Jonson at the founding of this great Imperium of Man? To protect mankind, to purge the alien, cleanse the unclean?

'We must act as a shining brand in the night, to lead the way for others to follow. We are the warriors of the Emperor, guardians of mankind. Roboute Guilliman called us bright stars in the firmament of battle, untouched by self-aggrandisement. Yet we, the Dark Angels, commit the supreme sin. We put ourselves before our duty. We have buried our traditions, masked our real history in legend and mysticism to confound others. We are not bright stars, we are an empty blackness, a passing shadow that serves nothing but its own purpose.'

He stopped again, feeling weary, and leant against the panel. He knew they would not listen, that in fact they could not listen, for he spoke against everything that made the Dark Angels what they are.

'Included in this log is a complete account of the disaster that has befallen Piscina and us. For this, I take sole responsibility. Our enemies know us too well. We have become an anathema to ourselves, as this plot of the Fallen demonstrates. Everything that has transpired has led us to this place and time, and there is nothing left but to do what we must. Ten thousand years ago, our soul was split. We tell ourselves that the two halves of us are the light and the dark. I have learnt a bitter lesson, that it is not true. It is a comforting lie, which keeps us safe from doubt, so that we do not ask the questions whose answers we fear. There is no light and dark, only the shades of twilight in between.

'If once there was a chance for us to redeem ourselves, it passed away ten thousand years ago. For a hundred centuries it has driven us, and consumed us at the same time. Not while one Fallen stays alive can we know peace within ourselves. But what then? What does it mean to be Dark Angels without the Fallen? We have come to define ourselves by them. Take them away and we are left without purpose. We have strayed far from the path, and it is my fervent prayer that you, the Grand Masters of the Chapter, the wisest of us, can find the true course again.

If not, then there will never be salvation, and all that we aspire to will come to nothing, all that we have achieved will be in vain. I beseech you not to allow this to happen. We are to make the ultimate sacrifice for the people of Piscina, and to safeguard our future. Do not make the deaths of my brethren be for nothing.'

Boreas switched off the log and walked away. As he reached the doorway, he stopped, another thought occurring to him, and walked back and reactivated the recorder.

'I have one more message to pass on. Walk that dark road down through the rooms of the interrogators, past the catacombs into the deepest chambers. Go to that solitary cell at the heart of the Rock and tell him this: *You were not wrong.*'

THEY GATHERED IN the chapel, their robes draped over their armour. Along one wall lay the bodies of the forty-two attendants and fourteen aspirants, each covered with a white shroud embroidered with the Chapter symbol. At the end, his shroud inverted, lay Nestor. The Dark Angels knelt in a single line in front of the altar, Zaul and Hephaestus to Boreas's left, Thumiel and Damas to his right. They each clasped a melta-bomb to their chests and bowed their heads. Boreas held the detonator, his thumb over the trigger stud. They had been unanimous – better to end the ordeal quickly, lest desperation set in as they starved to death and asphyxiated, and they showed weakness. This way was clean and instant.

'What is it that gives us purpose?' Boreas chanted.

'*War,*' the others replied.

'What is it that gives war purpose?'

'*To vanquish the foes of the Emperor.*'

'Who are the foes of the Emperor?'

'*The heretic, the alien and the mutant.*'

'What is it to be an enemy of the Emperor?'

'*It is to be damned.*'

'What is the instrument of the Emperor's damnation?'

'We, the Space Marines, the angels of death.'

'What is it to be a Space Marine?'

'It is to be pure, to be strong, to show no pity, nor mercy, nor remorse.'

'What is it to be pure?'

'To never know fear, to never waver in the fight.'

'What is it to be strong?'

'To fight on when others flee; to stand and die in the knowledge that death brings ultimate reward.'

'What is the ultimate reward?'

'To serve the Emperor.'

'Who do we serve?'

'We serve the Emperor and the Lion, and through them we serve mankind.'

'What is it to be Dark Angels?'

'It is to be the first, the honoured, the sons of the Lion.'

'Praise the Lion,' Boreas said, pressing the stud.

AFTERWORD
by Gav Thorpe

'MUCH ANTICIPATED' IS an over-used phrase, so I'll set-
tle for simply 'anticipated'. That is to say, since the first
printing of this novel went out of stock I've had a
steady stream of people asking when the book would
be published again. Perhaps not crowds of screaming
fans who might frenziedly celebrate the reunification
of a boy band (or, indeed, another instalment of the
life of a boy wizard), but nonetheless there's been a
gentle but persistent insistence that *Angels of Darkness*
should be made available again. So it is with a mixture
of pleasure and relief that this second printing is now
available, and the friendly pestering can stop – both of
me by fans, and of the poor staff at Black Library by
me!

I am very proud of this novel, for a number of
reasons. First and foremost, because of the way there
are two tales intertwined. Initially, I had conceived of
the interrogation of Astelan by Boreas to be presented

simply as shorter passages of transcript interlacing the 'present day' chapters of the book. However, as I discussed the novel with Lindsey, hard-working editor of BL, it became apparent that simply having lines of cold dialogue wouldn't convey the complex relationship that develops between the two characters. I am very glad that Lindsey made me think more about those scenes, because without them, *Angels of Darkness* would not be the novel it is, and would not have gathered such quiet respect amongst Warhammer 40,000 aficionados. Without that portrayal of Boreas in his prime as an Interrogator-Chaplain, the progress of his story in the other half of the book would be that bit flatter; less personal.

It was the changes in Boreas's attitudes as they are portrayed in that context that give me my second source of pride – *Angels of Darkness* achieves what I had wanted it to from the outset. To explain, when I was first approached by Marc Gascoigne to write a novel about Space Marines, I was hesitant. Could I create a story and characters about a group of inhuman, ultra-dedicated sacred warriors that was both engaging to readers on an emotional level as well as staying true to the well-defined and widely established nature of the Space Marines?

The fact that this book exists shows that hesitancy swiftly succumbed to my desire to meet a creative challenge. I wanted to create a story that would have the bolters blazing, ugly death feel of a true Warhammer 40,000 novel, whilst finding room for our protagonists to feel emotional conflict and spiritual angst. This meant finding a subject that would not humanise our Space Marine characters – because they are not human, they do not fall in love or get scared by big monsters or care very much about anything other than hot bolter death! The Dark Angels jumped out as an obvious choice, because they are so mired in their own secrets, their own designs, there were lots of conflicts of interest for me to explore. They had a *story* that I could help to tell a small part of.

Which nicely brings me onto my third and final reason for a certain degree of authorly smugness concerning *Angels of Darkness*. Once it was agreed that the Dark Angels would be our central characters, I wanted to both follow what had already been described in their background and history, whilst simultaneously turning everything people thought they knew on its head. This was because I wanted readers to wonder if they really did know what the 'dark secret' is.

Could they really believe what they already knew? Was that dark secret simply the rebellion of Luthor, or was there something even deeper, even more hidden than had been previously shown? Judging by the divided reactions amongst readers, especially those already fans of the Dark Angels, I know that *Angels of Darkness* has succeeded on that count.

Even now, years after the first printing, Astelan's testimony to Boreas crops up in conversations and internet debates about the nature of the Dark Angels and the Fallen. Can you believe the word of a traitor? For that matter, is Astelan really a traitor, or the true follower of the Emperor's vision? Do Boreas's actions and his eventual doubts, perhaps conversion even, lend credence to Astelan's arguments? Alternatively, does the fact that Boreas's own experiences of abandonment weaken his resolve and create an unwitting sympathy with Astelan? I could go on, to talk about the Old Legion versus New Legion conflict, or the catalytic role played by the shadowy gene-seed thief (who is the enigmatic Cypher, for those who haven't guessed), but there isn't space. I'm never going to say one way or the other, because it has always been my intent that readers get to decide and debate these issues for themselves.

All of which brings me to the end of this Afterword, save for one more shocking revelation. The part most-quoted from Angels of Darkness is probably:

> 'What was he waiting for?' Boreas asked quietly.
>
> Astelan looked into Boreas's eyes, read the curiosity that was now there.
>
> 'He was waiting to see which side won, of course.'

It's been a source of great interest and amusement to see just how much this has been simultaneously reviled and rejoiced. The cherished convictions of thousands were shaken by this dubious revelation. It fundamentally sums up the equivocation and secret agendas of the Dark Angels. But the thing is; I never planned it at all. It just came out as I was writing that scene. I remember it well, because I stopped dead in my tracks, hands hovering comically over the keyboard, and read it out aloud to myself. Wow, I thought, that's really going to get people talking.

So, everything else aside, perhaps that's the greatest achievement of *Angels of Darkness* – it even managed to shock me!

Cheers,
Gav Thorpe

ABOUT THE AUTHOR

Gav Thorpe worked for Games Workshop in his capacity as Senior Games Developer for many years, overseeing and contributing to the Warhammer and Warhammer 40,000 worlds. He has a dozen or so short stories to his name, and over half a dozen novels. He lives in Nottingham, UK.

WARHAMMER 40,000

THE ULTRAMARINES
OMNIBUS

'Great characters, truck loads of intrigue and an amazing sense of pace.' **Enigma**

GRAHAM MCNEILL
NIGHTBRINGER • WARRIORS OF ULTRAMAR • DEAD SKY BLACK SUN

ISBN 978-1-84416-402-5

LOYALTY AND HONOUR

THE HORUS HERESY

Mitchel Scanlon

DESCENT OF ANGELS

Loyalty and honour

The latest instalment in the best-selling
Horus Heresy series

ISBN 978-1-84416-508-7

'**Y**OU HAVE ALL been chosen to become part of the greatest warrior order the galaxy has ever seen. You will be stronger, faster and more deadly than ever before. You will fight in wars beyond counting and you will kill the enemies of mankind on worlds far distant from our beloved home of Caliban. But we will do these things willingly, for we are men of honour and courage, men who know what it is to have a duty that transcends personal concerns. Each of you was once a knight, a warrior and a hero, but now you are far more than that. From this day forth you will forget your past life. From this day forth you are a warrior of the Legion. Nothing else is of consequence. The Legion is all that matters.'

Zahariel gripped his sword hilt as the power of the Lion's oratory washed through him, almost unable to contain his elation at the thought of taking the Emperor's war to the farthest corners of the galaxy and being part of this brotherhood that stood at the brink of no less a task than the liberation of humanity's birthright.

'We are the First Legion,' said the Lion, 'the honoured, the Sons of the Lion, and we will not be marching to war without a name that strikes terror into the hearts of our enemies. As our legends spoke of the great heroes who held back the monsters of our distant past, so too shall we hold back the enemies of the Imperium as we set off into the great void to fight in the name of the Emperor.

'We shall be the Dark Angels!'

buy this book or read a further extract at
www.blacklibrary.com

ISBN 978-1-84416-559-9